Down and Out
in Manhattan
A Novel

Irene Magers

Shady Tree Press
New York, New York

Originally published with the title Cruise Ship Diaries, *Down And Out in Manhattan* is a
work of fiction. Names, characters, places, and incidents are the products of the author's
imagination or are used fictitiously. Any resemblance to actual events, locales, or persons,
living or dead, is entirely coincidental.

Published by Shady Tree Press
An imprint of iMg Books
136 East 64th Street, 7th Floor
New York, NY 10065
www.shadytreepress.com

ISBN-13: 978-0-9841211-3-7
ISBN-10: 0-9841211-3-7

Book Cover & Interior Design by Scribe Freelance
www.scribefreelance.com

Printed in the United States of America

Down and Out
in Manhattan
A Novel

for Geena
who brought the sunshine

acknowledgments

The author is extremely grateful to Mary Kaye, friend and mentor throughout each draft of this book. A veteran of more than forty cruises, Mary Kaye generously shared her firsthand shipboard experiences, giving the author the benefit of adapting her personal recollections, both horrendous and wonderful, into the story. Without Mary Kaye's input and encouragement, this book could not have been written.

Chapter *One*

"It's six o'clock...this is 1010 WINS road and weather report. It's 29 degrees in Manhattan. Snow mixed with sleet will begin during the morning rush hour. A stalled taxi is tying up traffic on the inbound Queens Borough Bridge. Overnight construction on the Triborough has been cleared. Two lanes on the lower deck of the New Jersey side of the GW Bridge remain closed. The Lincoln Tunnel is your best bet. And now...1010 news from around the world..."

Maggie grunted, hit the snooze button on her bedside radio, and turned over. She was awake; still, it was best to keep the alarm on. She was not one to take chances. She might go back to sleep and be late for work. Besides, the five-minute mute option was an efficient way of censoring the news that would put her in a foul mood even before she got up to face her own bleak existence, which was not enhanced by reports of disasters from around the world. It was galling enough that it was November, cold, dark, and a few days before the elections, which meant the airwaves were choked with candidates making exorbitant promises they wouldn't keep. Campaigns depressed Maggie like headline news, bad weather, and her dead-end job. Somewhere in her pursuit of life, liberty, and happiness, she had crashed and burned. At forty-four she felt as obsolete as the campaign flyers flapping on lampposts long after the elections were history and volunteers fanned out across the city, removing them before the fines kicked in.

"*A suicide bomber caused havoc in downtown Kandahar, killing fifteen. US troops are going door to door, rounding up insurgents. Marines have come under new attack in the northern regions of Afghanistan. There are reports of casualties. And now...1010 WINS Local news. A child of twelve was killed at the corner of 125th and*

Broadway last night. People reported hearing shots around midnight..."

Maggie threw off the covers and sat on the edge of her bed, putting her feet on the bare linoleum. Heat rising from the apartments below never quite reached the fifth floor and the jarring cold worked like a slap in the face. All right, she was wide-awake. *What's a twelve-year-old doing out and about at midnight?* she wondered, rolling her eyes and turning off the radio. She ran her fingers through her short-cropped brown hair, freshly tinted – a homemade job – done in a vain attempt to control some unruly gray intruders before they could gang up on her.

She glanced toward the lone window in her typical New York-sized bedroom, nine by ten, with just enough space for a small dresser at the foot of the bed. Her apartment was at the back of a brownstone with no view except from the living room where the window faced an adjacent roof and water tower. Her bedroom window faced a brick wall but if she looked down she had a bird's eye view of a narrow alley five floors below, a graveyard of old furniture and rusted garbage cans. No sunlight entered, but she could usually distinguish a dreary day from a pleasant one by studying the rim of light around the paper shade permanently rolled down after its spring broke last summer. This morning the rim was a dull gray. The weather today would be no better than the news. The forecaster knew what he was talking about. Okay, it was November and even if the sun tried again later it would only shed blue light, the general color of Maggie's mood. Widowed once, divorced twice, her life was a mess and she knew it but lacked the wherewithal to change anything. Most days she was simply too busy, and in the evenings she was much too tired to rearrange anything. Her life was the cluttered broom closet that no one ever straightened out.

Getting out of bed and planting her feet on the cold floor, she went through a rigorous stretching routine, after which her shoulders fell back into their normal position of defeat. As she now made her way through the short passageway of the apartment, she managed not to look at the wall mirror by the front door. Crossing the living room on a woven grass rug – a material that was wildly popular these days – Maggie walked into her galley-sized kitchen, promptly colliding with the refrigerator. She was tall, five foot eight, and her arms and shoulders were regularly black and blue from fighting the cramped spaces of her apartment.

Opening the refrigerator door, its bulb almost blinding her, she reached for some leftover Starbucks coffee. It was still in its *grande* cardboard cup, microwavable, and once heated, the burnt flavor she'd become addicted to would infuse her with a temporary high, reassuring her that she was alive, if not altogether well.

Sipping the hot black liquid, she eyed the clock hanging over the refrigerator. Its white plastic frame had yellowed with age but the mechanism was still dependable. She had time for breakfast. However, rummaging the cupboards, she realized she had forgotten to buy bread and cereal. Rustling a box of corn flakes, she decided they were no longer crisp, nor were there enough of them to waste milk on. Coffee would have to suffice. Perhaps one of her coworkers with something to celebrate would bring a box of donuts to the office. Coffee in hand, she walked back to the passageway and a hall closet where she flicked through the three business suits she wore on a rotating basis: brown, navy, and gray. She stubbornly refused to wear all purpose black.

Maggie was a paralegal at the law firm *Goodman, Barr & Noune*. The office was located on the corner of 59th Street and Madison Avenue and when the weather was pleasant, she walked the twenty-four blocks from her five-floor walkup on East 83rd Street. Otherwise, she took the Second Avenue bus in the mornings, returning home in the evenings via Madison Avenue. She avoided subways. The stale underground air made her nauseous and dried her skin. After forty, it was difficult to maintain a moist complexion, as difficult as it was to keep a waistline. Most of her coworkers belonged to a midtown gym that she resisted joining because of the cost. Why pay a stiff monthly membership fee to do Stairmasters when she climbed the five flights to her apartment daily, doubling up on weekends when she ran out to pick up *The New York Times* and buy groceries. Plus she always used the stairs rather than the elevator to the seventh floor of *Goodman, Barr & Noune*. Elevators made her claustrophobic and she avoided them like she avoided subways and people with open sores or deep coughs. Maggie took pride in good health and guarded her teeth. Likewise, she guarded her credit by paying her rent on time and making the required payments on her Macy's charge account. And she never fudged on her taxes. Her last marriage had disintegrated partially because she refused to sign a joint tax return that her husband had fooled around with.

A blast of cold air from the East River pummeled Maggie as she left the vestibule of her brownstone an hour later, buttoning her mohair coat over the navy blue suit, the warmest of the three. She wrapped a wool scarf securely around her neck and pulled a knitted cap down over her ears; still, the ensemble was no match for the wind and sleet. Luckily a bus came along just as she reached Second Avenue. She climbed onboard, holding her breath for a moment against the steamy heat evaporating from other passengers. She took an empty seat directly behind the driver, tried not to breathe too deeply, and absently perused the ads above the fogged windows. This was done mainly to avoid eye contact with her fellow passengers or, God forbid, conversation.

The ads on public transportation throughout the city were printed in both English and Spanish and generally addressed abortion, family planning, the advantage of learning English, along with a warning about panhandling. The ads weren't making much of an impact. Someone was wasting money big time. Invariably, a pregnant, non English-speaking woman walked the aisle, working the crowd with one outstretched hand; the other dragging a toddler with a face that could melt the most hardened New Yorker. Maggie usually dug into her pocket for a quarter, chalking it up to the price of the ride, all the while wondering how the woman came up with the bus fare. Ten people would have to fork over a quarter before she ran a profit.

The quality of life in the city had been better under Mayor Giuliani; at least the streets had seemed cleaner; fewer homeless lying around and less spit on the sidewalks. Wads of the glossy foamy globules now replaced the dog droppings of a bygone era because dog owners pretty much adhered to the pooper-scooper law. Maggie wondered about the health hazard of this new menace and, when walking, always kept an eyeball on the sidewalk, gingerly stepping around the sticky stuff, usually avoiding it. Spitting was a particularly bad habit, one that depressed her.

Her depression was not a new phenomenon. She had decided long ago that she was born depressed. Of course, if she thought hard and long, she could recall being a bit of an optimist at one point when, as a newcomer to the city, she had arrived from Wilkes Barre, Pennsylvania, with a college degree and a job offer in a mid-sized advertising firm. Deliriously happy, she rented a studio apartment on Lexington and 63rd and spent her free time, walking Manhattan, looking up at the skyscrapers while Frank Sinatra crooned inside her head: *"If I can make it here..."*

Determined that she would also make it here, she had done precisely that until everything changed the day her first husband's cancer was diagnosed as terminal. Maggie had been married a total of three times, but cared only remember the first, David Fitzpatrick, the love of her life and her only family when her father, a retired math teacher, died shortly after her marriage; her mother following him to the grave a year later.

An only child, Maggie was born Margaret Elizabeth Maghpye to middle-aged parents with plenty of regrets, they certainly didn't need another. However, since The Lord had seen fit to test their faith with an infant girl, they accepted their lot and dutifully brought her up as a God-fearing Methodist in their modest two-bedroom home where smiles came at a premium and laughter was the weakness of heathens. Growing up in the belief that she was the source of her parents' long faces, Maggie left home right after college when she could support herself.

A year after arriving in New York, she met David Fitzpatrick, a third-year law student. They married and settled in for the long haul. However, into their second year of bliss, a skin lesion on David's back changed dramatically. He ignored it; after all, everyone had moles, and he consulted a doctor only after his bled and proved to be a nuisance. The diagnosis, aggressive melanoma, came as a shock, almost as shocking as the aggressive billing that followed. They had no insurance. Maggie quickly depleted the cash her parents had left her and sold the house in Wilkes Barre, everything disappearing with the speed of light into a black hole.

"Caught too late," the specialists at Sloane Kettering said, shaking their heads and speculating that David's past summers as a lifeguard on Jones Beach before sunscreen became mandatory beach attire had put him on death row. When he died, Maggie was left drowning in sorrow and medical bills.

After the funeral, David's parents drove to Florida to recover from their ordeal. Two weeks later, when Maggie ran into one of his sisters in midtown, she learned that they had settled there. She wrote to them but never heard back. She telephoned each of David's siblings in Manhattan and regularly left messages, telling them that she was doing all right and hoped they were as well. Nothing was heard from any of them. She was puzzled. She had expected to keep in touch. Christmas approached and she held out hope that one of them would invite her for dinner. No one called. She spent Christmas Day at a donut shop on Columbus Avenue alongside a homeless guy with watery, vacant eyes. The staff had taken pity on him and let him in out of the cold. Maggie paid for his coffee and donut. She considered getting a cat that day, but changed her mind when she learned the price of the required shots. Veterinary bills were a liability she couldn't shoulder now that her savings were gone and she was in debt.

Less than a year after being widowed, she married again – on the rebound – and doomed from the start. Robert, an aspiring artist, was incredibly handsome but turned out to have married her in the mistaken belief that she could support the two of them until his paintings sold. The final crunch came when Maggie's advertising agency closed its door and she was laid off. Robert immediately began to grouse about money.

"Walk away from the medical bills!" he demanded. "The guy's dead and you're still paying Sloane Kettering!"

"Please, don't refer to David as *the guy*."

"All right." Robert shrugged. "Whatever you say. Just quit paying his bills. What's the hospital gonna do to you?"

"Ruin my credit."

"So what?"

"So *what?* We'll never be able to get another rental. Let alone buy a place."

"Who wants to buy a place? It'll only tie us down."

After weeks of arguing and Maggie not landing another job, the marriage cooled, not that it had been red hot in the first place because after the quick ceremony at City Hall, Robert lost interest in the physical side of their union almost as quickly. Painting took the juice out of him, he claimed, and not selling his work made him impotent. He began to spend more time at his studio downtown.

The day Maggie paid him a visit and took a look at his latest work, she realized why the paintings weren't selling. They were awful. Robert had given up on his colorful landscapes in favor of black dollops like the spots before your eyes that send you running to an ophthalmologist. After another heated argument, she removed herself and her stuff from their apartment. Robert's friend, an artist who had been a regular visitor during their marriage, mostly when Maggie was out, immediately claimed the space. Weeks later she spotted them hand in hand, walking up Fifth Avenue in the Gay Pride Parade. She hoped Robert's newfound happiness would have some positive influence on his work.

She filed for divorce. It was amicable.

She took an HIV test. It was negative.

Her next marriage four years later was undone by Henry's three children, aged six, eight, and twelve; each hating her vehemently for having stolen Daddy away from their saint of a mother, this in spite of the fact that Maggie hadn't laid eyes on Henry until after he had been divorced for two years. The alternate weekends when the children visited became a nightmare. When Maggie realized she'd be facing this small army of pint-sized combatants for a month each summer and on alternating holidays, she waved the white flag. She was not cut out for child rearing and certainly not someone else's, a crew with a perfectly good mother, unless one asked Henry.

The final straw came when she discovered that he had cooked their tax return. They split. She resigned herself to the single life and took back her maiden name, which had never caused her any trouble. Now, some twelve years later she was accustomed to living solo and although she could finally afford the shots, still resisted adopting a cat – the accessory of a lonely woman.

Chapter *three*

The bus had gone some twenty blocks down Second Avenue when it stopped abruptly behind a sea of red lights. Traffic was at a standstill. Sirens could be heard approaching the area. Maggie craned her neck and tried to listen as the driver opened his window and spoke to a police officer walking toward him.

"What's the trouble?" the driver wanted to know.

"Broken water main up ahead!" the cop shouted over the noise of frustrated motorists honking for attention.

"Where?" The driver leaned out the window and looked down as if he expected to see the officer standing knee deep in water.

"Next block. Water's coming this way. Judging from the size of the geyser, it could be more than one rupture. Once we clear the traffic ahead of you, you'll have go up to Third Avenue."

"Third? You gotta be kidding. That's a one-way street. Opposite to my route."

"Okay. Then go up to Lexington or Park until you can get back to Second. Probably around 57th."

"I better take Lex or the hoi polloi will revolt." The driver chuckled. "Busses on Park Avenue are about as welcome as parades."

Huddling his shoulders inside his yellow oilcloth cape, the cop dismissed the feeble stab at humor and walked away to attend to the escalating gridlock, all the while shouting into his walkie-talkie for reinforcements.

The driver shut off the engine but kept the heat on. "We'll be here awhile," he said, using the intercom. "Broken water main. Once I get the go-ahead we'll detour to Lexington."

A collective sigh went up among the straphangers. *Not again!* The ancient cast-iron arteries running beneath the city regularly busted a gut, spilling their bowels onto city streets, making them impassable.

Sitting idle with the heat on, it became unbearably hot inside the bus. People grumbled. Maggie loosened her scarf. It didn't help. She felt a headache coming on. Her stomach was empty. She wished she'd eaten the limp corn flakes.

"Sir, I don't think we need the blower," someone in the middle of the bus opined loud enough for the driver to hear. The heat remained on. Those standing in the aisle began to grow restless and when someone decided to pull the cord and leave, there was a sudden mass exodus. Maggie got up and joined the passengers jostling for the exits. She was approximately nine blocks from her office but figured it was better to walk and endure the sleet than suffocate in her seat. Besides, time was crucial. She could not afford to be late.

Stepping off the bus and onto the curb, icy water immediately seeped into her shoes. She heard several passengers curse as their feet, too, disappeared into the rapidly rising slush. The police officer was right. This was a major break. Water was running along the sidewalk like a river at snowmelt, taking a couple of dead rats along for the ride. Maggie shivered, wondering what else might be lurking under the murky surface. She bent her head and kept her eyes peeled for other vile creatures – dead or alive – as she sloshed toward the corner and higher ground. She prayed that her boss, Ms. Noune who lived in Westchester, was delayed this morning as well. Metro North trains were particular about racing along on icy tracks and generally proceeded with slow caution on a day like this. Maggie could picture Ms. Noune repeatedly checking her Tiffany watch while shuffling her expensive Gucci pumps on the blustery Irvington platform where she probably stood freezing to death despite her sheared beaver coat. A rail thin woman without an ounce of natural insulation, Ms. Noune felt the cold like none other and was bound to arrive in a foul mood today. Therefore, it was imperative that Maggie get to the office ahead her so she wouldn't be upbraided for being tardy. She picked up her steps, but the slow and shuffling herd around her thwarted her best efforts.

To make matters worse, her wool cap and scarf were stiff with clinging sleet and no longer offered any warmth. A mantle of ice lay across her shoulders. Of all the days to leave the umbrella at home, in the very least she should have worn rubber boots. Her feet were numb from being under water, and her shoes would surely fall casualty to the flood. Rotten luck. She had just spent eighteen dollars on new soles.

Trudging along, Maggie began to feel lightheaded and had to struggle for air. But it was impossible to stop and catch her breath, caught as she were in a solid huddle of pedestrians, one and all sidling up against the storefronts where the water wasn't quite so deep. Again, she wished she had eaten breakfast. There was a sharp twinge in the pit of her stomach and a dull hammer was pounding inside her head. She was exhausted and her workday hadn't even begun yet.

Wading ankle-deep along the flooded sidewalk, clutching her brown vinyl tote under her arm, she suddenly lost her footing on something slippery. Attempting to steady herself, she only managed to trip over another obscured object, which caused her to lurch sideways before losing her balance altogether and crashing against the window of a store. Her forehead took the brunt of the fall as it struck the metal frame of the plate glass. She felt her knees go soft and experienced a strange floating sensation a moment before the world turned upside down. On the periphery of her semiconscious state, she realized she was down for the count. But even as a black void enveloped her, she clung savagely to her purse. She'd heard of people being mugged while comatose.

"Are you all right?" someone was asking so close to her face that she could smell last night's garlic in his breath.

She forced her eyes open. Everything was a hazy blur, but she sensed that people were gathering around and were trying to help her back on her feet. She got up slowly, the hem of her coat hanging wet and heavy around her legs, her right hand groping under her left arm; she still had her purse. *Thank God!* As her vision returned, she shook off the helping hands and attempted to get her bearings by leaning her shoulder against the storefront. She felt a painful swelling on her forehead and forced herself to focus on something so as not to lose consciousness again.

Suddenly her eyes beheld a lovely sight. Her frozen feet and wet coat forgotten, Maggie gazed at a pink beach dotted with palm trees. Sunbathers sat under yellow umbrellas while waiters in white jackets approached, carrying trays of tall fruit drinks. The blue surf sparkled and in the distance a sleek white ship glided on the calm sea. Maggie felt tropical breezes caress her skin. She smiled.

I have died and gone to heaven...

A deep male voice brought her back to earth.

She turned toward the voice and saw the outline of a black uniform and yellow oilcloth cape. *A police officer?*

"Are you hurt?" he was asking her.

She shook her head.

"Officer!" Someone in the crowd held out a cell phone. "Shall I call for an ambulance?" Again Maggie smelled garlic and wondered why her nose remained so sharp when everything else felt so numb. In the next instant, alert to the fact that ambulances cost money, she spoke up before the officer could respond.

"No!" she said quickly. "I...I'm fine. Really!" The thought of an expensive trip to a hospital forced the blood upstream to her head. She immediately felt better, helped in part by the beautiful vision she'd seen: her private glimpse of paradise.

"Are you sure?" the officer pressed her.

"Yes. I'm perfectly fine. I don't know what came over me. But I'm okay now."

"All right." The officer turned to the crowd. "Break it up! Let's go!"

"Can I walk you home?" A young woman remained behind, holding her Burberry umbrella over Maggie. "Do you live nearby?"

"No. But thanks for offering." Maggie looked at the Good Samaritan dressed in a designer trench coat with a costly *Hermes* scarf protruding from the collar. This young person was spending her entire salary on clothes while sharing a studio apartment with four other women. Maggie was familiar with the economic realities of New York.

"Well, then..." the woman smiled before reverting to the standard aloofness of city dwellers, "good-bye." She walked away in sleek black boots that didn't mind the deep water.

Chapter *four*

"You're late!" Ms. Noune announced, coming out of her office just as Maggie was hanging up her wet coat and putting her vinyl purse into a drawer of her desk that was closer to Ms. Noune's door than the secretary's, befitting Maggie's position as a paralegal. However, whatever prestige she held over Vera, Maggie suspected the latter was better paid. Greatly inconvenienced, Ms. Noune consulted her watch with dramatic flair and scowled at the bruise on Maggie's forehead as if it were as offensive as a grease spot on her clothing. "You're late by half an hour!"

"I...I'm sorry. I'll make it up by staying tonight. The bus got stuck." Maggie felt demeaned, apologizing to the much younger woman, but after all Ms. Noune was her boss and, moreover, enjoyed educational seniority. Years ago, after failing to get another position in an ad agency, Maggie signed up for a six month course and became a paralegal, telling herself that once she could afford the tuition she'd apply to law school; that day never came. "There was a ruptured water main on..."

"I heard about that." In no mood to listen to excuses, Ms. Noune cut her off. She had suffered her own commute from Westchester on a cold train and just when she needed a shot of caffeine, neither Maggie nor Vera had arrived in time to make coffee, the lack of which made her more edgy than normal. She handed Maggie three folders, tapping a red manicured nail on a top sheet scribbled with illegible instructions. Maggie took the files; Vera's knowledge of hieroglyphics would come in handy today. "These cases have to be finished before lunch," Ms. Noune went on in a warning tone. "There's a preliminary hearing on Weiss vs. Goldstein in Judge Morano's chambers at one o'clock. Research that one first.

Find corresponding cases to support my arguments." Ms. Noune tossed her blonde shoulder length hair, pivoted on her heels, and disappeared into her office where her private phone was ringing. Her other line was ringing as well and Maggie saw her signal the secretary.

Vera picked up the receiver, informing the caller that Ms. Noune was in court this morning and couldn't be reached. "Would you like to leave a message," she purred sweetly to compensate for the white lie Ms. Noune always wanted her to use, believing it made her sound important.

Once Vera was off the phone, Maggie handed Ms. Noune's instruction sheet across her desk. "Be a sport and please type this for me," she said, grinning at the secretary, a twenty-something redhead with a ponytail sprouting from the top of her head like a fountain, which to the casual observer might be the source of the sprinkling of freckles across her nose. "If I work here till I'm ninety, I'll never decipher Ms. Noune's handwriting."

"No problem." Vera winked; she and Maggie were comrades-in-arms. "Give me ten minutes. You'll be in the library?"

Maggie nodded. "You're a peach, Vera. Thanks a million." She turned and trudged down the hall past the immaculate receptionist station, her wet shoes making squishy sounds on the carpeted floor, her stomach growling; no one had brought donuts today.

Chapter *five*

That evening after work, curious about the broken water main because it would affect tomorrow's commute, Maggie walked down to Second Avenue rather than take the Madison bus home. All things considered it had been a bad day. Her coat was dry but the hem was filthy. Her stockings had runs and her shoes were on life support. Her cap and scarf remained moist and smelled abominably of gamy wool. In her present state of dishabille, the finery in the windows of the fancy shops along Madison would depress her more than necessary, another reason to avoid the glitzy avenue tonight.

Work on the water main was going into overtime. A huge cave had been carved beneath the pavement where the water had been drained away, leaving only a few icy spots along the sidewalks. Portable flood lights lit up the intersection bright as day, making the side streets appear darker in contrast. There was no traffic in the area except foot traffic and, stepping around the blue wooden police barricades cordoning off the activity, Maggie continued along Second Avenue until she could cross the street and go down to First Avenue, pick up some food at a deli and take the bus home from there. The sleet had abated and except for an occasional ice patch, walking was no hardship.

She caught the sorry sight of herself in a store window and stopped a moment to reflect on the possibility of improvement. In her youth people said she was pretty. David had claimed she was beautiful. Now she figured she was average, at best. Her reflection in the window was not the flowery stuff poets wrote about. Her limp coat was a disgrace. So was her cap. She pulled it off and was running a hand through her hair, when suddenly she saw that same magical vision of this morning. Staring at it, she realized the dazzling image had not been a shock-induced ocular phenomenon. It was just a poster, a large photograph of a heavenly scene. The sleek ship slicing through the calm sea, the pink beach, the smiling people sitting under the yellow umbrellas were real and so were the waiters approaching with refreshments. This was merely a colorful publicity shot taken at a paradisiacal place. Maggie looked up and read the letters over the storefront: Agnes Perollo's Sea and Air Travel.

She shrugged. Her glimpse of *Civitas Dei* this morning had simply been a glossy advertisement for a cruise. Pretty and enticing, but something she could no more afford than the shops along Madison Avenue.

Chapter Six

The next day was a nightmare. Ms. Noune suffered a setback in the first round of Weiss vs. Goldstein when she learned that the judge had tossed out several key grievances. Her clients were bitter and Ms. Noune was angry, deciding that Margaret Maghpye's research had been inadequate.

Storming into the office of an associate, Steve Brace, Ms. Noune fully expected him to corroborate her complaint of shoddy fact finding. They shared Maggie's services and Steve would have to be solidly in her corner if she planned to reprimand her. However, after leafing through the file, he declared that the research had been thorough.

"You might have utilized it better," he suggested with a wry smile.

Laura Noune left his office, livid. This was a slap in the face. Steve Brace was only an associate, of course, but he was a Harvard man, which carried some weight around here. In fact, she'd been surprised last year when he was passed over and *she* had made partner. Of course, she suspected that her rise over him was due to her gender; all firms had to have at least one female in their letterhead. She also suspected that the senior partners, Mr. Goodman and Mr. Barr, were watching her and had perhaps already heard about the fiasco in Judge Morano's chambers. Somehow she would now have to divert the blame. One way to do that was to get rid of Margaret Maghpye; let the senior partners believe Maggie had screwed up. They wouldn't give it a moment's thought. Paralegals were a dime a dozen. There was no shortage.

But how did one fire an employee who'd been here for twelve years? Did Maggie have friends among the lower echelon in the firm? If unceremoniously dismissed, would some meddlesome soul begin to raise questions? Might Ms. Maghpye sue to keep her job, forcing Laura Noune to explain her action to the partners? It was probably better to work Maggie till she cried "Uncle" and quit on her own accord. She was a renter with no mortgage, and was definitely not on the hook at Bergdorf or Saks. She would get another job. Her type always survived. Laura Noune and her husband might not. They had gone out on a limb when they bought that four-bedroom house with a pool on Field Terrace in Irvington. Both were attorneys but neither one could afford to lose cases. Disgruntled clients might seek the services of competing law firms, of which there was no shortage either.

After leaving work at six-thirty, something again drew Maggie down toward Second Avenue. She was carrying a pile of cases to read at home, for although she had again stayed past her regular quitting time, she had not completed the enormous amount of research Ms. Noune suddenly required. Maggie hoped the extra workload signaled that a pay raise was in the pipeline. She was due for one. Perhaps Ms. Noune wanted to test her in order to justify it. Well, her boss could rest easy. Maggie would earn it. She didn't mind working at home. It didn't interfere with her social life. She didn't have any. She was a certified loner.

Stopping a moment in front of Agnes Perollo's Sea & Air Travel before cutting over to First Avenue, she again gazed at the wonderful window displays, captivated by the large center poster in particular. The balmy scene warmed her and the white ship on the tranquil blue sea beckoned her. There were several similar pictures displayed, smaller than the one in the middle, and each ship carried a lofty name: *The Caribbean Countess. Viking Princess. Ocean Star.* And why not? All were sufficiently imposing to warrant royal monikers.

Maggie stood transfixed in a pleasant reverie while an icy blast from the East River whipped at the hem of her coat, which she had meticulously brushed clean before going to work this morning. Oddly enough, she didn't feel the cold tonight; maybe because the bright, tropical scenes were so mesmerizing and so incredibly beautiful they took the sting out of the wind. The door to a beach cabana stood open, inviting her toward it. She heaved a deep sigh.

If only...perhaps if I get that raise...then maybe...

Chapter *Seven*

"Can I help you?" A prematurely gray-haired woman wearing a black *boucle* suit with a beige turtleneck, looked up from her computer the minute Maggie entered the store, the small bell above the door announcing her.

"Oh...?" The heat inside the travel agency felt so good and only now did Maggie realize that she had walked in out of the cold. "Uh...actually no. I'm just browsing," she uttered automatically, same as when shopping at Macy's till she found something to try on. Of course there was nothing to try on in a travel agency but surely one was allowed to browse. She bit her lips, shifted the weight of the files under her arm and studied some tropical scenes on a wall opposite the window, all the while wondering how best to extricate herself and politely leave.

"This is the perfect time of year to plan a getaway," the agent said in a perky voice. "Can I interest you in a warm weather cruise? The temperature in Nassau is in the eighties. A far cry from what we are expecting in New York tonight."

Maggie shuddered. She had heard the forecast.

"It'll break the record," Ms. Perollo continued. "Not since 1974 has it been this cold so early in November. It kind of makes one eager to escape, doesn't it? Think about it. For only sixteen hundred dollars you can spend seven days and seven nights, cruising the Caribbean with all you can eat in a choice of five world-class restaurants. Around the clock entertainment. First-run movies. Casinos. Exotic ports-of-call." After listing a number of additional amenities, Ms. Perollo closed the sales pitch with a wink, "The warm sun comes free with the package."

Maggie didn't know how to respond. She was still trying to think of a way to leave. She had to buy food for dinner. She had to catch a bus. Unfortunately, her silence acted as encouragement.

"A cruise is the ultimate vacation," Ms. Perollo said, now handing Maggie some material from a pile on her desk – visual aids did wonders in closing a deal. "It's an all-inclusive luxury floating spa and resort. Completely carefree. No taxis. No hassles with foreign languages. No getting lost in strange towns while trying to find restaurants or museums. Everything is at your fingertips onboard ship. If you ask me, the best cruise right now is on The Mexican Star where you get eleven days and nights for only seventeen hundred dollars. A real bargain. It's a relatively small ship. Only seven hundred passengers compared with the twenty-five hundred on most Caribbean cruises. Of course The Mexican Star has the same stellar entertainment. Being smaller it has only one dining room, but it's a beauty with three French chefs. It leaves from San Diego with ports-of-call in Acapulco, Salina Cruz, and Tapachula."

"It sails from San Diego?" Maggie sighed dreamily; she and David had spent their honeymoon there. She put Ms. Noune's bundle of folders down on an empty chair and leafed through the brochures Ms. Perollo had given her. "Hmm, what wonderful cabins," she mused out loud, studying one with a private deck and a cozy sitting area with sofa and chairs, wet bar, and a flat screen TV. The space looked larger than her entire apartment. There were also pictures of a mouthwatering deck buffet plus the aforementioned dining room with its French chefs posing in tall white hats. Another picture showcased a sparkling pool, people lounging around it in colorful canvas deck chairs.

If only...

"The flight from New York is included in the price, of course," Agnes Perollo said, seeing the dreamy expression on her potential customer. "It's truly a terrific deal. The best offered at the moment. But...uh, wait a minute. Let me just see..." Puckering her brow, she consulted her computer screen and hit some keys on the keypad. "Oh, dear! I was afraid of that. There are only a few cabins left and this close to the departure date they will go fast. But I can put a twenty-four hour hold on one. The ship leaves San Diego on November the 23rd. A few days before Thanksgiving. Is that a problem for you? Have you already made plans?"

Maggie shook her head and estimated that the roundtrip flight to San Diego alone cost five to six hundred dollars, making the cruise itself very reasonable.

"If you opt for a semi private cabin, you can do better on the price," Ms. Perollo added, figuring from the way this customer was dressed that she didn't have money to throw around.

"That would be nice." Maggie pretended to mull it over. Hey, who was she kidding? No matter how the cabin was sliced up, it was more than she could handle.

"Look, let me hold a spot for you. This Mexican cruise is very popular. In fact, I'll let you in on a little secret." Having sized-up this customer as a single woman, Ms. Perollo threw in some additional bait. "A disproportional number of gentlemen are booked on this cruise. The ratio is very favorable. Are you interested in meeting new people?" This question invariably hooked lonely women who knew perfectly well that "people" in this context was synonymous with eligible men.

Maggie played-out the string. "I'm not looking, but if a nice man were to approach me, I guess I wouldn't toss him overboard."

Agnes Perollo laughed and pressed her point. "Romance is as assured as sunshine on this cruise. Even if you're undecided now and book a cabin, you have nothing to lose. The reservation automatically cancels itself out after twenty-four hours unless you secure it with a credit card." She gave Maggie some additional literature dealing with the Mexican trip. "I hope you decide to take this one. It's tailor made for you."

Maggie added the new brochures to the pile she already held in her hands. "Do the cabins look like this?" she asked, pointing to the picture she had studied in detail.

"More or less. But this late in the booking, I can't guarantee which deck you'll be on."

"That's all right. As long as it's above the waterline," Maggie quipped, referencing her distaste of closed-in spaces. She was beginning to enjoy this charade. She had no intention of going on a cruise, of course, had absolutely no available funds, but it couldn't hurt to pretend for a few more minutes. The telephone wasn't ringing. This small agency did not appear to be busy.

"Here, take this material as well." Ms. Perollo gave Maggie some paraphernalia pertaining to cruise wear and information about sightseeing in Acapulco and other ports-of-call. Turning back to her computer, she said, "Give me your name and I'll hold a cabin."

"Margaret Maghpye." Maggie hoped the agent wouldn't also ask for her address and phone number; revealing that information would be more of a commitment and might be followed-up with annoying calls, such as those from telemarketers.

"Could you spell it, please?"

"M. A. R."

"Just your last name."

"Oh, sure. M. A. G. H. P. Y. E."

"Thank you." Ms. Perollo turned away from the screen and looked over the rim of her glasses at Maggie. "Stop in tomorrow by this time if you want to keep the reservation." She pushed her business card into Maggie's already full hands. "Or just call me with a credit card number. Don't forget, I can only hold the cabin for twenty-four hours."

"I'll stop in after work," Maggie promised, deciding she'd better take the Madison Avenue bus home tomorrow to avoid being spotted around here. There was no way she could take a cruise, something she didn't want to admit to Ms. Perollo's face. She had accepted the pretty brochures with the idea of keeping them on her coffee table at home, where she'd occasionally enjoy looking at them.

And maybe someday...

Chapter *eight*

Buoyed by fantasies of sandy beaches and swaying palm trees, Maggie climbed the five flights up to her apartment without the usual feeling that her feet were encased in cement. She unlocked the door, put down the bag of groceries she'd bought after leaving Agnes Perollo's agency, kicked off her shoes and stepped into the living room, putting the pile of travel brochures on top of the old TV, a relic she never watched because all she got was snow. Before the building was wired for cable she got a few good channels; now it cost sixty-nine dollars a month to watch the news and sitcoms. So far she had resisted shelling out good money for bad shows.

Shrugging off her coat, she hung it in the hall closet along with her hat and scarf before bending down to pick up the groceries. Suddenly an eerie sensation pricked at the back of her neck, dispersing her pleasant dreams of sunny days, blue seas and foreign ports. She felt a chill, not from the cold apartment, she was accustomed to the temperamental radiators; something else was amiss. She made a quick check of her belongings. She had her purse, gloves, groceries, the cruise information, the...

Ms. Noune's files?

With a shivering alarm, Maggie tore open the front door, praying she had put the files in the stairwell while unlocking the three dead bolts. She hadn't! There was nothing on the landing. Her heart sank, realizing that she had left the files at the travel agency. Dear God, she now clearly remembered putting them down on a chair next to Agnes Perollo's desk, and also remembered leaving without them; her hands full of travel brochures, her head so full of dreams of tropical places that she had neglected to be vigilant. Sweet Jesus! The files were highly confidential. How on earth could she have been so absent-minded? She was not in the habit of losing things. In a state of escalating panic, she opened the closet and grabbed her overcoat, sending some metal hangers clattering to the floor. Foregoing hat, scarf and gloves, she snatched her vinyl tote, stuffed her feet back into her shoes, and barged through the front door. Racing down the stairs, she realized she had forgotten to lock up. But never mind. She had nothing worth stealing and almost wished someone would take the old TV set off her hands.

Panting like a marathoner, Maggie reached Second Avenue. She stepped off the curb and into the street, stretching her neck, looking for signs of an approaching bus. She saw one but it was several blocks away and, unfortunately, a man in a wheelchair was waiting at her stop, which meant the driver would first have to lower a platform and hoist the invalid onto the bus before anyone else could board; an activity that took precious time. Maggie couldn't wait. Ms. Perollo might close before she got there. She would have to splurge on a taxi.

Minutes later she was banging on the door to the travel agency. No one answered. The place was locked. Agnes Perollo had gone home. A small light had been left on and through the window Maggie could see the files. She rattled the door in the desperate hope that perhaps Ms. Perollo was still in there somewhere. No such luck, and if she continued testing the door, an alarm might sound. Having left the files was bad enough; to compound that mistake by being arrested for breaking and entering was plain dumb. She would have to come back in the morning on her way to the office, which meant she couldn't work on the files tonight. She could imagine the scope of Ms. Noune's anger. After this offense any pay raise was dead in the water.

Defeated, Maggie went back home, taking some comfort in the fact that at least the files weren't lost. Plain as day, they were on the same chair where she had left them. They would be safe there until tomorrow morning.

Chapter *nine*

Business Hours:
Mon. through Fri. 10 am to 7 pm
Sat. 11 am to 5 pm
Closed Sundays.

Maggie stared at the small lettering on the door. She hadn't noticed the sign last night and wished Agnes Perollo's home number was on her business card so she could call her, explain the emergency, and ask her to please come and open up early. It was only 8:30. She had to make a quick decision. She could wait here till ten o'clock, retrieve the files and face Ms. Noune's wrath for again being late, or she could go to the office without the files and face her fury for their temporary misplacement.

Maggie concluded it was too cold to wait around. Better go to the office empty-handed, hide out in the law library, work on other cases, and basically keep out of Ms. Noune's sight until ten o'clock when she could use her coffee break to run back here. Once she had the files, all she had to do was concoct a story as to why she hadn't worked on them last night. She could claim a migraine, which might fly although it was well known that Ms. Noune believed any employee complaint of illness was imaginary.

"I need the McCormick custody case!" Ms. Noune exited her office and confronted Maggie in the process of taking off her coat. Maggie spun around. When she'd arrived moments ago and found Ms. Noune's door closed, she had cherished the hope that she was still on the Metro North train and hadn't arrived yet.

"The McCormick case? Yes, of course." Maggie dropped her purse into the drawer of her desk and turned toward the file room.

"Where are you going? The McCormick case is in that batch of files you took home last night. I need the transcript along with the Weiss vs. Goldstein case. Did you find the paragraphs where Mr. Goldstein contradicts himself? It's crucial. I'm due in judge's chambers at eleven."

"Right...uh..." Maggie began perspiring as waves of heat swept over her, her discomfort not helped by the fact that Ms. Noune looked impeccable. Didn't that woman ever sweat? Incredibly intense, prone to fits of anger, she looked cool as a cucumber, her herringbone designer suit without a hint of a crease or a speck of lint. Maggie cleared her throat. It was counterproductive to tell a fib about a migraine, which wouldn't explain the absence of the files, only the fact that she hadn't worked on them. She had no choice now but to come clean. It was not yet nine o'clock. It would be another hour before the travel agency opened.

"Actually, I don't have the files at the moment," she said, squaring her shoulders and facing her nemesis, all the while trying to keep her voice even.

Ms. Noune's finely penciled eyebrows jumped clear to her blond hairline. "What do you mean?"

"I don't have them. But I know where they are."

"Well, then go get them!"

"I can't until ten o'clock."

"Ten o'clock? I need them now. Where are they?"

"Uh..."

"Yes?"

"Well, unfortunately, I...I left them at a travel agency on Second Avenue last night. They are perfectly safe. Under lock and key. I'll pick them up the minute the place opens."

"You mean to tell me that confidential legal records are floating around some two bit travel agency?" Ms. Noune's voice rose, her blue eyes taking on the color of steel. Vera stopped typing, turned and gaped at the scene.

"No one's tampered with them. They're perfectly safe."

"Safe? You've got to be joking. You're finished here!"

"Huh?"

"You're fired! Clean out your desk. Your pay will be in the mail."

The dismissal felt like a punch in the stomach and suddenly Maggie couldn't breathe. She felt ill. She reached for the back of her chair to steady herself, determined not to go weak in the knees in front of Ms. Noune. "I'm s...sorry," she croaked, tasting bile in her mouth. "I'll get the files the minute the agency opens. I guarantee that no one has touched them."

"I repeat. You're finished here! Clear out your things and consider yourself lucky that I don't press charges against you for negligence!"

"Uh...uh, all right." Maggie's head swam and her legs trembled. *Fired...* Dear God, who would hire her now? The job market was super competitive. It had been twelve years since she'd last searched for a job and it was bound to be more of a battle now that she was older. Would Ms. Noune give her a recommendation? Obviously not. Would one of the partners? Probably not. Maybe Mr. Goodman, but after being fired it would take a lot of nerve to ask him. "I'd like to go and pick up the files before I clean out my desk," she said, fighting for composure. "It's the least I can do. Please..." She hated to grovel, but desperation had a way of making fools of people.

Ms. Noune looked as if she was about to spit, not a becoming expression for someone so well dressed. "*You* pick up the files? Over my dead body. Tell Vera where they are. I'll send a man from security." Ms. Noune turned on her heels and went into her office, closing the door behind her with a loud and decisive click.

Chapter *ten*

Numb and shaking, Maggie cleaned out her desk, stuffed her personal effects into her brown vinyl tote, gave Vera the address of Agnes Perollo Sea and Air Travel, and said goodbye.

"I know a good employment agency on Third and 42nd," Vera whispered as Maggie put on her coat. "My friend just got a job through them. The place is called Jobs Aplenty. Go and fill out an application. When they call here to verify your employment, I won't put the call through to Ms. Noune. I'll put the caller on hold and then come back on the line and pretend to be her. I can do a pretty good impersonation of her nasal twang. I'll tell them you left on your own and that you were terrific and we were very sorry to lose you."

"Thanks, Vera," Maggie said, tears burning the back of her eyes. It was painful to have a kind person, half her age, witness her humiliation. Struggling against a churning sea of emotions, Maggie took her tote, said a final good-bye to Vera, and turned to leave. As she walked through the outer office, she passed the receptionist with barely a nod and continued out through the gleaming doors of *Goodman, Barr & Noune* without a backward glance. Having been so unceremoniously dismissed, she didn't think it was necessary to observe protocol and walk around and say goodbye to anyone, especially not to the senior partners.

From force of habit she took the stairs to the street, her heart sinking with every step. Emerging into the blustery November morning, her mind was blank and an obstruction like a tennis ball was lodged in her throat. Swallowing convulsively, she hung the tote over her shoulder, buttoned her coat, fished out her gloves, and pulled her knitted cap down over her ears before walking slowly up toward Fifth Avenue. Catching the bus on Madison and going home was out of the question; weekends and evenings in that dreary apartment were bad enough. To go directly to the employment agency Vera had suggested was equally depressing. She couldn't bear to fill out applications or face an interviewer today. Being right back to where she'd started twelve years ago was a painful realization. She needed time to adjust. This morning she'd gotten the ax. Tomorrow was soon enough to feel the sting. It wouldn't hurt to take a day off.

Aimlessly, she trudged south along Fifth Avenue, melting into the throng of shoppers looking at the colorful store displays. The windows at Saks were dark, the glass covered, but there was activity and anticipation behind the brown paper, and it was only a matter of days now before it would be peeled away, displaying glittering holiday scenes unlike the inside of Maggie's head, which would remain dark and shrouded with the knowledge that she was down and out.

She had not felt this hopeless since the day David died.

Without purpose, she crossed Fifth Avenue, now walking back uptown past Rockefeller Center. It, too, was being prepared for the holidays. Autumn's faded chrysanthemums were being raked from the raised flowerbeds to make way for holly and trumpeting angels. The fifty-foot tree from someone's yard upstate had not yet arrived. Traditionally, it would be trucked in during the Thanksgiving weekend.

Thanksgiving...? Simone...?

Maggie stopped, stared absently at the pedestrians pushing past her, and decided to call Simone Carrel, friend since her first days in New York when they had lived in the same building. Simone was married, had three sons and a full time job. She and her brood lived in Queens but she worked in Manhattan, keeping books at her father-in-law's print shop on West 56th Street, where her husband also worked with the expectation of taking over the business. Maggie and Simone met at least once a week at various lunch places, where sandwiches cost six-fifty and service was sufficiently quick to accommodate their forty-minute lunch hour. On an occasional Saturday they'd go shopping or see a movie.

Stopping at what passed for a phone booth – a metal box on a stand – most of them vandalized with receivers dangling inches from the sidewalk, Maggie found one that still had a dial tone and called Simone at work, all the while thinking that maybe she'd get a cell phone once she got a new job.

"Hi! It's me!"

"Hey, Maggie! How's it going?"

28

"Not too bad. How about yourself?"

"Actually, I'm sitting here daydreaming. I really should quit my job and stay at home. You know, keep an eye on things and get to know the kids before they leave the nest. I've said this before, but the trouble that lurks when my back's turned can only be imagined by those tending toward the ghoulish."

"I won't even try," Maggie said, forcing an unnatural chuckle. She didn't feel like laughing. "Quitting your job sounds like a good idea. I'm thinking of that myself."

"Really? Ms. Noune has finally driven you nuts?"

"Yes..." Maggie's pride didn't allow her to admit she'd been fired; she certainly wouldn't mention it over the telephone. "I'm taking a long lunch today just to irritate her."

"Lunch? This early? You gotta be kidding. It's only...what?"

Maggie glanced at her Timex wristwatch. "Ten thirty."

"Okay, I can slip away. Let's meet at eleven."

This was precisely what Maggie had hoped for.

Half an hour later she and Simone were seated in a small booth at a deli on West 57th Street between Fifth and Sixth, eating pita bread stuffed with avocado, cheese, and bean sprouts; sliced tomatoes and dressing on the side. They had gotten a jump on the lunch crowd. By noon a long line invariably started to form. This place served organic food, which everyone craved nowadays.

Simone was a seamless talker, and after she ran out of stories and had nothing more to report about her family or shows she and Howard and seen, she reminded Maggie to come out for Thanksgiving dinner. It was a pleasant yearly ritual where Maggie took the train to Queens, carrying a large pecan pie from Eli's.

"Thanks Sim. But I might have to miss your feast this year."

"*What?* Why?" Simone sputtered, her mouth full. She looked bewildered, swallowed, and wiped her chin on a thin paper napkin she pulled from the chrome dispenser on the table. "If you're planning to accept another invitation, forget it! I won't hear of it. Our Thanksgiving won't be the same without you. It certainly won't be the same without your pecan pie."

"I'll have Eli's deliver one," Maggie grinned.

"I'm just kidding. We'll miss you. Not the pie. So what's up? Don't tell me you've met someone who's more fun than my family."

"No one can come close," Maggie said in all honesty, adding, "I'm toying with the idea of taking a trip. Maybe I'll go on a cruise." Even before she'd finished that flippant remark, she wondered how and why that crazy idea had suddenly tumbled out. Maybe it was just a need to pretend and to chitchat about something pleasant in order to postpone mentioning that she'd been fired.

"A cruise? Really?"

Nodding, Maggie avoided meeting Simone's gaze while allowing a subconscious wish to usurp her common sense. She was talking nonsense, of course, and wasn't thinking clearly, but who could blame her? It wasn't every day one was handed a pink slip. The jolt had obviously addled her brain and loosened her tongue. A cruise, even the thirty-dollar Circle Line trip around Manhattan Island, was out of the question.

"A cruise..." Simone repeated, a dreamy look in her eyes. "How fabulous! I can't remember the last time you vacationed outside the city. You've always claimed it's more fun to explore the home turf. Tribeca and SoHo, for instance."

"I still believe that."

"But now you're spreading your wings? Looking for new horizons?"

"I suppose so. Plus, I have some extra time on my hands."

"What do you mean?"

"Well, okay..." Maggie heaved a deep sigh. "I might as well tell you. I'm not just taking a long lunch. Truth be known, I have all day. I was let go this morning."

"You were *fired?*" Simone snapped her fingers. "Just like that!"

"Yes. Can you believe it? Twelve years with the same firm and suddenly I'm out on my ear."

"That's not fair. Can they do that to you? Did they at least give you severance pay?"

"I don't know. I'll find out once my check arrives."

"Well, if they don't include it you can sue."

"I don't want to. I want nothing more to do with Ms. Noune. Besides, how do you sue an attorney?"

"I don't know. But we could ask Howard. Why don't you come back to the print shop with me."

Maggie shook her head. "Thanks anyway. I'd rather fantasize about some pleasant adventure for the rest of the day. Tomorrow I will begin making the rounds of employment agencies, which will be difficult enough without the baggage of a lawsuit."

"May I ask what brought on this sudden dismissal?"

"I inadvertently left some files at a travel agency last night."

"They're gone?"

"No, they were still there this morning. The place was closed so I couldn't get them. Someone from the office will collect them." Maggie glanced at her watch. "I guess they've been picked up by now."

"So what's the big deal? That's not enough to lose ones job over."

"I didn't think so either. Maybe Ms. Noune was just looking for an excuse to get rid of me. She's never liked me. Bad chemistry or something like that." Maggie shrugged. "I don't really know. Things were different before she joined the firm and when I worked for Mr. Goodman. I wish he had never assigned me to her."

"And now before you take another job, you want a vacation. Is that it?"

"Yes. A restful cruise might knock a few years off my face. Going back into the job market is bad enough without looking like I'm about to apply for social security."

"Hey, watch it! You're younger than me." Simone ran a hand through her short hair done in a poodle perm, a style that went out of fashion long ago except she'd been too busy to notice. "At least you aren't going gray yet."

"Thanks only to those magic potions I buy at Duane Reade."

"Well, I could color my hair black every night and still wake up like this in the morning." Simone pointed to some gray stands. "What you see here is courtesy of my kids. Peanut butter in the sofa. Bloody noses. Fights with the riffraff next door. Lately it's girls calling at all hours. Not to mention my mother-in-law."

"I'd change places with you in a minute," Maggie sighed. "I always wanted to have a family. It just never worked out."

"Well, I'd like to trade places with you. I've never told you this but I envy your independence. You're free as a bird and you have an apartment in the city. Believe me, we only live in Queens because we can't afford Manhattan."

"It's not all it's cracked up to be."

"Says who?"

"Anyone paying the exorbitant rents."

"Funny you should mention rent. You know my niece Lisa from Pittsburgh?" Maggie nodded; Lisa, her brother and parents were regulars at Simone's Thanksgiving table. "She's moving here. My sister and brother-in-law promised she could try living in New York once she finished two years of college. That time has come. She'll be staying with us while she looks for a rental and a job. I hope neither takes too long. Our house is crowded as it is."

"If I take a cruise she can have my place while I'm away," Maggie offered.

"Really? You mean it?"

"Sure. Why not? Actually, even if I don't take a trip, and if Lisa is game to bunk on my sofa and maybe pay a little rent, she's welcome. It would help tide me over until I find a new job."

"Lisa would kill to be in the city right off the bat. She's not keen on commuting from Queens and it would also be a lot easier for her to look for work if she were right in the hub of things. What sort of rent are you paying these days?"

"Fourteen hundred a month. Do you think she'd be willing to pay a little of that?"

"Are you kidding? Her parents are paying her expenses until she's employed. They can afford it. They let her put three diamond studs in each ear and a gold ring through one of her eyebrows. That kind of self-mutilation doesn't come cheap. Here's the deal. Lisa will pay the entire amount if you take the cruise and she has the apartment all to herself. Once you return, or if you don't go, you guys can split the rent fifty-fifty until she finds her own place. How long is the cruise?"

"About two weeks."

"Perfect. Done!" Simone slapped her palm down on the table so hard that two waiters came rushing over. "It's okay, fellows," she held up her hands, "I was just making a point." They withdrew and Simone got back to business. "So where were we? Oh, yes. You've got yourself a temporary roommate. But, now tell me about this trip you're thinking of taking. I'd love to go on a cruise. I've often tried to sell Howard on the idea but we always end up spending our vacations in Florida. It's convenient and it's free because we use his parents' condo. So when do you leave?"

"A couple of days before Thanksgiving."

"Where to? The Bahamas?"

"No, I'm thinking of taking a Mexican cruise. It's longer than most of the Caribbean cruises. Extra days on board for approximately the same fare." As she was saying this, Maggie began to actually believe that she might go. This was no longer idle conversation or wishful thinking. Lisa covering some of the rent made it possible.

"More bang for your buck, huh?"

"I guess you could say that."

"Margaret Maghpye!" Simone laughed and pointed a finger accusingly. "Still practical to the bone."

Maggie smiled secretly. Simone didn't know just how practical she had to be. She was not one to bare her shortcomings, financial or otherwise, even to a close friend. At the time of David's illness, Simone had believed that insurance took care of everything and Maggie had never enlightened her.

Chapter twelve

It was two o'clock that very afternoon when Maggie walked into the travel agency on Second Avenue. Agnes Perollo was wearing the same black suit as yesterday but with a different turtleneck, a ghastly pea green color.

"Hi!" Ms. Perollo greeted her like a favorite niece. "You left some folders here last night. A uniformed individual picked them up this morning. He said he was from your office. I hope it was all right to let him have them."

"Yes, of course."

"Okay. So..." Agnes Perollo clasped her hands together and looked expectantly at her customer, "you've decided to take the cruise?"

"Yes."

After lunching with Simone, Maggie had gone to Central Park where she strolled around the frozen duck pond marking its southern boundary. Few people were in the park and the paths were empty except for a couple of hardy New Yorkers walking their dogs dressed in the latest canine winter couture. Maggie's wool coat never quite kept her warm and she had to walk briskly to compensate, which meant her feet hurt in no time flat. But, sitting down on an icy bench was out of the question, so was going home in the middle of the afternoon. As long as she was out and about she could hold onto the high she felt after having lunch with Simone. Spending time with Simone had been as pleasant as always and had today yielded an unexpected windfall: someone to help pay the rent, making a warm weather cruise a reality.

Maggie remembered Lisa as a sweet kid and felt pretty sure she wouldn't trash the place, although she apparently enjoyed mutilating her face. Maggie also figured the apartment would accommodate two people as long as Lisa was content with sleeping on the sofa and didn't demand much closet space. For a long time Maggie had planned to install coat and hat hooks behind the front door; now she had the impetus to do it. She also had the impetus to take a real honest to goodness vacation, especially in view of the fact that she was practically getting the trip for free. Instead of a month's rent payable to the landlord, she'd write a check to Perollo Sea & Air Travel, drawing the difference from her savings. Of course she would also have to spring for a swimsuit and assorted cruise wear, but she could charge those purchases on her Macy's account and make minimum payments once she returned.

Chapter thirteen

The American Airlines flight from New York touched down at San Diego's Lindbergh Field at 8:30 in the evening on November the 22nd.

After getting her luggage, Maggie went out to the passenger pick-up area and waited for the courtesy bus that would take her to the Holiday Inn where she would spend the night. The same bus would bring her to the harbor in the morning, this shuttle service being part of the cruise package. However, the hotel room was an extra and unavoidable expense since no flights from New York arrived in time for a 10 a.m. ship boarding. On the return, she had a red-eye back to New York, which would give her an entire day to see San Diego unless her savings were depleted by that time because after paying for the trip, Agnes Perollo informed her about the "extras," such as tips for the ship's stewards, payable at the end of the journey since no money changed hands during the voyage. All she could eat was included in the price, as were shows, movies, lectures, and classes. But cocktails, beer and wine, would be charged to her credit card, as would bus excursions in ports-of-call and shipboard gambling. Of course, Maggie did not plan to visit the casino. She was not the sort to get lucky. Her entire life was an unbroken chain of bad luck. No cruise would change that.

In fact, her decision to embark on this adventure was something she had begun to regret during the two weeks leading up to the trip, when she realized that along with new clothes, she needed to apply for a passport and pay double for rush service. Moreover, in a moment of vain frivolity, she had splurged on a salon haircut and highlights in order to look good on her passport picture. As it turned out, she looked true to character: insane. Her large blue eyes, by far her best feature, came out looking black and unfocussed while her mouth was twisted in a weird half smile; neither was helped by the professional hair style and color.

Tossing and turning in her bed each and every night, worrying about what she had done, she was unable to sleep and unable to eat. Instead of looking for a job, she was shopping for cruise wear. Her loss of appetite and sleep cost her a dress size, but at least she could now load up on all that free food and return to New York at her normal weight. The weight loss showed in her face as well. It was less round. Cheekbones she hadn't seen in years were again noticeable and, except for her passport picture, her eyes seemed brighter. Of course that was probably entirely due to angst.

By the time the courtesy bus pulled up to Pier 7 at the San Diego harbor the next morning, a line was already forming on the wharf where ropes guided passengers toward the large docked ship. The minute Maggie stepped off the bus among others who'd spent the night at the Holiday Inn, a steward tagged her luggage, explaining that it would be taken directly to her cabin. A wonderful convenience, she mused, and took a deep and leisurely breath of the sea air spiced with the smell of kelp and boat tar. The sun filtering through the morning mist felt warm on her face and as she gazed in wonder at the huge white ship, she felt an uncommon anticipation. Suddenly she wouldn't trade this moment for anything in the world. She felt as though she were just now waking up after a long sleep, fully rested, and eager to face the day. For the first time in years she felt light-hearted, giddy almost. And why not? She was about to board a luxury liner and sail the vast Pacific Ocean, embarking on a brand new and wondrous experience.

Considering the great number of passengers, check-in went smoothly. Everyone in the line was talkative, cementing friendships right and left. An elegant silver haired women who looked to be in her late sixties, dressed in a stylish beige summer suit – matching Ferragamo purse and shoes – stood in line ahead of Maggie. Inasmuch as the family directly in front of her had three children in tow, she quickly made her choice, turned around and introduced herself.

"Hi!" she smiled, offering her hand. "I'm Francine Wirth."

"How do you do?" Maggie shook her hand, now glad that she had squandered her Macy's credit on clothes, for surely her white cotton blazer over the blue twill slacks and red tank top made her look cruise worthy; only her brown vinyl tote might be considered out of place. "I'm Margaret Maghpye. But, please, just call me Maggie."

"Where are you from, Maggie?"

"New York City."

"Oh, my home town! I was born and raised there. My husband and I lived in New York until he retired and we moved to Florida. He loved the easy Florida lifestyle. Golfing and sailing. Sadly he didn't enjoy it for very long. I'm widowed now. I try to get back up north at least twice a year to see my son and his family in Connecticut."

"You lost your husband recently?"

"No. It's been quite a while. Twenty years to be exact. He died after a long struggle with melanoma."

Maggie sucked in her breath. She, too, had been widowed because of that disease. But inasmuch as she had married and divorced twice since then, she could hardly pass herself off as a widow and therefore didn't mention it. "Where in Florida do you live?" she asked instead.

"Boca Raton. But I spend a lot of time on these ships. I stopped counting after forty cruises."

"Forty!" Maggie said, surprised. "That must be some kind of a record."

"Hardly." Francine Wirth shrugged. "Some people retire to a life of cruising. Their cabin becomes their condo."

"I can't believe that." Maggie was again amazed.

"It's true." Francine Wirth turned and pointed up toward the mid deck where several people could be seen, leaning their elbows on the railing, leisurely perusing the boarding process. "See! There they are. They are watching their new neighbors move in. Personally, and as much as I enjoy each and every cruise, I couldn't do it full time. I'd miss my friends and my life in Florida."

"I was in Fort Lauderdale once. Spring Break during my senior year in college. Actually..." Maggie grinned sheepishly, "that's a time I'd rather forget about."

"We've all done things that are better forgotten," Francine said, looking over Maggie's shoulder and suddenly waving at someone back in the line. "Mildred!" she called out. "What are you doing way back there? Come on up! Maggie, would you mind if my friend cuts in?"

"Of course not."

Mildred, overweight and over seventy, elbowed her way through the line, carrying several small bags she didn't trust to the stewards. She was wearing a pink linen pants suit and a western-style hat, both of which would have looked better on Francine Wirth who was tall and slim with perfect posture.

Dropping her bags, Mildred embraced her friend before Francine did the introductions. "Mildred, this is Margaret Maghpye from New York City. Maggie, meet Mildred Fischer from Chicago."

"Hi!" Mildred smiled broadly and pumped Maggie's hand.

"How do you do?" Maggie said and suspected that the dark brown curls peeking out from under Mildred Fischer's hat was a wig. The strands were too thick and glossy for a woman her age.

"So, how many cruises have you been on?" Mildred removed her rhinestone-rimmed sunglasses a moment to study Maggie.

"This is my first."

"You don't say. Well, Francine and I are old sea dogs. We both took to the sea after we were widowed. We met on a cruise fifteen years ago and have averaged two or three every year since. Of course, enticing Francine to come along on this particular one," she winked at her friend, "required a bit of work."

"Nonsense." Francine waved her hand dismissively. "I was eager to come."

"No you weren't." Mildred wagged her finger. "You were hesitant because of the long cross country flight from Miami to San Diego. Don't deny it. But at least you traveled at a civilized hour. I had to get up at the crack of dawn this morning to catch my flight from Chicago. Maybe next time I'll come out the day before and stay with you at the Westgate. Was it comfortable?"

"Very," Francine said.

Mildred turned back to Maggie. "The trips Francine and I regularly take leave either from Miami or New York and generally sail in the afternoon. This early morning departure is a bit of change for both of us. Other than that we know the ropes. All the ships are similar. They differ mainly in the number of passengers they carry. If there's anything you want to know, just ask us."

"Thank you." Maggie was pleased to have run into such friendly traveling companions even before boarding.

While the two older women fell into reminiscing about past cruises, Maggie looked around the dock. Dapper white uniforms were everywhere; there seemed to be more ship personnel than travelers. Adjacent to the queue she was in, a special section was cordoned off for people boarding in wheelchairs tended by their spouses. One infirm passenger appeared confused, another looked impatient, and one was sleeping, her head lolling on her chests. All were elderly as were their companions, with the exception of one. The man was elderly, no question about that, but the woman with him was not a day over thirty. She was either a trophy wife or his daughter. After giving her a second look, Maggie decided she was the former because a daughter would show more concern. This woman never once bent down to inquire about his comfort. He sat unprotected in the sun, while she wore wraparound sunglasses and a wide brimmed hat to protect her flowing black tresses. Her red slacks were skintight; ditto her white crocheted sweater. Maggie could swear she was wearing a black bra under the tight sleeveless number, clearly a sign of poor planning, as were the strapless gold sandals on her feet, for how would she ever maneuver on deck in four-inch heels?

Francine Wirth noticed Maggie studying the mismatched couple.

"Mildred and I have sailed the seven seas with that gentleman," she said, nodding discreetly in his direction. "We really ought to go over and say hello. We knew his first wife. A lovely lady. He was widowed two years ago and we have yet to meet the new Mrs. McKiernan." Sniffing with obvious disapproval, Francine went on. "She looks young enough to be an adopted child. Maggie, would you mind watching Mildred's stuff a second?"

"I'll be glad to."

"Come on!" Francine took her friend's arm and the two women left the line and walked over to greet William P. McKiernan.

After chatting a moment with their infirm friend and the woman he introduced as his bride, Sheila, Francine Wirth waved Maggie over. Mildred returned to her assortment of small valises and to guard their spot in line, while Maggie left to be introduced to this May-December couple.

"Call me Bill," the old gentleman said, reaching for Maggie's hand. His was cold and bony, but his smile was warm and Maggie saw remnants of handsome features in his face. "Once at sea everyone's on a first name basis so we might as well cut to the chase." He turned in the wheelchair. "Maggie, this is my wife, Sheila."

Sheila McKiernan mumbled a faint greeting without extending her hand and dismissed Maggie with a flick of her dark eyes from behind the smoky lenses of the Armani sunglasses. Her husband could do as he pleased and be chummy with these women, she didn't consider any of them worth her time. The first two were too old, and the younger one looked as if she'd gotten her outfit from the Sears catalogue. The brown vinyl tote was hideous.

"Not a very friendly sort," Francine commented as she and Maggie walked back to their spot in line.

"I don't suppose it's easy being the caretaker of an invalid. How old is he?"

"Bill?" Francine thought a moment. "I'd say he's in his late seventies. I noticed that up close his wife did not look quite the tender age she appeared from the distance."

"True." Maggie laughed. "She's at least thirty-four."

"Which is young enough to be his granddaughter. I can't imagine it's a love affair. But I suppose his wealth proved irresistible. Maybe he wasn't an invalid when they married? He was perfectly fine the last time I saw him on a cruise through the Panama Canal to Acapulco. He had been widowed for several months at that time. He and his wife never had any children. Maybe that's why he decided to marry one. The fact that he married so quickly doesn't really surprise me. It was no doubt a case of self-preservation. I distinctly recall a great number of women hanging around his neck on the trip I just mentioned. Men are fair game onboard and women become vultures around one that's single. To keep from being eaten alive, he probably figured he'd better marry before taking another cruise."

"His new wife will definitely discourage all comers," Maggie grinned.

Chapter Fifteen

Maggie's cabin did not look remotely like those in the brochures that Agnes Perollo had given her. The size of an elevator, it had bunk beds, no sofa and no flat screen TV. Maggie turned to the white uniformed steward, a young stocky Mexican with a shock of black hair, who had shown her along the narrow corridor on Deck Four; a level above the crew's quarters, she now learned.

"I think this is wrong," she said to him. "See..." she pulled the crumbled brochure from her purse. "My cabin is supposed to look like this."

"*Si*." He smiled.

Glad he saw her point, Maggie said, "Okay. Then please show me to the correct cabin. This obviously isn't it."

"*Si*." He was still smiling.

It occurred to Maggie that he hadn't understood her. "Do you speak English?"

"*Si*."

"Good. Then please take me to my cabin. The correct one." She showed him her boarding pass so he could see her name spelled out.

"*Si*," he said again and pointed to something behind the door just inside the cabin. Maggie saw her luggage. The dock porters had brought it here. Maybe she was in the right spot after all.

"*Muy bien...gracias*," she mumbled unenthusiastically. She had lived in New York long enough to pick up some Spanish vocabulary.

"*Buenos dias!*" the steward said and left to assist other passengers stepping off the elevator at the end of the corridor.

Maggie walked into her cabin, leaving the door open for the person she was supposed to share it with. But though it had saved her some money, she now regretted opting for a semi private room. She pivoted on her heels and looked around. The porthole was not exactly below the waterline but in any kind of a storm it would be. She felt a touch of claustrophobia. All her life she had avoided elevators, now she was going to sleep in one. There was no cozy sitting area, only a small built-in desk with a small chair tucked under it. She opened a door, believing it to be a closet, but saw that it was a lavatory the size of the one on her flight coming out, except this one included a shower.

Half an hour later, after she had unpacked and greeted various passengers from adjacent cabins who peeked in to introduce themselves, she began to suspect that maybe her small space would remain private. No new luggage was brought in, and when she heard the ship's horns bellow and heard people heading for the elevator to be topside at cast off, she became certain of it. The thought of having the cabin all to herself took the sting out of her initial disappointment with its size and décor.

The Mexican Star was underway. Maggie felt a slight rumbling under her feet, reminding her that she was on a low deck and also that she was missing the departure. She took her cardkey, shut the cabin door behind her and, avoiding the elevator, raced up the four flights of stairs to the main deck to stand at the railing among her fellow passengers watching the harbor, the sprawling city of San Diego, and the mountains rising behind its cluster of tall downtown buildings, slowly melt into a blur before disappearing altogether in the lingering morning haze. Gulls followed the ship out to sea, shrieking and gliding over its churning wake.

Back in her cabin, Maggie was rearranging her clothes, making use of both slim closets, when several flyers were slipped under her door. She eagerly bent down to pick them up. One announced that everyone must don life vests and report on deck for a mandatory safety drill at eleven o'clock. Another flyer listed the daily activities onboard, such as tai chi, yoga, bingo, bridge, and various lectures. Evening entertainment included dancing in the Coconut Lounge, the gambling casino, chamber music in the Atrium, and two art auctions, dates to be announced. The theater on the B Deck would alternate between live shows and movies; their schedules would be posted daily. A separate map showed where the various facilities were located, including the infirmary, shops, spa, and hair salon. One flyer dealt with the meal service. Breakfast was available, cafeteria style, in the Promenade Lounge or poolside on the top deck. A full lunch buffet was served on the main deck between the hours of twelve and two, and for those passengers who hankered for a more casual fare, the aft deck barbecued hamburgers and hot dogs during the same hours. Afternoon tea was served in the Atrium, while ice cream was available around the clock at several stations.

Reading the flyers, Maggie realized that for the first time in weeks she was ravenously hungry. She was also experiencing a sudden and insatiable appetite for adventure and leisure in equal measure. She felt strangely clean and rejuvenated. But mostly she was relieved that three thousand miles separated her from *Goodman, Barr & Noune*; ice, sleet, snow, sidewalk spit, and the Second Avenue bus.

Dinner the first evening onboard required dressy attire and thanks to Francine's and Mildred's chatter on the dock earlier, Maggie had gleaned that "dressy" simply meant no jeans and T-shirts. Silk slacks and a blouse, a cotton dress, were acceptable. Gentlemen were required to wear jackets in the dining room at all times, a tie being optional. The flyer went on to say that there would be a Captain's Ball – date to be announced – where black tie was mandatory, and gentlemen were advised about a rental service onboard for their convenience. Maggie hoped that her yellow knee-length chiffon with the flounced hem was formal enough for the ball because there was no mention of any gown rental service for women. She would ask Francine Wirth at the first opportunity. The woman was a walking information booth and had advised Maggie to sign up for the eight o'clock dinner seating.

"Six o'clock is much too early to eat," she'd explained just before they boarded the ship and split up, heading in different directions to their respective cabins. "That's when the families eat. The children make an awful racket."

Maggie had followed Francine's recommendation and now carefully observed the dress code as well, walking into the dining room on this first evening, wearing the sleeveless yellow chiffon with a white cotton bolero jacket so it wouldn't appear too formal. Originally two hundred dollars, the dress had been on sale at Macy's, and when she'd hesitated buying it – worrying about it being sleeveless – the salesgirl assured her that her arms were not the least bit flabby like other women her age. Maggie wasn't sure what the girl figured her for and didn't take it as a compliment, but bought the dress nonetheless.

The dining room looked spectacular and almost took her breath away. Shimmering white cloths, tall candles and flowers in the colors of the rainbow decorated every table. It was exactly like in the brochures. A uniformed steward wearing white gloves showed Maggie to her table where five other women were already seated. After introductions were made and as the first course, a succulent crab salad was served, Maggie glanced around the room for Francine and Mildred. She had expected to sit with them, figuring they would have saved her a spot; they had neglected to tell her about assigned seats.

When she spotted them at the captain's table, she realized of course that they were part of a well-heeled and frequent travelers clique. The McKiernans were seated there as well. Their table of ten had an equal number of the sexes, whereas all the other tables were predominantly women, including Maggie's. Men were not as plentiful as Agnes Perollo had claimed. But that was just as well; Maggie was not here to meet a man. She was long done with that part of her life. However, it appeared she couldn't escape the subject because once the women at her table felt at ease with each other – about the same time the rack of lamb was served – they spoke of nothing else.

One in particular, a rail thin woman of an indistinguishable age with a platinum bouffant hairdo, who introduced herself simply as Dorothy from Ojai – which she explained was north of Los Angeles – had apparently spent the first day at sea doing research and was delighted to now share the fruits of her labor. Looking discreetly around the dining room, she pointed to several widowed males, and with less enthusiasm nodded toward some divorced specimens she suspected were saddled with alimony payments, which made them eligible but not desirable.

"There are a number of gay passengers as well," she announced under her breath, nodding in the direction of the captain's table where an extremely handsome young man had his arm draped across the back of the chair of the elderly woman next to him. "I'll bet a hundred dollars he's gay. Why else would he be traveling with a dowager? I met the two of them while boarding. He's not her son. They are from Savannah. Their cabin is on the top deck, same as going first class, only no one calls it that anymore."

Rose Burke, a mousy little woman someone had once named Rose in the hope she would blossom, was, like Maggie, from New York and turned to her, saying, "It's always like that. I've been on a number of cruises. The good-looking men are invariably gay. You've got to identify them right away so you don't waste your time. Two men traveling together is a dead giveaway. See that gentleman over there at the table on our left?"

Maggie twisted her neck to look; the man was heavyset and balding. "What? You think he's gay?"

"No. But how old would you say he is?"

Maggie shrugged. "Sixty?"

"Yes, that's what I think." Rose Burke pursed her thin lips while her fingertips pushed at her sagging chin as if willing it to defy gravity. "Of course that makes him a good ten years older than me." She wasn't fooling Maggie; the gentleman in question was not a day older than Ms. Burke; if anything, it was the other way around. "I spoke with him earlier at the lunch buffet," Rose went on. "He's traveling alone. He's divorced...no children. But just so you know, I spotted him first him. I've got an exclusive." Rose Burke was in real estate back in New York. "If I don't make the sale in a day or two, I'll put him into multiple. Okay?"

Maggie assured Rose Burke, who'd never been married, that she needn't worry about any competition from her. "He's all yours. Once widowed and twice divorced, I've had it up to here with men." Maggie ran the edge of her hand across her chin.

Rose Burke gave her an odd look before turning her attention back to Dorothy from Ojai who was leaning across the table, still dispensing delicious gossip.

"The gentleman in the wheelchair at the captain's table is William P. McKiernan from San Francisco," she was saying. "Rich as Croesus, he'll probably die a pauper the way his new wife spends money. I saw her in the jewelry store earlier. Barely out to sea, she was already fishing."

"No fool like an old fool." The trite cliché came from a woman at the far end of the table.

Not wanting to gossip, Maggie didn't mention that she had met the McKiernans, but couldn't help herself from discreetly craning her neck to study the raven-haired Sheila, a beauty, no question about it. On the wharf this morning she had looked exotic, this evening she looked amazing. Her skin was flawless and she showed plenty of it, especially around the deep décolleté of her exquisite blue strapless dress where a long double strand of olive-sized pearls ensured a certain degree of modesty. She was talking animatedly with the captain and other men at the table, while her husband spoke mostly with Francine. He looked dapper in a navy blazer, gray trousers, blue striped shirt and red silk ascot. His thinning hair was more white than gray, but the candlelight in the dining room was kind to his face. He didn't appear quite as elderly as this morning. Momentarily glancing up from his plate, he caught Maggie staring.

She quickly looked away. But not so quickly that she missed seeing him smile at her.

Old flirt, she thought and now concentrated on her food.

"You've got to request a table change," Francine confronted Maggie at the breakfast buffet the following morning, a perfect morning, not a cloud in the sky, and the calm sea sparkled in the sunlight. Smoked salmon, scrambled eggs, and croissants on their plates, they went out on deck to enjoy their breakfast at one of the many small round tables set up around the pool, which was not open for swimming during the breakfast hour. A steward followed with orange juice and coffee. "I saw you with that dreadful gaggle of women last night."

"I was assigned to that table," Maggie explained, thinking it was sweet of Francine Wirth to keep tabs on her; she didn't seem the mother hen type, more the consummate socialite. She had worn a stunning red silk dinner suit last evening, and this morning she was wearing designer slacks and a pin-tucked white blouse with an exquisite broach on its collar.

"Yes, seats are assigned, but everyone is entitled to make a change," Francine said. "It isn't advertised or there'd be a regular game of musical chairs. Go see the dining room steward right after breakfast. Demand another table. A larger one. One with eight people. Make it very clear that you don't wish to sit exclusively with women. Insist there be at least two men at your table. Oh, look! Speaking of the devils! There's Bill McKiernan." She waved him over.

"Good morning, Francine! Hi Maggie!" he said and wheeled himself up to their table. He was wearing dark Bermuda shorts, a white polo shirt and brown leather sandals. His arms and legs were deeply tanned attesting to his love of warm weather cruises. A waiter appeared instantly with tray of food from which he could choose.

Francine moved over to accommodate his wheelchair. "I was saving this spot for Mildred," she said. "But it's yours now. God knows when she'll show up. She's fond of sleeping late."

"Sheila sleeps late as well," Bill said. "She skips breakfast and goes right to the Pilates class. Me? I'm up with the cows. I can't remember the last time I slept past five in the morning." He settled in, took a plate of fruit, and turned his attention to Maggie as the waiter poured coffee. "So, my dear, how many of these cruises have you been on?"

"This is my first."

"Really?" He raised his eyebrows in surprise. "Then let's hope it will be memorable. Seeing that Francine has taken you under her wing, I know you won't lack for intelligent company. What do you do on shore?"

"Sightsee, I guess."

He smiled. "No, I meant, what do you do back home? When we met on the pier in San Diego yesterday you said you were from New York."

"Oh, I see. I'm a paralegal."

"Which firm are you with?"

"Goodman, Barr and Noune. Actually...uh, I quit to take this cruise," Maggie quickly added, hoping the little lie would end the subject of her pathetic job situation. Thankfully, she was spared further inquiry when Mildred arrived, carrying a cup of coffee, spilling it as she set it down on the table. Instantly, a blur of white uniforms materialized to clean up the mess and bring her a new cup.

"Really, Mildred!" Francine scolded. "It's nice to see that you're up early for once. But you've got to eat something. You can't subsist on coffee. Just look at your hand! It's shaking. Why you insist on trying to diet on a cruise is beyond me. For heaven's sake, have some breakfast!" Francine turned and told one of the attendants to bring Mildred a plate of scrambled eggs and a cheese Danish.

Maggie chuckled. Maybe Francine was a mother hen under her fine exterior after all.

That evening the dining room steward showed Maggie to a new table, a table of eight, two men and six women, and she had to admit it was a more interesting mix. It was certainly interesting to watch the women make fools of themselves over the slim pickings; a ratio of six-to-two was not one that favored her sex, nor did it bring out the best in them. At one point she thought it'd come to blows between Ms. Olson from Seattle, a single mother of a college-aged daughter, and Ms. Rasner, a retired high school teacher from Kansas City. Both were knocking themselves out over the same man, a nice looking individual in his fifties. Listening to their competitive banter, Maggie learned that Dr. Hellman was a dentist from Cleveland, recently divorced with two grown sons and a thriving practice, making him a real catch unless alimony payments were choking him. As the meal and conversation progressed, it seemed that he preferred Amanda Olson. Dressed in a little black sleeveless number with a matching headband holding her blond hair in place, she looked prim and proper. Should she ever get to Cleveland, she would impress Dr. Hellman's family and friends.

The other gentleman at the table, Paul Hopkinson, was in his late seventies and hard of hearing; something the ladies forgave him once they discovered he was a widower, no alimony payments, and collected rent from several buildings he owned in Minneapolis. His sterling résumé stoked the ardor of the rail thin Dorothy with the big hair, who had also requested a table change, landing at this one with Maggie. Tonight, instead of gossiping about the men on the ship, Dorothy simply smiled at Mr. Hopkinson and let him do all the talking. It worked. By the time dessert was served, she and Paul had decided to attend tonight's movie together. Dr. Hellman was all but in bed with Ms. Olson, while Claudia Rasner was left scouring the room for other possibilities. The two remaining women at the table had discovered that they were both bridge players, which immediately forged a bond.

With no other prospects in sight, Claudia Rasner decided to latch on to Maggie. "Do you gamble?" she asked, getting up from the table at the conclusion of the meal, her eyes still roaming the room for better company.

"Gamble? Good heavens, no!"

"You should. It's loads of fun." Claudia wanted to go to the casino but didn't want to walk in alone. There were bound to be plenty of gentlemen at the roulette tables and once she established herself as a player, she'd ditch Maggie. "I always set a limit of twenty dollars. When that's gone, I stop."

"I suppose twenty dollars isn't too much to lose."

"Exactly. Think of it as entertainment. In Manhattan you probably spend that much on a movie." Claudia had heard about prices in New York, a place she couldn't afford to visit on a teacher's pension. Having seen two kids through college, she took early retirement last year when, at the age of fifty-five, she sustained a back injury coaching girls' lacrosse. Following surgery and while laid up in the hospital, her husband – also a high school teacher – began fooling around with the medical insurance adjuster. After her hospital stay, arriving home unexpectedly one afternoon when her twice-weekly physical therapy session was canceled, she discovered their affair, which aggravated her back to its pre-operation level. The doctor prescribed a brace and her sister prescribed a trip to get away from it all. Heeding the latter's advise, Claudia signed up for this cruise, nixing the brace because, God forbid, anyone mistake her for an invalid. However, without it, she needed pain killers. Her doctor gave her a prescription and authorized the ship's physician to refill it as needed.

"If you include popcorn and a coke," Maggie had to admit, "I suppose a movie in Manhattan will amount to twenty dollars." She went on to explain that she had looked forward to seeing tonight's film, *Open Range*, not a first-run movie by any means, but she'd missed it years ago when it played on the big screen at the Zeigfield on West 54th Street.

"Okay, tell you what..." Claudia Rasner was ready to bargain and reached for her brown silk jacket hanging on the back of her chair; it matched her skirt and went well with her curly, reddish hair, "I will go see the film with you. Afterwards we will stop in at the casino for a few minutes."

The movie lived up to Maggie's expectations. Its hero, Kevin Costner, portrayed Western bravado with a lovable side, and the glamorous Annette Bening played a middle-aged spinster with courage. The kid in the film was irritating, but the story had a happy ending; even Robert Duvall survived. Maggie liked that, although in her own experience it was never so.

Keeping her promise, Maggie now accompanied Claudia to the casino. Walking in, she was surprised to find Francine playing Black Jack; she hadn't figured on her being a gambler. Of course after forty cruises anyone could develop bad habits, and who was to say gambling was bad? Maggie realized that her stern Methodist upbringing hadn't altogether left her and, in a fit of belated rebellion, doubled her limit and signed for forty dollars worth of chips.

Plastic in hand, she and Claudia strolled up to a roulette table. Maggie placed a bet on number seventeen and won. When she tried it again she lost. After a few more spins, she lost interest in the game. Claudia stayed and continued playing while Maggie went over to a felt-covered card table. After watching how the game went, she tried her hand. No luck. There went another handful of chips. She joined Francine at the Black Jack table. Half an hour later all her chips were gone. Preparing to leave the casino, she looked around for Claudia and saw her signing another chit.

"What about your limit?" Maggie whispered, coming up to her.

"Don't be a fool. I'll win it back," Claudia hissed and seemed to resent Maggie's presence. Her green eyes were unusually bright. She took a swig of scotch; drinks were free in the casino and numbed the pain in her back. She might be able to skip a pill tonight.

"I doubled my limit. It's gone so I'm leaving," Maggie said, turning her back on the charged atmosphere in the casino. She had not enjoyed losing forty dollars and vowed this would be her first and last time. Gambling was obviously something one had to acquire a taste for, like eggplant and avocados, and she wasn't about to initiate any new and expensive cravings at this point in her life.

"Any luck tonight?" a familiar voice behind her asked as she was walking out.

Maggie spun around. "Oh, Francine! I didn't win if that's what you mean. How did you do at Black Jack?"

"Terribly. I should have switched to another game but most of the tables were too crowded. I like some elbow room if I'm going to drop two hundred dollars."

"You lost two hundred dollars?" The amount shocked Maggie.

Francine shrugged. "My limit. I never allow myself to lose more than that in any one evening. Maybe I'll have better luck tomorrow. If not I'll stick to the slot machines." She nodded toward the one-armed bandits in the vestibule outside the casino, being fed nickels and quarters by women putting in coins and pulling the handles with robotic movements all the while waiting for bells to go off.

At the far end of the corridor, music spilled out from the doors to the Coconut Lounge. As she and Francine passed by, Maggie glanced into the jungle milieu. People were dancing on a square of parquet in the middle of the room while others lounged in safari chairs, sipping tropical drinks at tables shaped like bongo drums. Bamboo and fake palm trees completed the scene. Continuing toward the large and airy Atrium Lounge, where a chamber music concert was imminent, they spotted Mildred at the bar and joined her for a few moments before all three settled down in the leather club chairs to enjoy the concert, which turned out to be as good as any Maggie had attended back home at Alice Tully Hall. When the musicians took a break, she checked her watch, surprised to discover that it was past one o'clock. She was not used to such late hours. She got up and excused herself.

Leaving the Atrium, passing the card room where six separate bridge games were in full swing, Maggie admired the stamina of the players as she headed toward the stairs leading down to her deck. Dead tired, she wanted nothing but a good night's sleep. However, just before starting down the steps, she felt a refreshing sea breeze wafting in from the promenade and suddenly the air inside the ship felt stale. She decided on a quick walk before going to bed.

She stepped out on deck among other strollers similarly inspired. The night air was balmy and the sky was sprinkled with a million stars. Stretching her neck, she leaned over the railing to look for the moon but the deck above acted as a ceiling obstructing her view. She turned and walked toward the midship stairs. Taking hold of the banister, she climbed to the top deck where a soft breeze – as light as one set in motion by butterfly wings – caressed her face; a far cry from the stiff wind blowing off the East River back home. She walked past the pool covered with a taut plastic sheet this time of night but the late hour notwithstanding, people were lounging in the canvas chairs, talking quietly and enjoying the moonlight. She spotted Dr. Hellman and Ms. Olson holding hands and sipping wine, oblivious to everyone else around them. Maggie sighed; it was a night made for romance and her two dinner companions were clearly experiencing the magic of the full moon.

All at once she felt a chill, a cold shiver ran through her body, leaving an empty, forlorn ache in her chest that soon gnawed at her innards, the harbinger of her familiar bouts with sadness. But determined not to let it swamp her tonight, she took a deep breath and tried to neutralize her personal darkness by counting her blessings. She was on a beautiful ship. She had made new friends. Tomorrow would be another day of continued luxury and leisure, no work, no chores, no bus to catch, no slush to ruin her shoes. The wind was gentle, the temperature warm, and it was impossible to believe that tomorrow was Thanksgiving Day. Imagine basking in a tropical paradise instead of riding the drafty train to Queens, dressed to the teeth in woolens, yet freezing to death.

Instantly, Maggie felt ashamed. Simone was a dear friend and Maggie was grateful to be part of her family every Thanksgiving. Several years ago, Simone had started inviting her for Christmas as well; something Maggie's pride wouldn't allow her to accept. Each year she fabricated an excuse until Simone stopped asking, the result being that Maggie always spent Christmas Day alone, careful not to answer the telephone and alert anyone to her status. During the afternoon, she would take a walk along the East River to Gracie Mansion, cross through Carl Schurtz Park, and return home sufficiently hungry to eat the take-out dinner she'd bought the day before at the prepared food counter at Eli's. Every year it was the same routine and the same menu. Two slices of white turkey, mashed potatoes topped with a dollop of gravy, stuffing, green beans, and cranberry jelly on the side. The miniature pumpkin pie came in a separate plastic container.

She stopped at the ship's railing and gazed, spellbound, out across the moonlit black sea. The twinge in the pit of her stomach was loosening its grip as pleasure in her surroundings slowly returned. Iridescent foam rode the crest of each gentle wave and the misty wind-borne spray tingled her face pleasantly. This was something she had never experienced. It was far better than being in love, an emotion that would only disappoint. She no longer envied Amanda Olson.

She let go of the railing and continued strolling toward the bow of the ship, the deck narrowing as she went. There were no passengers or stewards serving drinks along this last stretch. She had the space all to herself and felt on top of the world. Simone was right when she'd accused her of being a loner. Maybe she did prefer her own company to anyone else's. One thing was sure, she felt less alone here on this deserted deck than on the ground floor at Macy's during their Fourth of July sale.

Suddenly she sensed the presence of someone else and stopped walking the minute she discovered that she was *not* alone. Spotting a figure up ahead, she realized that a man was resting his elbows on the railing and leaning over, quietly studying the sea, the moonlight glinting on the silvery steaks in his otherwise dark hair.

Holding her breath trying to determine if she ought to proceed along the deck or turn back, she noted that he was a fine looking individual, his profile ruggedly handsome. Lean and long in the limbs, he was wearing faded jeans and an open collared shirt under a linen blazer; Clint Eastwood in his prime came to mind. She wondered why she hadn't seen him among the ship's passengers. If she had, she certainly would have remembered; one did not forget such an imposing individual. But, be that as it may, she decided to leave. Since he had chosen this isolated spot, he obviously wished for solitude, precisely like she did. All right, he could have the bow to himself tonight. He had gotten here first. She turned and walked away. After a few steps, she looked back over her shoulder just to make sure she hadn't imagined him. She hadn't. He was still there. But he was no longer staring into the sea. His head was turned toward her. Okay, he had spotted her and was relieved to see her leaving. She picked up her steps and fled.

How refreshing, Michael Sanders was thinking to himself, seeing the woman run away and glad he wouldn't now be forced into idle conversation. He'd been warned about pushy females on the cruise and was not about to cross paths with any of them. Since boarding the ship, and except for his dealings with Captain Vicente Reyes and the ship's navigator, he was for all practical purposes a stowaway and planned to keep it that way.

Chapter nineteen

The following morning, passengers awoke to hot, sultry weather and the sea was calm as a pond. The ship wasn't moving. When people began questioning why, one of the ship's officers explained over the loudspeaker system that they had dropped anchor during the night for routine maintenance in the engine room. To recompense for any inconvenience, cocktails today would be courtesy of Commodore Vicente Reyes. The whispering stopped as people quickly sidled up to the various bars, ordering mimosas and Bloody Marys for starters.

After attending a morning Pilates class, Maggie climbed the outside steps to the top deck, hoping to find a bit of a breeze to help her cool down before she went to her cabin to shower; then off to a lecture before lunch. The classes were free and she was determined not to miss a single one. This morning she had to splurge on a thirty dollar straw hat in one of the ship's many shops, a hat she could have bought for a fraction of that at a street vendor in New York, but it was a necessary purchase; she was not accustomed to the strong sun and burned easily.

Due to the stifling humidity hovering over the idle ship, youngsters had free reign of the top deck deserted by adults seeking refuge indoors. Some children were playing shuffleboard; others swam under the supervision of one of the nannies the ship provided. The pool was reserved for children during certain hours each day; otherwise it was for adults only. Passing the noisy youngsters, Maggie continued along the railing toward the bow, enjoying the sight of the massive expanse of ocean and hoping the man from last night was somewhere else. She didn't want to run into him again. For reasons she couldn't fathom, seeing him had disturbed her sleep and she didn't want him to now spoil the solitude of this beautiful day. Personally, she was glad the ship was anchored; the heat didn't bother her, she was in no hurry to go anywhere, and this delay would provide everyone with extra time onboard, something she found far more desirable than free drinks. She stopped and looked toward the shimmering horizon. The ship was out too far to see land; still, somewhere in the distance the pink beaches of Mexico awaited her and she could almost feel the warm sand between her toes.

She continued walking and was passing a row of empty deck chairs, when she saw someone in a wheelchair up ahead. Pulling the brim of her new hat down over her eyes against the glare, she realized it was Mr. McKiernan sitting unprotected in the sun, head bent and asleep, which would never do in this temperature. An immobile person of his age could suffer heat stroke in no time flat. She rounded the wheelchair and faced the elderly gentleman.

"Bill!" she cried. "Isn't it too hot for you out here?" She touched his shoulder to rouse him.

He raised his head and opened his eyes. "Oh, Maggie!" he said and righted himself in the confines of the chair. "Hot, you say? Yes, I believe you're right. I must have dozed off. I'd better find some shade." He tried to move the wheelchair but it wouldn't budge. "Hmm, that's strange," he said, struggling with the brake. "It seems to be stuck."

"Here, let me help you." Maggie worked the brake. "Something is jamming it," she said after a moment of trying to free him. "No, wait a minute. There's a device here on one of the wheels."

"Oh, of course. That's a security lock in case the chair is left unoccupied. My wife must have clicked it inadvertently when she left me here earlier." At the mentioning of his young wife, he smiled, but it was a mere stretching of the lips, the kind mourners give each other at funerals.

"Does it need a key? Do you have it?"

"Let's see…" Bill patted the pocket on his blue polo shirt and checked both pockets in his white linen trousers. He shook his head. "No. Sheila probably has it." He fished out a handkerchief and wiped his brow.

"Where is she? I'll go get her."

"Don't bother her. She's in a Pilates class. She always stays for both sessions."

Maggie frowned. There was only one session each morning, and Sheila McKiernan had not been there today. "Maybe I can try to loosen the wheel manually," she offered, bending down and jimmying the mechanism. After a while, the chair moved.

"Oh, good!" Bill sighed with relief. "Thank you, Maggie. You're kind to trouble yourself. May I ask for one more favor?"

"Sure."

"Can you help me into the shade? I feel a little faint. This chair is different from my own." Maggie noted his hands were shaking and she wondered how long he'd been out here, hatless, in the blistering sun. The scalp under his thinning white hair was turning an angry pink. "This is the cruise line's regulation chair. It conforms to the narrow corridors and cabin doors. My own chair wouldn't fit. We had to put it in the ship's storage room."

"Maybe you ought to go to the Atrium. It's air conditioned and you can have a cold drink." Maggie figured Bill needed more than shade at this point.

"Yes, that would be nice. Actually, on second thought, I'd rather go to my cabin. Would you mind helping me? Do you have a moment?"

"Of course. Just tell me where it is." Maggie turned the chair around, pushed Bill McKiernan out of the burning sun, and headed for the elevator banks.

Ten minutes later, after he'd had a glass of water and was lying comfortably on the sofa in his enormous cabin, Maggie left, realizing that these quarters looked exactly like the ones in Agnes Perollo's brochure, complete with a large private deck, which made her wonder why he had bothered going topside.

That evening as she was dressing for Thanksgiving Dinner, putting on her yellow chiffon dress and holding her hair in place with a blue headband that complimented the blue flowers in her shawl, Maggie realized that the professional highlights were blending in nicely, giving her generic brown hair an overall blond shine. It had been worth the expense. Before buying the straw hat, her face had gotten a bit of color, which meant she didn't need to apply blusher. She also noticed the dark circles under her eyes were fading. Had the sun done that bit of magic as well? Leaning into the mirror, fastening a cluster of small pearls in her ears that David had given her, Maggie realized that for the first time in years she didn't recoil from her own reflection. In fact, what she saw was not at all displeasing.

There was a sudden knock on her door and she opened it to an unfamiliar steward standing in the narrow corridor, obscured behind a huge vase of pink roses from the ship's florist.

"For me?" she said, surprised, as he handed them over. She was not in the habit of receiving flowers.

"*Si.*"

"But why? I mean who sent them?"

"*Si.*"

"*Gracias*," she shrugged, closing the door on another English-challenged steward.

Putting the vase down on the desk, admiring the roses, she knew who had sent them even before she found the small card tucked between the fragrant blooms.

Chapter
twenty

Chrysanthemums in the colors of autumn decorated the dining room for the traditional American Thanksgiving feast. Before sitting down, Maggie walked over to the captain's table to thank Bill McKiernan for the roses.

"They're beautiful. You shouldn't have..." she said, bending down and speaking to both Bill and Sheila, figuring the bouquet had been sent with the latter's knowledge. However, it immediately became clear that Sheila was not aware of the flowers because she gave Maggie a startled look an instant before her eyes narrowed.

"Enjoy them, Ms....ah..." she said, but instead of trying to remember Maggie's name, curled her lips, adding, "You may go now. Our table is about to be served."

With that rude dismissal ringing in her ears, Maggie retreated, regretting her diligence. So much for protocol. She should have waited and thanked Bill tomorrow morning at breakfast. His wife was never around then.

Maggie reached her own table and sat down only moments before Captain Vicente Reyes rose from his seat and gave a little speech marking the Thanksgiving celebration. Toasting the holiday, he ordered the waiters to pour wine for everyone; the ship was once more under way but drinks were still complimentary for the remainder of the night.

After dinner, melodies from the Roaring Twenties enticed Maggie into the faux jungle milieu of the Coconut Lounge. Francine and Mildred showed up shortly and came over to where she was seated at a bongo table with Rose Burke and Ronald Cohen, the gentleman Rose had set her sights on that first evening at sea and had now apparently snared. Claudia Rasner sat with them as well; she looked pale, leaving Maggie to wonder if she was losing at the gambling tables.

"So, Bill sent you flowers?" Francine said to Maggie in reference to the little scene she'd witnessed earlier in the dining room. Dying with curiosity, she and Mildred each pulled up a chair, nodding their greetings to the others at the table.

"I wish he hadn't," Maggie said.

"Why did he?" Francine wanted to know.

"His wheelchair got stuck this morning on the top deck. I helped him back to his cabin. It was no big deal. He certainly didn't need to send flowers."

"I'm not surprised. He's a gentleman from the old school." Francine signaled a waiter for a bottle of champagne in an ice bucket. "His type does not ignore an act of kindness." Rose, Ronald Cohen, and Claudia were drinking margaritas and declined to switch, leaving Francine and Maggie with the entire bottle because Mildred decided to order a stinger. Drinks being free probably accounted for the liberal way everyone indulged.

For the lack of enough men to go around, women danced with each other and seemed to enjoy the exercise. Maggie found it depressing. Francine sniffed and called it "vulgar."

Shortly Paul Hopkinson came into the Coconut Lounge with Dorothy on his arm. He was obviously also a gentleman of the old school, because he made it his business to dance with as many single women as possible – making sure no one was a wallflower – including everyone at Maggie's table, except Rose Burke who refused to leave Ronald's side for fear that another woman might spirit him away. Maggie and Paul managed a respectable fox trot, but it was Francine and Paul who drew everyone's attention with their rendition of the Charleston. The entire dance floor emptied as everyone watched their fancy footwork, giving them a rousing hand afterwards. Having enjoyed the applause, Paul kept Francine on the floor for another dance at which point Dorothy cut in, reclaiming her date. Mildred was the only one not dancing. Neither man nor woman could entice her to the floor. She knew her limitations. She was now on her second stinger and was in no condition to set foot on the slippery parquet. She soon excused herself and went to bed.

After Mildred left, Francine checked her watch, a clear indication she was growing bored with the Coconut lounge. "It's too late now to catch Private Lives," she said to those at the table. "We've missed the first act. Any other suggestions?"

"How about the art auction?" Maggie said. There was an auction house a few blocks from her apartment in New York and, although she'd never considered attending, this cruise put new experiences into a better light. Once out of her daily rut, unfamiliar activities began appealing to her.

"Good idea!" Francine said. "We can walk in anytime. In fact, it's better to arrive late. They always save the best items for last. Who is game?"

"We're playing cards at eleven," Rose spoke up for herself and Ronald Cohen, Dorothy and Paul were still dancing, and Claudia made a sour little moue without divulging her plans.

"All right, Maggie, it's just you and me." Francine got up and, leaving a half bottle of champagne behind, walked out with Maggie.

The auction was held in a conference room on the Purser's Deck. Neat rows of chairs faced a podium where the auctioneer was pounding his gavel. Signing in, the latecomers were each handed a numbered paddle and a sheet listing the artwork offered. Seeing the minimum bids in parenthesis, Maggie knew she would not be participating.

Francine bid on a gorgeous watercolor and won. The next painting, a still life of fruits and flowers, sent a great number of paddles waving. Finally the gavel went down, and a spotter went over to a blond woman in the front row. Maggie craned her neck and saw that Amanda Olson was the winner. She also saw that it was Dr. Hellman who signed the slip.

The next item was a bucolic Danish landscape circa 1920, which Francine wanted for her son's house in Connecticut. "There's a perfect spot over the fireplace in his study where Anne has hung a mirror," she whispered. "One never hangs a mirror in a library," she added with a snort of indignation.

Maggie suspected that Francine was not in harmony with her daughter-in law's decorating taste and wondered what the latter would do if presented with a painting not to her liking. Art was a very personal thing and Francine was stepping on delicate terrain, but was saved from tripping when a gentleman from Atlanta outbid her. And when the auction eventually came to a close, she owned only the watercolor. "Oh, well," she shrugged, leaving it to be packaged and shipped to Florida. "I'll get an oil painting for my son's library in Acapulco. I know of a number of good galleries there."

It was past midnight when they left the auction and walked up the stairs toward the Atrium where Francine spotted someone she knew from Florida and from previous cruises.

"Finally! There's Doug Collins!" she cried. "Poor man. He's been under the weather since leaving San Diego. I've seen neither hide nor hair of him. He always feels queasy the first few days at sea."

"Seasick?" Maggie asked, surprised. "It's been so calm."

"He has an inner ear weakness and stays in his cabin until he adjusts to the swells, benign, as they've been. I'm glad to see he's finally up and about. Come on. Let me introduce you."

"If you don't mind, I think I'll just get some fresh air and go down to my cabin."

"All right. You can meet him tomorrow." Francine said goodnight, turned and walked into the Atrium, cheerfully waving at Doug Collins who was surrounded by no less than four women. Maggie grinned. Francine was in for a battle of the sexes.

Maggie stepped out onto the promenade and walked toward the stern of the ship, again appreciating the perfect conditions. Agnes Perollo had not exaggerated the weather. Feeling revived by the ocean breezes, she decided to go up to the top deck for the panoramic view.

As she climbed the outside steps, she spotted Sheila McKiernan deep in whispered conversation with one of the ship's officers. They were standing in the shadows of one of the lifeboats, and the manner with which her body leaned against his impeccable navy blue uniform, gold stripes glinting in the moonlight, indicated they weren't discussing tomorrow's menu. Maggie wondered if Bill McKiernan was asleep in their luxurious cabin, oblivious to his wife's socializing. It was none of her business, of course, and after the episode in the dining room she had resolved to never again be caught in that woman's radar.

Reaching the stern on the top deck, a designated smoking area, Maggie could smell the smokers long before she saw them clustered into conversations groups shrouded in a haze of tobacco. Holding her breath, she hurried toward the bow of the ship, reminding herself to henceforth make use of the midship stairs.

No sooner had she passed the covered pool when she spotted the man from the night before up ahead. Stopping in her tracks, she swore under her breath with disappointment; his very presence here inhibited hers. She had hoped to be alone. Except for her cabin, it was difficult to be alone on the ship and as much as she enjoyed the company of her new friends, she needed to be by herself once in a while. This man made that small pleasure impossible. In fact, she almost felt guilty being here as if she were an intruder on his turf. Of course no part of the deck was anyone's private property, he had no claim on any area, even this remote one. She noticed that he was in the exact same position as yesterday, leaning over the railing and peering into the water as if searching for something, or as if he were preparing to jump and was looking for a good spot.

Well, get it over with, she thought uncharitably. If you're suicidal and stupid enough to jump, don't worry, I won't sound the alarm or throw you a life preserver. Swallowing her irritation with little grace, it occurred to her that perhaps this Clint Eastwood look-alike was some sort of a fish watcher. Like a bird watcher on land, trying to identify a rare avian species, he might be trying to identify some strange marine life skimming the water's surface late at night.

While standing still and deciding what to do, she studied him and realized that if not for his change of clothing – no jeans tonight – but a sports jacket with slacks, shirt and tie, she could swear that he had never moved from this spot. Again she thought it odd that she never saw him anywhere else on the ship. It carried seven hundred passengers, and although she basically stuck with the friends she'd made early on, she recognized all the others and knew quite a few by name. This passenger must be at the six o'clock dinner seating or else he took meals in his cabin. Maybe he was seasick during the day, confined to his berth, only to emerge at night when no one was around to watch him retch. That said it was time for her to leave. It was none of her business what he did, or why. She turned, leaving the deck to its lone occupant and ignoring what she took to be the sound of his voice. Was it her imagination, or did she distinctly hear him say, "Hello." No, more likely he'd said, "Go ahead...make my day!" Okay, she was leaving. Without looking back, she hurried toward midship.

Michael Sanders had indeed said hello, but it was lost on this woman who, for two night in a row now, seemed determined not to come within ten feet of him. Why? He showered daily and wore clean clothes. A puzzled grin tugged at the corners of his mouth as he watched her disappear. She was wearing sensible low-heeled shoes, he noted, and the breeze lifting the flounced hem of her dress displayed shapely legs. Up close she was probably a pretty woman. But she sure didn't want him to discover that. The females onboard ship had a reputation for being aggressive. She was obviously not one of them and her shy deportment intrigued him, even as his attention was once again focused on the sea, trying to look beneath its black surface.

Chapter
twenty-two

Dead tired by now, Maggie reached the elevator banks and, dismissing her dislike of small enclosed spaces, pushed the button for a ride down to her deck. When she stepped into the lift, she was surprised to find Bill McKiernan sitting in his wheelchair, facing the back and wearing only a pair of blue striped pajamas. It wasn't like him to be seen in public like that.

"Hi!" she said, rounding the wheelchair as the elevator door closed. He appeared dazed. She touched his shoulder. He remained unresponsive. When the lift stopped on the Atrium deck and a noisy group got on, he took no notice of them.

"Bill, where are you going?" Maggie asked after the elevator had stopped twice to let everyone off and they were again alone, continuing down toward her deck. She maneuvered his wheelchair around. It wasn't locked, the wheels were fine; however, looking closely at Bill it was clear that *he* wasn't. His face looked pasty. His eyes were unfocussed. Maggie feared he might have suffered a stroke, in which case he needed a doctor, and quickly.

She looked for an emergency button on the elevator panel but saw only the red fire alarm which, if pressed, would rouse the entire ship. She knew there was a hospital onboard, but it hadn't occurred to her to learn its location because she didn't expect to become ill.

The elevator stopped on her deck. The door opened and she stuck her head out, hoping to see a steward, but the corridor was deserted. It was awfully late, of course, and the staff was entitled to some sleep. But the ship's doctor would have to be on call no matter the hour.

"Mr. McKiernan," Maggie bent down, addressing the pajama-clad man by his last name, which under these circumstances seemed more appropriate. "I'm going to my cabin to get a map. We need to get you to the infirmary." As she was saying this, she pulled the wheelchair out from the elevator so he wouldn't go back up again, alone. She wondered how long he had been riding the lift aimlessly. And where was Mrs. McKiernan? Still with the officer? If not, and if she had gone back to her sumptuous cabin and found her invalid husband missing, wouldn't she worry about his whereabouts and go looking for him?

Pushing the wheelchair down the narrow passageway, Maggie reached her cabin and, sliding the keycard into the slot, opened the door and backed in, wedging the wheelchair in the door so she could keep her eye on Bill. She switched on the lights and quickly found the map and just as quickly located the ship's hospital. Three flights up. Turn left. Follow the signs.

Okay, now back to the elevator.

Suddenly there was a screech. Maggie looked at Bill. He appeared as dazed as when she'd found him and had clearly not cried out. She poked her head out into the corridor and saw Sheila step from the elevator, followed by two of the ship's officers.

"There he is!" Sheila McKiernan shrieked again. "That woman has him!" Storming forward, she snarled at Maggie. "What do you think you are you doing? What sort of trick are you turning?" Maggie blanched with the insult. Sheila turned back to the officers. "What kind of a ship is this?" she demanded to know. "You allow hookers?"

The two men looked at Maggie, not quite sure what to think. She didn't fit the image of a lady of the night, but Mr. McKiernan *was* wedged in her cabin door, wearing pajamas, and several people on the decks above, when questioned about the missing VIP wheelchair passenger, indicated they'd seen Ms. Maghpye riding down with him.

"Arrest her!" Mrs. McKiernan ordered in a high-pitched voice, pointing a two inch lacquered nail at Maggie and not caring whose sleep along this peasant deck she disturbed.

Since no one was caught between the sheets, arrest seemed a bit extreme, and the most senior of the two officers attempted to calm the distraught wife. She had enlisted their help in finding her husband; they had found him and it was now time for cooler heads to prevail.

"Look..." he said in a lowered voice, cognizant to the fact that passengers were sleeping in adjacent cabins, "we will deal with this in the morning." He didn't believe any sordid activity had been in the making. Throughout the cruise he had seen Ms. Maghpye in the company of Mrs. Wirth and it was highly unlikely that she would consort with someone unsuitable.

The other officer agreed with his colleague. "We'll make a report to Captain Reyes first thing in the morning," he said.

"Mr. McKiernan needs to see a doctor *tonight*." Having recovered from Sheila's humiliating accusation, Maggie finally spoke up and held out the map. "I was trying to find out where the..."

"You took my husband to your cabin to find a doctor?" Sheila hissed; she didn't look attractive when angry, her face was hard, the kind that wouldn't age well. "Looks to me like you were planning to *play* doctor."

The words stung. Maggie realized she'd been a fool to get involved. She should have left the poor man on the elevator. Again tongue-tied, she spread her hands, appealing to the good judgment of the officers.

"Let's get Mr. McKiernan up to his cabin," the senior man said, taking command of the wheelchair. He nodded to his colleague. "Alert Dr. Madrasso!"

The younger man reached for a small apparatus attached to his belt.

Maggie noticed an abrupt change in Sheila's face. There was a sudden gleam in her dark eyes. "Dr. Madrasso?" she purred. "Yes, of course. We must send for him at once." She licked her red lips and flicked her long black hair over her shoulders as she now walked toward the elevator ahead of the officers and without giving Maggie a backward glance.

Chapter
twenty-three

Worrying about the officers' report and a potential summons to meet with Commodore Vicente Reyes, Maggie didn't sleep well the rest of the night. During breakfast the following morning, she immediately told Francine and Mildred the entire story. Both shook their heads in disbelief and volunteered to accompany her if there was to be a meeting with the captain.

An interview never took place. Apparently, when Dr. Madrasso examined Bill last night, he discovered that he had mixed scotch with a prescription medicine and had, furthermore, taken a sleep aid, leaving him dazed and confused. Alone in his cabin he suddenly craved a change of scenery and had wheeled himself into the elevator, only to promptly forget his destination. Several people admitted they had seen him riding up and down, some now expressing remorse at having ignored the elderly gentleman, explaining they didn't realize he was in distress. "I thought maybe he had Alzheimer's and was enjoying the ride," one woman blurted.

Maggie spent the rest of the day poolside, loafing in a canvas deck chair, reading and avoiding Sheila McKiernan, which meant staying away from the spa and the shops. She was reading a book she'd borrowed from the ship's library and, resting her eyes between chapters, enjoyed studying her fellow passengers. Rose Burke and Ronald Cohen were sitting in the shade of an umbrella, playing cards. Wearing swim trunks, Ronald displayed his expansive girth with no self-consciousness whatsoever, whereas Rose had wisely deferred from putting on a bathing suit. Instead, she was wearing a sundress, which unfortunately didn't conceal legs blue with varicose veins. Maggie saw several women edging up to their card game, pretending interest, but obviously just itching for an introduction.

Although Rose had staked proprietor's rights with Ronald Cohen, claim jumpers circled around just in case.

Maggie's eyes leisurely wandered on to a group of weight-watchers gathering in the shallow end of the pool. The women were wearing similar bathing caps decorated with pretty plastic flowers sold in the ship's gift shop. However, their less than graceful exercise routine and the white salve smeared across their collective noses spoiled the picture. At the opposite end, two women with salon lacquered coiffeurs and no caps held on to the side of the pool, kicking their legs under the surface while warily eying the group at the shallow end, lest they send up a spray of water. None of the women at either end were swimmers. Of course the minute a gentleman slipped into the pool, a furious ripple ensued, as everyone became Esther Williams.

That evening after dinner, Maggie went to the Atrium with Francine and Mildred. She finally met Doug Collins and learned that he was a stockbroker and a widower, which made him very desirable to the single ladies. Maggie also learned that one look from Francine vanquished any woman edging up to Doug with romance on her mind. Maggie was impressed and wondered how she managed that withering mien, and why? For although Doug was attractively slim with a head of thick gray hair, and probably Francine's age, Maggie couldn't imagine that she was saving him for herself. Francine was not the lovelorn type.

Claudia Rasner joined the group, was introduced to Doug Collins and chatted with him just long enough to realize he was too conservative, not her type, after which she asked Maggie to come with her to the casino. When she hesitated, Claudia suggested they first see tonight's movie, a trade-off that had worked once before.

Maggie was relenting just as Bill McKiernan wheeled himself over, smiling his greetings to everyone in the group. She hadn't seen him all day and he hadn't been at dinner, but looked none the worse from his wanderlust of last night. She wondered if he had any memory of it.

"Doug!" he said. "Glad to see that you finally got your sea legs." Bill knew Doug Collins from former cruises and the two men shook hands.

"Do you know Claudia Rasner?" Maggie asked Bill.

"By sight only. We've not been properly introduced." He smiled and offered Claudia his hand. "Hi! I'm Bill."

"Nice to meet you," she said, eager to escape Maggie's collection of friends, each older and more infirm than the next. "I'd stay and chat but Maggie and I are on our way to catch tonight's film."

"Maggie," Francine stopped her before she could leave. "If I miss you later, don't forget that Mildred and I will be on the first shore boat tomorrow. You'll have to get up early if you want to join us. We'll be going to Centro. The old historic part of Acapulco. Whatever you do, don't go to La Costera Miguel Alaman. It's lined with hi-rise hotels. Nothing but steel and glass. We see enough of that back in the States."

"Okay, thanks for the warning. Centro definitely sounds more interesting. But don't look for me early. I probably won't leave the ship till mid morning. Is the beach at Centro nice? Is the sand pink?"

This was a color Mildred was familiar with; she wore various shades of it every day. "I don't think so," she said, puckering her forehead. "I believe some beaches in the Bahamas are pink. Or is it in Jamaica?" She turned to Francine. "Do you remember?"

"I'm not a beach person. You know I never sit in the sand. Not even in Florida where it's practically in my front yard."

Mildred shrugged and turned back to Maggie. "Sorry, we can't help you. But I know about the shopping. The stores in Centro are *prima!* You can buy the most beautiful silver jewelry. And belts with aqua stones to die for. My son's wife placed an order with me. Not to appear partial, I'll have to get a similar belt for my daughter whether she wants it or not. Plus I need souvenirs for my grandchildren."

"Mildred morphs into bag lady the minute we go ashore," Francine laughed. "Wait till you see her haul her purchases back to the ship. She'll need a shore boat all to herself."

"Don't forget to bargain," Bill McKiernan chimed in, looking at Maggie and Claudia. "The shop keepers expect it. They enjoy it. Mexican vendors have no respect for you if you don't haggle."

The ship arrived in Acapulco during the night, dropping anchor outside the harbor. When Maggie didn't see her friends at the breakfast buffet, she realized Francine had not been kidding when she said they were taking the first shore boat. She wondered how Mildred had managed to get up so early; the love of shopping must have gotten her going.

In order to avoid spending money on food in Acapulco, Maggie ate a substantial ham and mushroom omelet, adding an extra croissant and cheese Danish to pack and take ashore. Claudia joined her for breakfast, carrying a plate of plain toast. She looked sullen, popped a pill with her orange juice, and claimed to have no interest in sightseeing. Maggie suspected that after she left Claudia in the casino last night, she had continued to lose and was blowing a hole in her teacher's pension.

It was ten o'clock before Maggie, wearing her swimsuit under a pair of beige slacks and a plaid camp shirt, was ready to go ashore. Hanging her brown vinyl tote and beach towel over her shoulder, she started down the steps attached to the side of the ship and immediately experienced a moment of vertigo; this was like climbing down the outside of a tall building. The shore boat bobbing in the water below seemed awfully small and, clutching the rickety rope railing, she wondered how Francine and Mildred being twenty years her seniors had managed this descent. Perhaps it took practice. One thing was sure. Bill McKiernan was not going ashore. This port-of-call was not wheelchair accessible.

As Maggie stepped into the tender, taking a seat among the three dozen passengers already seated, including several youngsters hanging over the side, trying to touch the water, she glanced back up at the ship and was surprised to spot the man she had seen on the top deck several nights in a row. She took a second look just to be sure and could have sworn that they made eye contact. Of course she was only imagining that, for surely the distance was too great. She wondered if he was studying the shore boat, counting heads, determining if it could hold one more person. When it left and he was still standing at the railing, he must have decided to catch the next one. Maggie turned her back on the ship and looked toward Acapulco as the tender sped into the harbor where another large cruise ship was docked and sleek yachts in all sizes were moored. Her heart swelling with anticipation, she placed her tote and beach towel between her legs and held on to her straw hat to keep it from flying off in the wind. She marveled at being here and was tempted to pinch herself. It was too good to be true.

When the tender pulled up to the pier servicing Centro, she stepped off and immediately headed for the beach. The sand was not pink, but it was beautiful and, kicking off her sandals, she spread out the ship's towel, stepped out of her slacks and pulled off her shirt. Her green swimsuit was a conservative maillot with a skirt panel in the front; she was not bold enough to don a bikini. Of course, looking around, she saw women much older and bulkier than she, wearing them. Suddenly she felt slim, trim, and youthful. In short: wonderful. The beach was hers to enjoy. Acapulco was hers to explore. She had all day and most of the evening because the final shore boats didn't return to the ship until ten tonight.

Sitting down, crossing her arms over her knees, Maggie enjoyed the view and the solitude. Beyond the harbor, The Mexican Star sat white and shining on the calm sea, exactly like on the posters in Agnes Perollo's window. Young men in white shirts and Panama hats were selling refreshments to sunbathers from various concessionaires along the boardwalk. The crescent shaped shoreline was a mix of rocky areas and stretches of sand. Acapulco was a city of considerable size, much larger than she expected, with neighborhoods spreading up into the hills, where some of the residential homes appeared to be clinging to the cliffs by prayer alone. Across the bay, she saw the tall buildings of Playa Icacos that Francine had mentioned and was glad to be in Centro; the old town was more her liking. The architecture was quaint with a beautiful Moorish cathedral dominating the square.

Gazing back out across the water, Maggie saw a paraglider being towed behind a speedboat, soon lifting off to a dizzying height. She shuddered. She knew that people from the ship had signed up for this particular sport while other passengers had signed up for the bus ride to La Quebrada to watch the death defying cliff divers; equally terrifying to Maggie's way of thinking. She couldn't imagine paying good money for the privilege of being scared silly. She planned to simply enjoy Centro, its beach, and surrounding neighborhoods.

Wondering if she could safely leave her tote while she went for a swim, Maggie figured that if she didn't go out too far, she could see her belongings from the water. Still, as a precaution – after all, the ship had warned about pickpockets – she walked over and asked a group of fellow cruise passengers sitting nearby to keep an eye on her things for a few minutes. All her important stuff was in that purse: passport, wallet, camera, keycard, and her pearl earrings. She hadn't bothered to make use of the ship's safe-deposit boxes because, except for the pearls, she had nothing of value that would warrant taking up space in the Purser's Office, including her Timex watch, which she now removed and threw into the bag; she didn't think it was waterproof.

The bay was wonderful and Maggie would have stayed in the water till her skin wrinkled, but she didn't want to impose for too long on those safeguarding her tote bag. Walking out of the surf, she waved her thanks and, shaking sand from the towel, dried her hair and sat down, letting the sun do its job on the rest of her.

After an hour of lying on the beach and before getting a burn, she pulled on her slacks and buttoned the shirt over her swimsuit, made room in the tote for the towel, and prepared to walk around town. She would come back for another swim later when the sun was lower in the sky. Now it was time to see the sights. But first she stopped at a souvenir kiosk to buy postcards and stamps. She wanted to send cards to Simone, Vera, and Lisa. Sitting down on a bench near the fishing pier, she wrote her greetings and dropped the postcards into a mailbox as she strolled the perimeter of the old harbor square.

At one point during her walk, she got an eerie feeling as though she was being watched. The hair rose on her scalp. Turning her head carefully from side to side without appearing suspicious, she saw a young man who did, in fact, seem to be following her. Unless she was mistaken, he was the same person she had seen loitering at the kiosk where she'd bought the postcards. Testing him, she casually kept walking, stopped short, and quickly looked over her shoulder. Sure enough, she saw him stop as well and now make a great pretense of bending down to tie his shoelaces. Was he mocking an American tourist? Was he a local mimic practicing his art? He didn't look scruffy, she didn't think he was a pickpocket; nonetheless, she kept her tote close to her body. She was from New York. She was crime savvy. She knew the ropes.

Melting into the crowds of tourists on the sidewalks, she had forgotten him about the same time she spotted Doug Collins, Francine, and Mildred having coffee at a brightly painted outdoor café on the opposite side of the street. They saw her as well and waved her over. As she approached, she sucked in her breath because – looking beyond the threesome – she caught sight of the individual she'd seen late at night on the top deck and again this morning at the ship's railing. He had come ashore and was having a beer at the bar directly behind her friends. Up close and in broad daylight, wearing khakis with a green striped shirt, sleeves rolled up to the elbows, he was the spitting image of Clint Eastwood.

Maggie took off her straw hat and ran her fingers through her hair to give it some lift. She regretted not wearing lipstick and wondered if the swimsuit under her slacks made her look bulky. But why this sudden concern with her appearance? Except for the fact that they were on the same cruise, this man was a total stranger and far too handsome to pay attention to a plain woman. She gave herself a mental heads-up to reality and punched the hat back down on her head, no longer caring if it flattened her hair.

"Sit down, Maggie." Francine pointed to an empty chair the same time she waved the waiter over. "How about some coffee?"

"I'd love some." Maggie sat down and hung her tote across the back of her chair.

"So what have you been doing with yourself all morning?" Mildred wanted to know.

"I went to the beach and had a wonderful swim. How about you?"

"I've been shopping." Mildred grinned and pointed to the bags under her chair.

"Mildred is giving the local economy a shot in the arm," Francine remarked.

"Speak for yourself." Mildred now reported that Francine had spent the morning scouring galleries for pricey paintings.

"Art can be a good investment," the latter said in self-defense.

"Paintings?" Doug shook his head and turned in his chair, giving Maggie a front and center view of the red and white checked Bermuda shorts he wore with a yellow and green striped golf shirt. As if this collaboration wasn't bad enough, he was wearing laced business shoes and black socks. "Stocks are a far better investment," he was saying. "German stocks in particular. Their heretofore sluggish economy is showing signs of life." Although he was directing his comments at Maggie, he didn't look upon her as a potential client; indeed, he simply found it difficult to look away. The sun had tinged her face pink and, framed by unruly hair peeking out from under the perky straw hat, was incredibly appealing. Her blue eyes were unusually bright and he wished himself twenty years younger. "I feel a turnaround is coming. It has already begun in Asia where the economy..."

"All right! Enough shop talk!" Francine held up her hands to silence him. "One can't hang a stock certificate in the living room. Anyway, on a more pressing subject. It's time for lunch. Who's hungry?"

Both Mildred and Doug responded in the affirmative.

"I'm not hungry yet," Maggie said. "I want to walk around first." She put down her empty cup and fished into her brown vinyl tote to pay for the coffee.

"Put that away!" Francine ordered before Maggie could dig out her wallet. "Doug is paying." She nudged him.

"Of course. I never let a pretty lady pay. *Three* pretty ladies," he quickly amended.

"Thanks." Maggie smiled and prepared to leave.

"Don't be tempted to drink from any public fountain," Francine warned her. "No matter how clean it looks. The local population is immune to the water. Don't let that fool you."

"Good advice," Doug nodded. "And when you buy bottled water, test the cap. Be sure it's factory sealed. Some shop keepers fill the empties people leave behind with tap water and resell it as purified."

"One can't be too careful," Mildred added. "That goes for the food as well. Don't eat anything raw. But seriously, why don't you come and have lunch with us? We are going to Casa Mer out on the main pier. It serves a fabulous lobster Newburg."

"I'd love to," Maggie said, "but I won't be hungry for hours. I had a late breakfast. And there's so much to see. I want to take a tour of the cathedral and hike into the hills. I'd like to get a closer look at those homes on the cliffs. The ship's pamphlets claim some are owned by Hollywood movie stars."

Francine nodded. "By all means, go ahead. This is your first time in Acapulco. Enjoy yourself. We'll see you back onboard tonight. Don't miss the last shore boat. The ship doesn't wait for anyone. You'll hear four long blasts from its horns at a quarter of ten. That'll be your final warning."

"I'll remember." Maggie hung her tote over her shoulder and was off. Crossing the narrow coble-stoned street, she again felt as if someone was watching her. But instead of goose bumps on her neck, this time it gave her a warm pleasant feeling. She glanced around and caught the eye of Clint Eastwood's double still sitting at the bar behind her friends and close enough to have heard their entire conversation. She quickly looked away and tried to remember if she had said anything silly. But why should that matter? She was flattering herself to think that he might have been sufficiently interested to eavesdrop.

Chapter
twenty-six

After visiting the historic cathedral which Maggie learned was built in the 1930s, a date that didn't exactly make it ancient, she spent the next hour, walking the narrow downtown streets of Centro and perusing the colorful merchandise in the many shops without being tempted to buy anything; no one was expecting her to bring back souvenirs.

Strolling past quaint restaurants with whitewashed adobe walls and red tiled roofs, she saw groups from the ship, having lunch. She waved but kept walking, only stopping to chat a moment with Dorothy and Paul sitting at a sidewalk table in the shade of a leafy palm.

Continuing on, she spotted Amanda Olson and Dr. Hellman by a street vendor where Dr. Hellman was buying her a turquoise necklace. At the other end of the long display table, Rose Burke was looking at silver bracelets and Maggie saw her choose some bangles with matching rings. She wondered where Rose's companion was. Had Ronald Cohen remained on the ship or had another woman snatched him away, leaving Rose to console herself buying fancy trinkets? Maggie didn't stop to find out. There was too much to see and she didn't want Rose tagging along, delaying her.

As she turned away from the row of vendors, she spotted the same young man she'd seen earlier; this time he was studying piñatas hanging in bunches among the souvenir shops. It seemed unlikely that a local would be paying tourist prices, and again Maggie thought that perhaps she was being followed. But for what possible reason? She shrugged. She was being paranoid.

Leaving the kiosks, she was crossing an intersection against a light that wasn't working, when she spotted Clint Eastwood's twin walking solo along the opposite sidewalk. Considering the great number of single ladies from the ship milling about town, she was amazed twelve of them hadn't circled their wagons around him. And just so he wouldn't think that she had anything on her mind, she stopped at the curb and busied herself buying a bottle of water from a boy with a donkey cart. Checking the seal on the cap before paying, she glanced around and saw that her mystery man had disappeared.

Walking away from the tourist-congested areas, she found a shady bench on a quiet side street and sat down to drink some water and eat the croissant and cheese Danish she'd brought along from the ship. Setting out again, and as the day wore on she became increasingly adventuresome, soon heading up into the foothills in the hope of seeing the fabulous cliff homes. Her camera was in her tote bag and she planned to take pictures of the coastline, the harbor, and the ships from up high where she could get a panoramic shot.

The pavement eventually became gravel, then a winding dirt road with multi family homes on both sides of the street. Scores of children were playing on the stoops to the buildings where laundry hung from lines strung between open windows. Small bodegas sold comestibles and local women traded gossip while they pinched the tomatoes and examined freshly baked tortillas. Maggie loved the ambiance. This was the real Mexico. Acapulco was for tourists. She snapped a couple of pictures, took a sip of water, and put the bottle and the camera back into the tote. Her only disappointment was that she hadn't come to any of the homes of the movie stars. Maybe she had taken the wrong road into the hills or hadn't gone far enough yet. Perhaps they were out of sight behind some of the high walls she passed. But thoroughly enchanted with the local flavor and although the neighborhood was now becoming increasingly rundown, she continued walking. The flat-roofed houses along this stretch had once upon a time been painted white, little of which remained, the red adobe showing through. One structure had suffered a fire, its scorched door dangling on a rusty hinge, while others looked abandoned. There were no vegetable stands by the side of the road and no children played in the street; it seemed like a no man's zone, a deserted neighborhood.

Walking in the shadows of these neglected buildings, Maggie began to feel vulnerable and stopped to look over her shoulder to confirm that the young man wasn't following her. There was no sign of him. Good. She chided herself for any absurd fear.

She passed a pottery shop and kept going, barely glancing at the wares. The pottery was plain terra cotta, not glazed with pretty colors to attract tourists; besides, the shop was closed. A flock of large, squawking birds startled her as they suddenly flew across her path and into the top of a cluster of palm trees up ahead, their colorful wings a foil for the deteriorating surroundings. Again Maggie felt slightly uneasy and suspected that perhaps she had ventured too far away from the main hub of town. She looked around and walked past a man sitting in the doorway of a shabby house. He appeared to be deep into his siesta yet something told her that he remained vigilant under his sombrero. She kept going, deciding that she would soon and very casually turn around and go back; it was not her style to turn tail and run. She was from New York.

When she happened upon an alley where some men were arguing, their dispute coming to blows, she knew that she was in the wrong place. It was high time to get back to town. A build-in sensor, a warning, stiffened the hair at the back of her neck. Self-preservation told her that this was as far from Acapulco as any tourist ought to go on foot and alone. She had probably gone too far and now wished for Rose Burke's company. She should have let her tag along.

Chapter
twenty-seven

Pivoting on her heel, Maggie started to walk back downhill, soon passing the small pottery shop. Though closed, it indicating commerce the kind she was familiar with. She felt better about her surroundings.

Concentrating on the dirt road, which would shortly become graveled, then paved as it led down into Acapulco, she kept her eyes straight ahead. The way seemed awfully long suddenly and she was surprised that she had come this far earlier. Rounding a bend in the road, she happened to look out across an empty lot and in between some trees saw the sparkling blue bay in the distance. She remembered that she had wanted to take a panoramic picture. This was the perfect spot for it.

Crossing the vacant lot, mesmerized with the vista, she failed to notice some stealthy movement behind her. She heard no footsteps in the soft dirt. She saw no one dart out from between two adobe structures; however, before she could dig out her camera, she felt a tug on the vinyl tote a nanosecond before it was wrenched from her shoulder, replaced by a cold draft in the empty space it left under her arm. Startled, she spun around and saw a young man running back up the street, carrying her purse.

A sick feeling swept over her. It threatened to topple her. Her knees felt weak. She couldn't breathe. Nonetheless, her brain processed the fact that this was the same individual who had followed her earlier today. Stunned, she watched as he sprinted away and although instinct told her to pursue him, she couldn't. Shock had turned her legs to jelly; they wouldn't support a chase. She couldn't move. Rooted to the spot, she saw him turn a corner and disappear.

Standing in a paralyzed stupor, Maggie looked around. No less than two people on the far side of the road had witnessed the crime and although her traumatized expression now appealed to them for help, neither one stepped forward or showed any interest in chasing the thief. The woman in the doorway simply turned and disappeared inside. On a stone stoop next door, the man crossed his arms over his chest and went back to sleep under his sombrero.

Never before had Maggie felt so alone, so helpless, *and* so stupid. She rummaged her head for some Spanish vocabulary that might rouse the sleeping man, but came up blank. She couldn't put a coherent thought together, definitely not in Spanish. She could only agonize over the realization that her wallet, passport, camera, keycard, and pearl earrings were gone. She almost sank to her knees in despair at having been so careless and exposing herself like this. What on earth had inspired her to walk so far away from town? She, a New Yorker, should have known better. The tropical sun must have addled her brain.

Again she contemplated pursuing the thief. Of course by now he was long gone and it could prove dangerous to try to catch him. Suppose his trail led into a blind alley; cornered, he might resort to violence. Again she berated herself for venturing into these unknown hills, an idiot's errand. This was a new low. She wished she had never left the ship this morning. She should have concerned herself with Claudia's low spirits and stayed with her, then none of this would have happened.

Tears of bitter frustration stinging the back of her eyes, Maggie realized she could do nothing now except continue back down the road toward Acapulco, find a police officer and report the crime. But how would she get back on the ship without her passport and keycard? In these days of heightened security, everyone was checked and rechecked. Picture ID was a must. Of course Francine, Mildred, and others could vouch for her and she was clearly listed on the ship's roster, but it was a sobering thought to have to admit to this colossal lapse in judgment. Flyers had cautioned disembarking passengers about falling victim to crime. Having been duly warned, Maggie had nonetheless stepped right into a trap. A few hours on foreign soil and she had become the consummate dim-witted tourist, a bad joke, tonight's object of embarrassing gossip onboard ship.

Chapter twenty-eight

Half running, half walking, blinded by angry tears, Maggie passed the bodega selling fruits and vegetables where she had happily snapped pictures earlier. It was now closed for the afternoon siesta, but even if it had been milling with customers, she would have taken no notice of it. She didn't see anything or anyone, certainly not the lone individual walking toward her until she ran straight into him, almost knocking him down. Without apologizing, and trying to get past him, she was pushing him out of the way when a deep male voice – definitely American – stopped her.

"In a hurry to return to the ship?" he said with a mocking lilt.

Maggie was in no mood for wisecracks. "No!" she blurted heatedly and still dazed and traumatized wiped the back of her hand across her wet eyes. "I have to find someone who speaks English." Again she tried to get past this person who seemed to be deliberately blocking her path.

"Whoa!" He grabbed her arm before she could run off. "I speak English. You won't find anyone else around here who does."

"Oh?" Maggie pulled her arm free. "Then please tell me where I can find the police."

"They're not in this neighborhood. Every available officer has been assigned to the downtown area. Tourists falling victim to crime is bad for business. Shops and restaurants depend on law enforcement to keep tourists safe and eager to spend money."

"Well, *dammit!*" Maggie usually didn't swear but she was in a terrible bind. "I just became a victim. My purse was snatched. Not downtown. Right up there."

She pointed at the winding road from whence she'd come, finally looked at the American, and immediately fell silent. Having been robbed in broad daylight was bad enough. Having to explain herself to Clint Eastwood was the final straw. She wished herself dead. "Oh, God!" she moaned. "I feel like such a fool."

"It's not your fault."

"Oh, but it is. I walked right into a trap."

"Well, maybe we can do something about it," he said, taking her elbow and starting back up the road. "Show me where it happened."

"*What?*" Maggie sputtered aghast and jerked her arm free. "Go back up there? Without the police?"

"We might as well. No officer will bother with a purse snatching. Perhaps he'll write up a report. But that'll be the end of it."

"Sounds like back New York," Maggie muttered under her breath.

"You're from New York?"

"Yes. So I ought to know better than expose myself to a thief," she bit off tartly. "That's what you're thinking...isn't it?"

"No. I was thinking that you showed true New York hubris when you started out."

"Huh?"

"I saw you at the café with your friends earlier today. I overheard you telling them that you wanted to explore the hillsides. Something I was planning to do as well. Of course I was surprised when I saw you start up into this seedy neighborhood."

"You followed me?"

"At a polite distance. Now I wish I had followed you more closely. I might have seen the thief and perhaps given chase."

"Perhaps?"

"Well, yes, depending on how big and strong he looked."

Despite herself, Maggie grinned.

"By the way, I believe we are on the same ship," the American said, offering his hand. "My name's Michael Sanders."

"I'm Margaret Maghpye." She shook his hand without admitting that she recognized him. "My friends call me Maggie."

"All right, Maggie," he gave her a crocked smile. "Let's go catch a thief. In the very least we might find some of your belongings. Thieves usually discard what they can't turn into cash."

"They dump passports and credit cards?" she said, hope rising.

"Sometimes. Of course there's a black market for those items nowadays. Let's just hope the bandit is a small-timer looking for cash and with no experience in the world of forgery and criminality."

As they started to retrace her steps, Maggie wondered if she ought to tell Michael Sanders about the young man she'd seen around town, the person she was sure had snatched her purse. Of course if she mentioned that, she'd look even more foolish for having thrown caution to the wind and venturing out of bounds.

"Here. This is the spot," she said after a while, stopping at the scene of the crime. "This is where he came up behind me. I was looking out across that vacant lot toward the bay and didn't notice him until it was too late." She turned her head; the man on the far side of the road was still reclining on the stoop, his sombrero over his face.

"Where did he go from here?"

"I didn't really see. He just ran further up the road and disappeared into thin air."

"He must have ducked into a building or rounded a corner."

"Yes. He disappeared around a corner but I don't know which one. It happened so fast. Maybe it wasn't a real corner. It could have been a path between some buildings."

"Okay. Let's keep going until something jogs your memory."

"Come to think of it, I do remember a pottery shop. When the thief ran back up the road, he turned right just beyond it."

"Good. A point of reference."

Continuing up the road, Maggie wondered if they might find someone willing to provide leads. Locals might not give her the time of day but in this male-dominated society they might be willing to speak to Michael Sanders.

"Do you know any Spanish?" she asked him.

"Yes, but if you're thinking of asking for assistance, forget it. The thief is obviously a local. We are outsiders. Gringos. They wouldn't lift a finger to help us. Nor would they accuse one at their own."

"That's not very comforting."

"Unfortunately that's how it is. They're dirt poor and only know us as tourists spending more money in one day than they earn in a year. We're the quintessential Ugly Americans and fair game."

"I should have thought of that. I guess I take the grand prize for stupidity."

"Don't be so hard on yourself. It happens all the time. You're not the first and you won't be the last."

"But I'm from New York City. I should know better."

Michael Sanders grinned. "On that count you are guilty." The way he said it, his indictment sounded like a compliment.

"There!" Maggie stopped and pointed. "That's the pottery shop. See that cluster of palm trees? He rounded the corner just beyond that."

They reached the spot and saw that it led into a narrow wheel-rutted road and a sorry collection of wooden shacks with flimsy corrugated tin roofs. An old swaybacked burro harnessed to a cart by one of the dwellings, was nibbling on the grass growing between the wheel ruts. Past the donkey, they could see children playing around a puddle of water.

"I guess he could be just about anywhere in there," Maggie said, hope of finding her belonging vanishing. "After what you said a minute ago, knocking on doors won't do us any good."

"That's true." Michael nodded. "But let's not give up so fast." Maggie realized she was an incurable defeatist. "What does your purse look like?"

"It's a brown vinyl tote. About this big." She held out her hands. "It's old and worn. The thief won't get a penny if he tries to sell it."

Michael took several long strides along the rutted road. Maggie followed him.

"Is that it?" he said moments later, pointing toward a brown bag propped up against some trash bins.

"Oh, my God! Yes! I don't believe it." Maggie ran over, grabbed her tote and held it against her chest, praying it still contained her important documents. She was preparing to search the bag but before she could open it, Michael came up behind her and took her arm.

"Come," he said with a sudden urgency in his voice. "You've got your purse. Let's go!" He pulled her none too gently back to the corner and down the street, ignoring her protests with his rough handling. He didn't relent until they were past the pottery shop and then some.

"Okay," he finally said, stepping behind some yucca trees by the side of the road, away from any probing eyes. "Open it."

Maggie cried out in surprise when she found her passport and wallet. Riffling through the latter she saw that the money was gone, no surprise, but at least her credit cards were still there along with the keycard to her cabin.

"I guess the thief just wanted the cash," she said. "And my camera and earrings." Shaking her head sadly with that particular loss, she pawed the empty tote bag. "What do you know? He took my reading glasses. The ship's towel along with a half empty bottle of water is also gone. What on earth would he want with that?"

"A water bottle and a towel?" Michael frowned. "Let me see your purse a minute." She handed it to him. "The fact that it was left in such a conspicuous place," he mumbled while feeling around the lining, "can only mean they hoped you'd come looking for it. It's almost as if they were counting on it."

"They?" Maggie said. "It was a lone thief who stole my purse."

"Could be. But I'm beginning to suspect more is at play here. Come on, let's get out of here."

Holding the tote, Michael left the shelter of the yucca trees and hurried down the road, not stopping until they came to a crumbling garden wall along an arroyo on the bay side of the street where he determined there was no chance of being spotted. Pulling Maggie with him, he disappeared behind the wall and now proceeded to empty the bag, handing Maggie her passport and wallet. "Keep those in your pocket," he said before starting to tear at the lining.

"Hey! What are you doing?" she cried, watching as he ripped out the bottom and the sides of her tote which was, admittedly, old and ugly; still, she was attached to it and needed it more than ever now that her cash was gone. "Hey! Stop! Wait a minute!" She grabbed at his arm. "What do you think you're doing? First I'm robbed. Now you're ruining my purse!"

"Look! Look at this," Michael Sanders said as he withdrew his hand, showing her a fistful of sealed plastic envelopes. "I believe this is heroin."

"What?" Maggie took a step back. He was looking at her with a grave expression. "Hey, wait a minute. You don't think...*what?* You think that stuff's mine? Good God! You think I'm a druggie?"

"No." Michael dropped the envelopes back into the tote. "It's my guess that you were singled out as a mule. They steal your purse and, figuring you'll come looking for it, plant the stuff after removing most of your belongings so you won't notice any difference in the weight. The thief obviously had the help of a fast-working seamstress to fix the lining. Unknowingly, you'd be transporting an illegal substance back to the States. Professional drug runners are constantly dreaming up new methods. But this is the work of a rank amateur. It's an old ploy that has been done many, many times. You've probably been watched since leaving the ship. Perhaps before leaving the ship."

"Someone *was* following me earlier today," Maggie finally admitted. "A young man. I'm sure he was the one who robbed me. But why me?"

"Your tote's the perfect size. They couldn't pull this on someone carrying a small purse. Plus you walked around alone. The perfect victim. When you strolled up into these hills, your stalker probably couldn't believe his luck."

"All that watching...all that trouble for a little bit of heroin?"

Michael raised his eyebrows with her naiveté. "Pure, uncut, I would estimate this batch is worth two hundred thousand dollars. Not bad for a day's work."

"Oh, my God! Well, what are we waiting for? Let's take it to the police. Maybe we can help them bust up a drug ring. I can describe the suspect."

Michael shook his head. "If we go to the police we'll be locked up and languish under lock and key until long after the ship leaves."

"Why? It's not our heroin. We're turning it over. Isn't that the proper procedure?"

"Back in the States that would work. Here it's a different story. The police might decide it's simpler to hold us rather than bother the real culprits who are notoriously eager to assassinate meddling officers. The authorities certainly don't want any descriptions. A lot of the fellows on the force are involved in the drug trade."

Maggie was suddenly afraid. She had read about Mexican jails, and she had read about vicious drug gangs. She stared at the white envelopes in her bag and glanced over the old garden wall, but except for a stray dog inspecting some garbage left by the side of the road, no one was about. People were still inside, enjoying their siestas, and Michael had wisely picked a very secluded spot. But although her important documents were returned to her, she wished she'd never gone back for her purse. "Suppose we hadn't taken the bait?" she said.

"The thief would employ an alternative plan and have someone drop your bag off at one of the ship's shore boats. To throw off suspicion, he'd send a youngster who'd claim to have found it. Your passport and keycard inside would make identification ridiculously easy and the bag would be delivered to your cabin. The lining intact, you'd never suspect a thing. You might grumble about your lost valuables, but you'd be grateful to have your passport and credit cards."

"It's unreal. I don't mind telling you that I'm scared. What do we do now? Should we just throw everything away? Leave it here?"

"No. Some children might find it."

"Is it better to drop it in a trash bin in town?"

Michael shook his head. "Same problem. Locals regularly sift through the trash. The trick is to take the stuff off the market. Dispose of it once and for all."

"Okay." Maggie liked that plan. "Let's sprinkle it here in the dirt and cover it up."

"Yes, that's what I was thinking. Afterwards we'll have to go to the beach for a good dunking." Michael grinned despite the seriousness of the situation. "Would you be game to go swimming in your clothes?" When Maggie looked puzzled, he explained. "Drug-sniffing police dogs can detect minute traces. Once we open the sealed bags and discard the contents there will be powder residue on us. Salt water will get rid of it."

"I thought you said the police is corrupt. Why would they bother us?"

"Some officers are corrupt. Others take pride in catching tourists who might have bought drugs. It proves they are vigilant. We don't know who's who. They wear the same uniform."

"Are you in law enforcement back home?" It occurred to Maggie that Michael Sanders was awfully knowledgeable about the drug trade and crooked cops. Plus, he had immediately suspected her purse and recognized the substance in the plastic bags.

"No."

"No? So what do you do?"

"I'm retired."

"From what?" she persisted.

"The airlines," he said, his voice a steel trap closing the subject.

Okay, Maggie had no further questions.

Michael produced a key from his pocket and now began puncturing the bags, handing each to Maggie so she could dispose of the white powder under the chaparral.

"I'll take the empties," he said and, using the heel of his shoe, dug a hole in the soft ground. He dropped the bags into it and kicked dirt and grass on top. "Give me the tote. We better bury it as well." When Maggie hesitated, he said, "Look, your purse is extremely valuable to some unsavory characters that don't know it's empty. I'm sure someone on the ship has been assigned to keep an eye on it. They're obviously planning to reclaim the contents after you disembark in San Diego. It could be ugly. Believe me, you are a lot safer without the bag."

Though Maggie hated to lose it, she saw Michael's wisdom and allowed him to give the tote a decent burial.

Half an hour later, walking along one of the main streets in town, heading for the beach and that all-important swim, Dorothy and Paul came up behind them, Dorothy tapping Maggie on the shoulder. She nearly jumped out of her skin, expecting to see a police officer demanding that she stand still while his dog sniffed her clothes.

"Maggie! Aren't you going to introduce us to your friend?" Dorothy purred, mentally comparing the tall, good-looking individual to her own beau. Paul Hopkinson was a rich widower but the man with Maggie was much younger and had all his hair. Dorothy would trade escorts in a heartbeat.

"Oh, of course." Maggie breathed a sigh of relief not to be staring down an officer of the law, crooked or not. "Dorothy and Paul, this is Michael Sanders."

Without extending his hand, Michael nodded to both of them.

"Do you live in Acapulco?" Dorothy asked. She hadn't seen Mr. Sanders on the ship and figured Maggie had gotten lucky on land.

"No."

"Mr. Sanders is on the cruise with us," Maggie said.

"Really! How delightful! Where are you from?" Dorothy persisted.

"Los Angeles." Michael was anxious to be rid of these people. As much as both he and Maggie had brushed themselves off, he knew the white powder still clung to their clothes and hands, invisible, but not undetectable to the heightened sense of a trained beagle. They could not afford to stand about and waste time on social niceties; especially now that he spotted a police officer walking his dog along the opposite side of the street; too close for comfort.

"Los Angeles!" Dorothy exclaimed. "I'm from Ojai. We're practically neighbors. Strange, I haven't seen you on the ship." She turned to Paul. "Paul, have you seen Mr. Sanders onboard?"

Paul Hopkinson shook his head. "Are you at the eight o'clock dinner seating?" he asked and inched closer, peering through his glasses at Michael, trying to recognize him.

"No." Michael looked beyond Paul's shoulder. The police officer was crossing the street at the intersection up ahead. He and his dog were coming this way. "Look, I think we ought get out of the sun," he said and started the process by casually strolling over to the other side. Dorothy and Paul followed with Maggie.

The opposite side of the street was even sunnier, and as Dorothy squinted up at Michael, she wondered what purpose had been served. She would never know, because he took Maggie's arm and left her and Paul standing on the sidewalk with barely a nod of good-bye. To her credit, Dorothy recognized the brush-off and didn't pursue him except to say, "It's been nice meeting you, Mr. Sanders. Enjoy the rest of your shore leave. You, too, Maggie."

"Thanks, I will." Maggie turned and smiled.

"See you back on the ship," Paul Hopkinson called after them. "Say, Mr. Sanders! Do you play bridge?"

"No."

Chapter *thirty*

That evening, after the buffet supper, sparsely attended since many passengers were dining ashore, Maggie went to the Atrium Lounge to hear a concert and splurge on a glass of wine. In view of everything that had transpired today, she felt she needed it. And she needed to fill the void that Michael Sanders left once they parted company after returning to the ship early in order to get out of their wet clothes. She had looked for him at the buffet supper; he wasn't there, which didn't surprise her. Nursing her wine, she had listened to the first part of the concert without really hearing the music; her mind was elsewhere; mostly on the enigmatic Michael Sanders.

Once his wife left for the casino, about the same time the musicians took their first intermission, Bill McKiernan abandoned his cluster of friends and, holding a whiskey sour in one hand, used the other to wheel himself over to the bar where Maggie was perched on a tall stool. Francine and Mildred were both confined to their respective cabins. After returning from Acapulco they had gone directly to bed, suffering intestinal disorders.

"Too bad about Francine and Mildred," Bill said as he came up to Maggie. "I heard that Doug has a touch of the same sickness."

"Yes." Taking her wine glass, Maggie slipped off the barstool and sat down in a club chair to be at eye level with Bill. "Something they ate ashore got the better of them. I saw Francine right after she came back onboard. She stayed on deck awhile, watching our departure and hoping the ocean breezes would work a miracle once we were at sea. She looked awfully pale but insisted she'd only eaten thoroughly cooked food."

"Doug blames the lunch they had at Casa Mer," Bill said. "But I can't imagine they became ill from anything that fine old restaurant served." He shrugged. "Oh, well, they'll feel better tomorrow. We've all had Montezuma's revenge at one time or another. I have eaten at Casa Mer in years past without incident and would have done so again today if not for this damned thing." He shifted in his wheelchair with a measure of impatience. "Thankfully, our next port-of-call has a longer deepwater pier. So unless another cruise ship gets there ahead of us, forcing us to drop anchor rather than dock, I'll be able to wheel myself down the ramp. I'm looking forward to that. Too bad we arrived into Acapulco late and lost our spot. I suppose we never quite made up the time we spent at sea with engine trouble."

"I guess not," Maggie said, remembering that she hadn't minded the ship being idle Thanksgiving Day. Of course that unscheduled delay cost Bill and other wheelchair-bound passengers the chance to go ashore in Acapulco, because there was no way a wheelchair could be lowered into the tenders. Climbing up and down those rickety steps was difficult enough for a mobile person like herself. "What put you in a wheelchair?" she suddenly asked, the words slipping out before she could determine if it was proper to pry. As far as she knew not even Francine had posed that question.

If Bill was uncomfortable with the query, he didn't show it. "A case of bad luck," he said with a negligent shrug. "I tripped stepping from my golf cart. The fall broke my hip. The fracture turned into a major ordeal because the operation went badly. Two additional procedures only made matters worse when I contracted a terrible infection in the hospital. So here I am. For all practical purposes a cripple. After this cruise, if my doctors can guarantee a reasonably good result, I'll have more surgery. Maybe a hip replacement? But enough of my tales of woe. Tell me, did you enjoy Acapulco?"

"Yes, it was wonderful." Maggie told Bill about her morning on the beach and exploring the town and the hills during the afternoon. She carefully left out the purse-snatching incident because Michael Sanders had urged her not to mention it to anyone.

"People gossip," he had cautioned while riding back to the ship in the tender. "Word could reach those assigned to watch you. If they learn that you thwarted their business dealings, they might take revenge."

"Won't they know it when they see I no longer have the tote bag?"

"They'll see you don't have it, but they won't know why. Cell phones don't work well from the ship so they won't be able to communicate with those on land. They'll think you never retrieved it and that their cohorts didn't make use of any substitute plans."

"Where's your wife?" Maggie asked Bill and dismissed her musings about today's misadventure.

"In the casino. Tomorrow is her birthday and someone put a bug in her ear, telling her that if she played the numbers of the day and the year she'd get lucky at midnight." Bill chuckled and checked his watch. "She went early to warm up."

"I can't believe she took that kind of talk seriously. Sounds to me like the advice one gets from a two-bit fortune teller."

"Yes." Bill smiled. "It just gave her an excuse to gamble."

"You don't gamble?"

"No. The casino is too crowded for a wheelchair. The atmosphere is entirely too flashy. As I get older my tastes get simpler."

Except in choosing a wife, Maggie thought because there was nothing simple about Sheila Mc Kiernan. The woman was Lorelei, a siren song that hopefully wouldn't lead her husband to shipwreck.

"You're not wearing your pearls this evening," Bill said, taking a sip from his glass.

"My pearls?" Maggie's hands flew to her earlobes. He was an observant old gentleman. "I can't believe you noticed," she said.

"Of course I noticed. I've never seen you in the evenings without them. The jewelry a woman wears tells a lot about her. My wife likes to sparkle. The brighter her jewelry the better. It's her personality. She craves attention. Pearls, when she wears them, must be huge. Yours, on the other hand, are dainty and understated. You don't try to draw attention to yourself. You ought to. You're a very attractive woman. Always wear earrings. More than any other jewelry they catch a man's eye. Of course, many things about you catch a man's eye. Even the eye of an old fellow like me." He winked at her.

Maggie felt uncomfortable. She didn't like receiving compliments on her appearance, a social dance she wasn't accustomed to. Besides, she knew perfectly well that there was nothing about her garden-variety looks that warranted it. Disingenuous praise from Bill McKiernan seemed inappropriate and far too personal, more so than receiving flowers. Was he flirting with her or just flattering her? Neither scenario pleased her and not sure how to gracefully accept his attention, she revealed today's incident without thinking. "Actually," she said, "my pearls were stolen."

"Stolen? Where? How?"

"I didn't mention it earlier, but someone snatched my purse in Acapulco. The earrings were in it. Please don't tell anyone. I feel so stupid falling victim to a petty thief." Again remembering Michael's warning, she pinched her lips together to keep from saying anything more; an expression Bill interpreted as sadness with her loss.

"I won't breathe a word," he promised. "I hope you didn't also lose your passport," he added solicitously.

Maggie shook her head. "The passport was in my pocket." This was partially true; after all, it had been in her pocket during the latter part of the day.

"That was very fortunate. It can be a trial to replace a passport while traveling."

"Believe me, I've learned my lesson. Next time I go ashore, I'm making use of the safe in the Purser's Office."

"Good." Bill finished his drink and put the glass down on the table next to his wheelchair. "Maggie..." he said, "I need a favor. As I said a minute ago, tomorrow is my wife's birthday and I want to give her something special. It's not pleasant for her to travel with an invalid. I'd like to make it up to her with a piece of jewelry. You have excellent taste. Your pearls indicated that. Would you mind helping me choose something for Sheila?"

"I'll be glad to."

Bill glanced at his watch. "Would it be an imposition to do it now?"

"No. Not at all."

"Wonderful! Later I might be too tired and go straight to bed. Ideally, I'd like my wife to have her present first thing in the morning. I want her to wake up and find a little surprise on the night table. I would have bought something earlier today but, as you know, the ship's duty-free jewelry store is closed when we're docked. Besides, my mind is not as sharp as it used to be. Things pop into my head and leave just as quickly. I tend to forget. At home I retain a valet to remind me about dates and appointments." Bill glanced at the musical instruments on the raised platform. "Of course I don't want you to miss the last part of the concert on my behalf."

"It doesn't matter," Maggie said, finishing her wine. "There'll be another one tomorrow."

Out at sea, in international waters, the jewelry store stayed open till all hours and the salesperson was delighted to see customers, especially once he recognized the wheelchair-bound passenger.

"*Buenos noches!*" he said, smiling broadly from behind the counter and stepping forward to hold the door open. "You come see *bello joyeria*?" He was about to give a conspirator's wink to Maggie, figuring she was the recipient tonight of the elder gentleman's largesse, but was stopped in the nick of time when Bill McKiernan said, "I need a birthday surprise for my wife. My good friend, Ms. Maghpye, has graciously agreed to help me choose something special." He patted Maggie's arm fondly before turning his attention on the trays inside the glass counter. "Perhaps a necklace? May we see some of those?"

"*Si, Senor* McKiernan!" Arturo Rivas beamed and all but rubbed his hands together before fumbling with a key and unlocking the small sliding door. "Many pretty ones. Yes?" He pulled a velvet-lined tray from a shelf and placed it on the counter. "*Muy bonito.* No?"

Bill Mc Kiernan pursed his lips as he inspected several pieces. All were diamonds with other precious stones worked into the designs. "Let's have Ms. Maghpye try on that one," he said, pointing to a lavish diamond and emerald choker with ruby cabochons worked into the design.

After the salesman fastened it around her neck, Bill asked her to move around in the shop so he could determine how the light caught the color in the stones. "What do you think?" he asked her.

"It's exquisite," she said earnestly, silently deciding the necklace looked like a miniature Christmas wreath around her neck. "Maybe it is a bit over the top? A bit much?"

"Which means it will suit Sheila." Bill McKiernan chuckled and had Maggie try on several other pieces including a simple double strand of graduated diamonds. "That's lovely," he nodded as Mr. Rivas fastened it around her neck, "but it needs something. Let's see how it looks with a pair of earrings." He leaned forward in his chair and pointed to another tray under the counter. "They don't have to match. My wife prefers to mix her pieces. She doesn't wear sets."

Maggie tried on several pairs of earrings, but Bill McKiernan kept coming back to some teardrop sapphires suspended on diamond studs. They were clearly his favorite. "What do you think?" he finally asked her.

"They're simple and eye-popping at the same time," she said, thinking: *Wow!*

"Hmm, a contradiction. Perfect!" Bill told Arturo Rivas to wrap up the earrings as well as the pricey Christmas wreath. He signed for his purchases and, putting the two packages in his lap, wheeled himself back to the elevator.

"Enjoy whatever is left of the concert," he said as Maggie exited on the Atrium deck. "I'll be going up to my cabin now. I'm happy the shopping is done. You were an enormous help. Thank you!"

"I enjoyed it," Maggie said in all honesty because the glittering stones had felt deliciously warm against her skin.

Chapter thirty-two

Maggie listened to the string quartet's last number without ordering another glass of wine. After losing the cash in Acapulco she had to watch her expenditures more closely than ever. She also watched each and every steward, wondering who the "contact" was. Again she appreciated Michael Sanders' wisdom in disposing of the tote; even empty it'd be like waving a red flag in front of a bull. She'd have to make do with her small white evening bag for the rest of the trip. Its size made it useless to drug smugglers, an added measure of comfort the next time she went ashore.

At the end of the concert, Dorothy and Paul came into the Atrium and pulled up some seats next to Maggie.

"Where's your gentleman friend?" Dorothy asked, craning her neck, looking around the crowded lounge. "The one we met in Acapulco."

"I have no idea," Maggie said, trying to sound unconcerned; she certainly didn't want to give the impression she was smitten. "We came back in the same shore boat, then parted ways. I think he likes to keep to himself."

"Ah-hah, a loner? That's too bad. I'd be nice to have him around. He's awfully attractive. He reminds me of some actor." Dorothy turned to Paul. "Who does Mr. Sanders remind you of?"

"Can't say offhand," Paul shrugged, his attention turned to the approaching steward. He ordered brandies for himself and Dorothy. "Maggie, will you join us and have a brandy?" he asked.

She shook her head.

"Well, a loner or not..." Dorothy was still fascinated with the elusive Michael Sanders, "Sheila McKiernan will soon enough try to bring him out of his shell. I suspect she's running out of officers." Maggie realized she wasn't the only one who had noticed Sheila's amorous adventures. "Perhaps Mr. Sanders is in the Coconut Lounge," Dorothy went on. "There's a *Can-Can* contest later. Everyone is going. We're going, aren't we, sweetie?" She reached over and playfully pinched Paul's knee as he was signing for the drinks.

"I thought we had a bridge game," he said, handing the pen and pad back to the steward.

"Oh...yes, I forgot. Well, cheers!" Dorothy sloshed the amber liquid gently around in her glass and touched the rim to Paul's before taking a sip. "We're playing with the Harrisons," she said to Maggie. "Good players. Otherwise a bit tiresome. They're from St. Louis," she added as if that explained it.

Maggie shortly took leave of Dorothy and Paul and went to the casino, curious to see if Sheila McKiernan was actually experience a winning streak. Walking into the charged atmosphere, she spotted Rose Burke and Ronald Cohen playing Black Jack; apparently they were still an item. Maggie noticed that Rose was wearing an inordinate amount of silver jewelry. That salesman in Acapulco must have convinced her it was a magnet for the opposite sex.

Maggie pushed through the crowd to where Claudia Rasner was playing roulette. At the buffet earlier tonight, Claudia hadn't wheedled her about going to the casino, and it appeared that her newfound independence worked in her favor. She was winning. Her face was flushed and her green eyes were overly bright, which Maggie hoped was due to luck, not pills. Crossing the room, she saw Sheila McKiernan stationed at another roulette table – one with all men – so win or lose she was in her element. Her dark hair was pulled back and tied into a knot, the coiffure exposing glistening gold earrings the size of doorknockers. The spaghetti straps on her black satin dress hung lazily off her shoulders while the hem barely covered the essentials, bringing to mind a seventies' miniskirt and making the come-hither message crystal clear. In a fit of petty contempt, Maggie wished she had talked Bill into buying Sheila some gaudy and cheap baubles.

Maggie left the casino. In the corridor outside the doors she stopped a moment to watch several women working the slot machines, but mostly she was trying to talk herself out of going up to the top deck. She ran out willpower about the same time that one of the players got lucky and coins flowed from the slot machine.

Michael Sanders was not in his usual spot. Maggie had the space all to herself and remained standing there for a few minutes, enjoying the view and the solitude but missing his company.

thirty-three

Dressing for dinner the following evening, she again put on her yellow chiffon with the flounced hem, now deeply regretting that she hadn't brought along an additional dress. She wished she had something new to wear, everyone had seen this one, and she wanted to look special because tonight was the Captain's Ball. She had worn rollers while showering and after using the blow dryer had teased her hair, giving it added volume. Primping in front of the mirror, trying to further improve on her appearance, she tried not to think about Michael Sanders, but couldn't help wondering if he would attend the festivities later.

She was finishing her grooming with a final touch of lip-gloss, when there was a knock on her door. Opening it, she saw a deck steward she didn't recognize, but she immediately recognized the small square box in his hands.

"What's this?" she asked, surprised, as he gave it to her.

"*Si.*"

Maggie sighed. "This...this can't be for me," she said, shaking her head.

"*Si!*" He suddenly seemed to remember something and pulled a letter from his pocket, giving it to her.

"Thank you." Maggie closed the door, put down the box and ripped open the envelope, frowning as she now read the note written on the ship's stationery.

My Dear Maggie,

Please do an old man a favor and wear these earrings tonight at the Captain's Ball. They are yours to keep. My wife pointed out that she has several similar pairs

*and sees no reason to have duplicates. She was, however, extremely pleased with the
necklace. You and I made a wonderful choice.*

Again, thanks for your kind assistance.

*Cordially,
Bill Mc Kiernan*

Dumfounded, Maggie sat down on the lower bunk, turning the box over and
over in her hand, not opening it and thinking that even if Sheila McKiernan had a
hundred similar earrings, she could easily exchange these for some that were
different.

Finally lifting the lid, Maggie stared at the sparkling stones on the velvet
cushion. She had never owned anything like this. Her mother had not believed in
jewelry, no family heirlooms were passed on to her, and she'd assuredly never had
the money to buy any for herself. This was way out of her league. She came to a
snap decision. She could not accept such an outrageously expensive gift. She closed
the box and put it into her small white purse. It wasn't yet eight o'clock. She had
time to return the earrings to Bill before dinner.

He was not in his usual pre-dinner spot in the mid deck cocktail lounge, where
the theme suggested an old English library. However, his wife was there, standing
at the oak bar surrounded by men in tuxedos, the required attire for tonight.
Maggie saw that Sheila was wearing the new necklace and noted that it went well
with her exquisite green *tulle* gown. She had a drink in her hand and her guttural
laughter could be heard above the din in the room, she was obviously in high
spirits; still, an inner voice told Maggie not to approach her. The memory of the
rude dismissal in the dining room the night Maggie had thanked her and Bill for
the flowers, was too fresh in her mind. So, although Bill's note had clearly said that
his wife didn't want duplicates, she might not know that he had given the earrings
to Maggie. And suppose he was not quite himself – not *compos mentis* – as he
wrote the note. Perhaps he'd suffered a moment of confusion and hadn't really
meant to give them away. Yesterday he admitted that his mind had some worn
spark plugs. Maybe he had mixed his medication with scotch again?

Maggie left the cocktail lounge and went straight the McKiernans' cabin,
where she found Bill putting the final touches on his evening clothes with the help
of the ship's valet. Bill dismissed the man the minute Maggie appeared, telling him
to return in five minutes. The valet returned at the same time Maggie left the

cabin still in possession of the earrings, along with Bill's assurances that he had, in truth, bought them with her in mind. "I never meant to give them to my wife," he explained. "Sheila didn't reject them. She never saw them. That was just a little ruse I employed to make it easier for you to accept them."

Amazed with his generosity, Maggie rushed back down to her cabin, put on the earrings, and combed her hair behind her ears to give the glittering stones maximum exposure. Admiring her reflection in the mirror, she couldn't help wonder if there were strings attached to this fabulous gift. But, mulling it over and over in her mind, she shook her head. The man was close to eighty and in a wheelchair. He had a beautiful wife. What could he possibly want from someone as plain and unsophisticated as Maggie?

Despite wearing the tired yellow chiffon, Maggie walked into the dining room, feeling positively radiant. And when she sat down, no one at her table could ignore her. Dr. Hellman narrowed his eyes and gave her a speculative look, forcing Amanda Olson to move forward in her chair, blocking his view to derail any budding interest. Paul Hopkinson, smiling benignly, wondered at the unusual sparkle in Maggie's blue eyes without making any connection to the earrings. But, seated next to him, Dorothy's jaw dropped to the floor at the sight of the blinding stones; the diamonds alone, she surmised, were a carat each, the sapphires double that. Itching to know if the illusive Mr. Sanders was Maggie's benefactor, Dorothy knew one thing for sure: the stones were genuine. She recognized the real McCoy, even while the two bridge players and Claudia came to the conclusion that they were paste.

At one point during dinner, Maggie turned toward the Captain's Table. Francine and Mildred were still confined to their cabins, taking only broth and ginger ale, but she wanted to catch Bill's eye and show him that she was wearing his gift.

He saw her and looked pleased.

Smiling at the old gentleman, Maggie only wished that Michael Sanders were here to see her shine.

At the conclusion of the six-course meal, passengers headed en masse for the Atrium – the only public space on the ship large enough to accommodate the ball. The room looked enchanting tonight. The leather club chairs were gone and crystal spheres suspended from the ceiling sent flickering strobe lights across the revelers. Bunches of helium balloons trailing long streamers tied into bows looked like floating bouquets. The center of the room had become a dance floor surrounded by small round tables with pink cloths and white roses. The orchestra played soft music from the raised platform, and instead of their regular attire, stewards wore blue satin breeches with velvet waistcoats; the ship's officers were in full dress uniform. The scene resembled a Strauss opera extravaganza.

Mesmerized, Maggie walked in with the idea of remaining only a short time because she was not silly enough to think that anyone besides Paul Hopkinson and Doug would ask her to dance. Admiring the ball gowns on parade from the dining room, she saw Sheila pushing Bill's wheelchair, a job usually left to a valet. Perhaps the new necklace made her more attentive to her husband tonight. Watching her, Maggie wondered how she had managed to pack that voluminous *tulle* gown; it must have required an entire steamer trunk. In fact, how had any of the women managed to pack such fabulous dresses to be worn for one evening only? Amanda Olson's gown was a floor-length mauve satin with puffy sleeves, Dorothy wore layers of blue lace, Rose Burke was in a beige shirred column, and Claudia was nowhere to be seen, she and her finery having disappeared right after dinner. Maggie questioned if the casino was open and allowed to compete with the Captain's Ball.

Circling the room, missing Francine's and Mildred's company, she found an empty chair at a table with Doug and several women taking full advantage of Francine's absence.

Commodore Vicente Reyes opened the ball with a pretty speech and a toast to the attractive ladies on his ship, after which he walked over and asked Bill McKiernan if he might have the honor of dancing the first waltz with Mrs. McKiernan. Smiling, Bill gave his consent, and the captain now escorted Sheila – who looked like a queen at her coronation – to the floor. The orchestra broke into the opening number and all eyes were riveted on the captain and Mrs. McKiernan until an appropriate interval had passed and it was deemed time to join in. The parquet soon became so densely packed that the dancers swallowed even the beautiful Sheila.

Waiters walked around, pouring champagne, and spirits were high. Doug danced twice with Maggie, after which he took each of the other ladies at his table for a spin. Paul Hopkinson was on the floor with Dorothy and it appeared that she wasn't letting him make the rounds tonight; therefore, Maggie didn't expect another dance. But never mind; she'd stay a little while longer to enjoy the festive décor, free champagne, and the romantic music, her feet cheerfully tapping the rhythm under the table.

Suddenly someone was tapping her on the shoulder. She turned around and found Michael Sanders bending over her.

"Care to dance?" he whispered.

Maggie nearly jumped up from her seat and, grinning with eagerness, took the arm he offered and walked with him to the center of the floor, now more than ever wishing she was wearing a real ball gown, one that made rustling noises like the ones heroines wore in romantic novels. But at least she was wearing high heels, and the minute his arm went around her waist, and his warm hand found hers, she forgot everything but the music and her handsome dance partner. Michael looked amazing in his black tuxedo with snowy white cravat, and of course it didn't take long for others to notice him. While dancing with their respective escorts, both Rose and Amanda were staring. The captain was now dancing with the dowager, and Sheila was doing some fancy footwork with the first officer but, even so, she spotted Michael, narrowed her eyes and all but devoured him. She ignored Maggie, which was just as well because had Sheila looked too closely, she might have wondered why someone on a low deck was wearing high-end jewelry.

The dance was over much too soon. Michael walked Maggie back to her table where two women sat idle and looked hopeful, ready to spring into action. But, holding the chair out for Maggie, he simply bent down, his lips so near her ear that it felt like a kiss.

"Thank you, Maggie," he whispered. "I enjoyed that." Then he was gone as abruptly as he had come, leaving her to question if she had imagined the whole thing.

Chapter thirty-five

Without Michael the ball lost its luster. Maggie remained a while longer but eventually left the Atrium, her mind in turmoil. She had let him get under her skin, which would never do because in her experience there were no happy endings, most assuredly not for a shipboard romance bound to sputter and die once the ship returned to port. It was pointless to engage in foolish dreams; besides, she had sworn off romance long ago. She walked out onto the promenade for some fresh air that would knock some sense into her.

Standing at the railing, the breeze tossing her hair, she began to wonder if Michael had retreated to his usual spot topside. The music coming from the ballroom, and couples taking a break from the dancing, leaning against the railing and each other, murmuring, laughing and sipping champagne, eventually stripped away all of her defenses, letting curiosity triumph. She decided to go up and see if he was there. She wouldn't approach him or in any way intrude on his privacy; only take a quick look from the distance.

The night air was crystal clear and after reaching the top deck, Maggie felt sure she was high enough to where she could raise her hands and touch the stars. The sea was as black as the sky, the iridescent foam riding the waves mirroring the celestial pinpoints of light above her.

A feeling of contentment washed over her. She would have to go back many years before hitting the high she was experiencing this very moment. Each day on the ship proved to be more wonderful than the previous. This was as close to heaven as she would ever get in an upright position. She filled her lungs with the briny sea air, turned away from the railing, and continued walking past the covered swimming pool.

He was there!

Standing in the same darkened area at the bow of the ship, he was staring intently into the sea exactly like he'd done on those other evenings, except tonight his black tuxedo melted into the darkness around him, making him less visible. Maggie took a few more steps before remembering that she hadn't come to encroach on his space. She stopped, turned, and headed back toward midship.

"Maggie?"

At the sound of her name, she spun around.

"Maggie? Is that you?" Squinting against the lack of light, Michael waved her toward him; her yellow dress was unmistakable; it glowed in the dark.

His voice sent pleasant shivers dancing on her spine, which might also be due to the brisk night air, of course. "Michael?" she said, feigning surprise and walking up to him, pretended she hadn't been here before. "Hmm, so this is the bow..."

"Oh, come now," he laughed, his teeth white like the spray on the waves. "You've been here before. Several times. I saw you here last night."

"You did?" Maggie felt her face turn beet red and blessed the darkness. She glanced around; she positively hadn't seen him here last night. "Where were you? I mean...I didn't see you."

"I was up there." Michael turned and pointed toward the bridge. "Captain Reyes occasionally invites me to inspect the navigational equipment."

"You're a navigator?"

"No. Just curious about pinpointing our location."

"Why? You don't trust the officers in charge?"

"I trust them explicitly."

"You just like to pitch in. Is that it? Help out. Like yesterday in Acapulco when you came to my rescue. Are you some sort of modern day Don Quixote?"

"No." Michael grinned at the comparison. "I have no lofty goals. Being on the bridge is not a happy assignment. Not one I would choose. This is not a pleasure cruise."

"I don't understand."

Michael's face suddenly changed and his voice became low as he said, "It's not necessary that you do."

Maggie forged ahead. "If this is not a pleasure cruise...what then? Are you working under cover? Are you involved in security? You can tell me. I can keep a secret. Besides, you hold a club over me. You found heroin in my purse. Suppose I lied. Suppose that stuff was mine all along."

Michael shrugged. "I don't think so. Besides, the minute I handled the envelopes, I became your partner in crime." He raised a censorious eyebrow. "I believe we agreed not to speak of it. At least not until we're back on American soil."

"I'm sorry. You're right." Maggie glanced over her shoulder, happy to see that no one was around. "It was silly of me to blurt it out."

"Nothing about you is silly, Maggie," he said. "And you don't surround yourself with silly people either. You chose your associations wisely. Francine Wirth, for instance."

When Maggie registered surprise that he might know Francine, Michael explained himself.

"I had the pleasure of speaking with her at a small cocktail reception Commodore Reyes hosted in his quarters the first night out from San Diego."

That said a mouthful. Maggie figured one had to be a frequent traveler or know the captain particularly well to be invited to a private gathering in his cabin. Yesterday in Acapulco Michael had told her that this was his first cruise, which narrowed the options. She decided to press him.

"You know Captain Reyes personally?"

"We play golf occasionally."

"Where?"

"In Los Angeles."

Okay. That fit. Yesterday he had told Dorothy that he lived in Los Angeles. Captain Reyes probably lived there as well. "Since this isn't a pleasure cruise, is it a business trip?" she now asked him.

"No." The word was punctuated by a period, *plunk!* She could almost hear it. Okay, so much for pressing him. She leaned her elbows on the railing, looked out to sea, and remained silent.

"Your earrings are lovely," Michael said, after a while of studying her profile and the way the wind blew her hair in an unruly dance. "It's a good thing they weren't in your purse yesterday. I assume you left them in the ship's safe."

"Oh!" Maggie's hands flew to her ears. "No, these earrings are brand new. A passenger gave them to me."

"A passenger?" Michael frowned, puzzled.

"Yes. Bill McKiernan. Since you know Francine Wirth, you must know him as well. Maybe he and his wife were at that private reception you just mentioned?"

"Yes. They were there."

"Well, I can tell you that Bill is the most generous soul on earth," Maggie said, dreamily. "Last night, once we were at sea, he asked me to help him choose some jewelry that was supposed to be a surprise birthday gift for his wife. He had me try on lots of pieces before buying her a fantastic necklace and these earrings. Well, imagine my surprise when the earrings were delivered to my cabin just before dinner tonight. Of course, I tried to return them, but he wouldn't hear of it. Still, I'm saving the box just in case. He might change his mind and want them back later. I saw the price tag in the store. They cost twenty thousand dollars!"

Michael whistled. "That's a pocketful of change. But I'm sure they are yours to keep. Bill Mc Kiernan is a well-known philanthropist and generous to a fault. He's frequently written up in the California papers. He gives money away right and left. To him twenty thousand is petty cash."

"I hope you're right," Maggie touched each ear reverently. "I'd love to keep them. But so far I don't dare consider them anything but a loan."

Activity on the bridge above caused Michael to look up. Maggie looked up as well and saw an officer frantically signaling from behind the glass.

Michael tensed. "I have to go," he said without explanation. "Good night, Maggie."

Before she could respond, he was gone. Agile as a cat, he climbed the steps to the bridge and disappeared from sight.

Maggie walked down to her cabin. She undressed and went to bed.

A while later something woke her from a deep sleep. She felt the ship slow down and then stop altogether. Without the hum of machinery it became very quiet in her cabin.

What was happening? More trouble in the engine room?

When the rumbling vibrations shortly resumed, she knew they were under way again.

Chapter thirty-six

The Mexican Star docked at Salina Cruz at one o'clock the following day. The ship's sightseeing guide in hand, Maggie disembarked with Francine and Mildred; both had recovered their health sufficiently to explore this port-of-call.

Francine walked off the ship in a crisp seersucker jacket with navy slacks and a pristine white shirt. Mildred's clothes were invariably wrinkled. She had a fondness for linen, which collapsed in the heat. For today's excursion she was wearing linen slacks with a drawstring waist and a pink T-shirt with the "Guess" logo stamped in rhinestones across her ample chest. The color suited her, but the outfit was designed for a bulimic sixteen-year-old; it was a wonder she had found it in her size. Maggie was in a pair of comfortable jeans and the same plaid camp shirt she had worn in Acapulco. Every stitch of clothing she'd taken along on the cruise, except the yellow dinner dress, was machine washable and she made good use of the self-service laundry on her deck.

Today she was planning to stay close to her friends, no venturing about on her own. Likewise, she carried no valuables in her small white bag except for some Mexican currency she'd signed for in the Purser's Office this morning when she placed the earrings in a safe deposit box after first showing them to Francine. Mildred had not been at breakfast and there had been no sign of Bill either.

"I'll probably give them back to him at some point before the cruise ends," Maggie told Francine as they sat alone at their regular poolside table. She went on to explain about Bill's note, as well as her initial attempt to return the earrings to him.

"Why would you want to do that?" Francine said, examining the dazzling stones.

"They were awfully expensive. Sooner or later he might have second thoughts." To Maggie's way of thinking, twenty grand was not pocket change, no matter how rich Bill was.

"He won't. I know Bill. Keep the earrings and enjoy them. But be sure to put them in the ship's safe before we go ashore today."

Maggie had done so immediately after breakfast, and as she now walked down the docking ramp, following behind Francine, Mildred, and Doug Collins, she remembered Bill saying that he was looking forward to going ashore at this port-of-call. She glanced around but didn't see him among the disembarking wheelchair passengers. There was no sign of Sheila McKiernan either.

"I wonder where Bill is." Maggie tapped Francine on the shoulder. "He was eager to go ashore today. This ramp makes it possible for him."

Francine stopped and looked around. "Hmm, that's right. I don't see him. And he wasn't at breakfast."

"He probably ordered room service," Mildred said over her shoulder without stopping. "I did. But I couldn't really eat. I'm still weak from that sickness we caught in Acapulco."

Ahead of them, Doug overheard their comments and stopped at the bottom of the ramp to give the ladies a hand as they stepped onto the wharf. Wearing a pair of multi-striped shorts, a white business shirt with cufflinks, a Marlins baseball cap, and black knee socks – this time with tennis shoes – Maggie had to struggle to smother a grin. The fact that Doug was slim was all that saved him from presenting a comical figure. "I saw Dr. Madrasso in the elevator earlier," he now said. "He got off on Bill's deck."

"Did he tell you he was going to Bill's cabin?" Francine asked.

"I didn't inquire."

"So you're just speculating?"

"My stock and trade." Doug grinned.

"Maybe he is waiting to disembark after the first crush of passengers have left," Maggie said. "He told me he doesn't like crowds."

"Then he should be on a different cruise ship. One with half the people. Of course his wife enjoys this one." Mildred rolled her eyes. "More passengers, more officers."

"Hush!" Francine didn't want to participate in any sordid gossip and leveled her indignant gaze at Mildred. "This is really none of our business."

Walking along the pier with her friends, Maggie suddenly heard someone shout her name. She felt a pleasant tingling because she recognized the voice. Stopping and turning back toward the ship, she saw Michael Sanders raise his hand above the crowd on the gangplank, his exit hampered by the slow moving passengers in front of him.

"Hey, Maggie! Wait up!"

"Say..." Francine stopped in mid stride, her eyebrows in a questioning arch. "It seems that gentleman is chasing you. How refreshing. It's usually the other way around. Who is he?"

"I think he's a navigator or something." Maggie waved her hand, indicating she'd wait. "His name is Michael Sanders. He's a friend of the captain."

"He was at the ball last night," Doug was quick to report. "I saw him dance with Maggie."

Deciding that he looked familiar, Francine watched the stranger's approach with great interest. "Maggie, did you strike up a romance while Mildred and I were confined to our cabins? Have you been holding out on us?"

"Absolutely not!" Maggie protested loudly. "Believe me, there's no romance."

Michael Sanders strolled up to the group and as Maggie made the introductions, he told Francine and Mildred that he'd had the pleasure of meeting them at Captain Reyes' cocktail reception the first night out from San Diego.

"Yes, of course," Francine said, now realizing why he looked familiar. "You were that quiet gentleman. You said you were from the Los Angeles area, but not much else. You didn't appear to enjoy yourself. Were you still getting your sea legs?"

"No. I don't get seasick," he assured her.

"What deck are you on?" Mildred asked. "You're not at the eight o'clock dinner seating, are you?"

"No. I take meals in my cabin. I share quarters with First Officer, Raul de la Vega."

"Oh, so you're on the bridge deck," Doug observed with envy because he was one level below Francine and Mildred – an inside cabin without a porthole – galling enough without now discovering that he hadn't been included in the captain's reception. Of course, he'd been struggling with seasickness the first two days; still, he would have been gratified by the opportunity to decline the invitation. Glaring at the interloper stealing his thunder, he wished Mr. Sanders would move along. Doug was looking forward to squiring the ladies around Salina

Cruz and didn't want any competition. On the other hand, perhaps Mr. Sanders had money to invest; he looked like the type who had a portfolio.

"I was hoping you and I might spend the day together," Michael said, now speaking directly to Maggie.

"I'd like that." She turned to face her friends. Never before had she been so popular. Imagine having a choice between three perfectly wonderful people and Clint Eastwood. Wait till she got home to New York and told Simone about this. "Would you mind?" she asked the group.

"Of course we mind," Francine snapped, her attempt to appear ruffled foiled by the glint in her eyes. "But we'll manage. Run along you two. Have fun."

Taking their leave, Maggie and Michael wound a separate path through the crowd of shore-going passengers, many heading for the busses parked along the harbor to take them on various guided tours arranged by the ship.

Maggie had not signed up for any of the tours and neither had Michael. They did, however, visit some popular attractions the ship recommended, such as the aquarium where, among a number of exotic exhibitions, they watched several young performers frolic among sharks in a giant pool. When a particularly large shark became too inquisitive, the swimmers quickly scrambled up and over the side. It was awhile before they went back in, and only after the fish had been fed.

Toward evening, Michael and Maggie found a restaurant off the beaten path, where they enjoyed an excellent seafood dinner in an enclosed courtyard lit by colorful paper lanterns. Purple bougainvillea had the run of the adobe walls and a trio of musicians performed soulful Spanish ballads from a second story balcony. The place was full, they were lucky to get a table and, glancing around, Maggie recognized no one from the ship; the diners were all well dressed locals. She now wished she'd taken along her white jacket to wear over her camp shirt and jeans. Of course Michael was also in casual clothes – khakis and a polo shirt – but paired with a tan linen blazer, he fit the milieu better than she. As usual, she was the dandelion in the grass.

She removed her glasses right after reading the menu because one stem was broken; something she hoped Michael hadn't noticed. Her good pair had been in the vinyl tote and lost to the thieves in Acapulco. Luckily, she had taken this second pair along on the cruise, but the stem should have been repaired long ago. Why hadn't she thought of it before leaving New York? Why did she never think of anything until after the fact? About the only thing she remembered to do – the only thing she managed to accomplish in a timely fashion – was to get up in the mornings, go to work, and return home. But not even that had been good enough. She was fired. And why did her back have to be up against the wall before she made a simple decision such as having her glasses fixed? She was jobless before she took a vacation. She spent money only after she'd lost her income. It was cockeyed. She did everything backwards – upside down – and lacked the brio to get on an even keel and stay there. Her life was a mess, the proverbial unmade bed where she slept comatose – an emotional invalid – inattentive to simple matters such as keeping her belongings in good repair. Bill Mc Kiernan was stuck in a wheelchair, resisting another operation; she was stuck in a lackluster routine, resisting life. And tonight, why had she blabbed to Michael about her humdrum existence?

By the time coffee and dessert arrived at their table, and without really knowing how it had come about, Maggie had spilled her pathetic tales of woe, giving far too many details to each of Michael's questions. It was a mistake to talk too much about oneself. She should have stuck to yes and no. Black and white. And, having exposed her sorry circumstances in full color, she now felt embarrassed; again after the fact. Why hadn't it occurred to her to lie a little? She could have thrown in a master's degree. A couple of years of law school. Rich parents who left her a bundle. Michael would never know. Their friendship would end with this cruise. Even the hot and heavy romance between Amanda Olson and Dr. Hellman might not survive on land. Shipboard friendships were instant, fraternization was easy, but Cleveland and Seattle were two thousand miles apart, the stretch between New York and Los Angeles was even greater. Once everyone returned home, reality would set in, the distances would prove insurmountable and not worth the trouble.

When the bill was presented, Michael insisted on paying, even though Maggie dug into her purse and lightening fast placed a fistful of Mexican currency on the table. He wanted none of it and forced her to put it away.

As they left the restaurant she wondered miserably if he had covered the tab because he now knew that she had no job. Again a wave of mortification swept over her. She should have kept her mouth shut. She should never have told him about being fired or about Lisa sharing her apartment. And why had she bothered to explain about her doomed marriages? In fact, why had Michael been so nosey? Come to think of it, why had he wanted to spend the day with her when there was a boatload of better pickings?

Chapter thirty-eight

Walking silently along the narrow streets leading toward the harbor where The Mexican Star lay docked, bathed in floodlights, a scene so warm and welcoming that Maggie couldn't wait to get back on board, into her cabin, and the blessed refuge it offered. The entire cruise was a wonderful escape, but all too temporary with just a handful of days remaining. Once the ship reached Tapachula, its return to San Diego with only one port-of-call would pass much too quickly. All too soon she'd be back in New York, visiting employment agencies, filling out forms, answering inane questions and remembering to use the buzz word "challenge." Interviewers loved hearing that word; it made them think the applicant enjoyed working overtime without pay. By this time next week she'd be squirming in her seat while some smart-ass agent half her age passed judgment on her résumé.

"What would you be doing right now if you weren't on this cruise?" she asked Michael after a while and in a desperate bid to put off thinking about next week. They'd reached the harbor square teeming with tourists and locals alike, and the question might rattle some skeletons in his closet. Tit-for-tat, any flaw in his résumé would definitely make her feel better.

"I suppose I'd still be with South World Airlines," he said absently against the music of a roaming Mariachi band before correcting himself. "No...no, I guess I wouldn't."

"Because you took early retirement?" Maggie remembered he had said he was retired when the subject came up in Acapulco.

"Retired? Actually, I resigned."

"Resigned?" A stickler for details, Maggie asked him why.

"I could no longer fly."

"So, you're a pilot?" She was finally getting somewhere. When he nodded, she pressed ahead. "Why couldn't you fly?"

"My focus was off. For the safety of the passengers I decided to ground myself."

"You were ill?"

"I suppose so..." Michael's steps slowed, he appeared distracted and stared into space a moment before he took Maggie's elbow and indicated they sit down on a bench near the wharf. "I was never diagnosed as physically ill," he said, dropping down next to her, "though I'm sure the line between the physical and the mental is often indeterminable."

"You mean you were stressed-out?" Maggie asked almost happily; this was her comfort zone, something she could relate to. "Depressed? Burnt out?"

"Yes."

"You want to talk about it?"

"Not really." He turned and looked at her with a grimace that crinkled the corner of his eyes. Her heart skipped a beat. Why did crows' feet look so attractive on a man? "But I suppose I owe it to you."

"You don't owe me a thing. On the contrary. *I* owe you dinner. In Tapachula I'll buy." After all, she wasn't totally destitute, not yet anyway. She'd get a job as soon as she returned home, even if she had to work at Macy's. Besides, the act of inviting him for dinner at their next port-of-call served to reclaim some of her lost pride.

"I prefer the old-fashioned way."

"Women feel strings are attached if a man always pays," she countered."

"I don't operate that way," he said, a crocked smile on his lips even as his gray eyes became shrouded with something unpleasant.

It occurred to Maggie that the prawns he'd eaten back at the restaurant might be giving him indigestion. Was he becoming ill like Francine and Mildred? She was glad she'd ordered swordfish, well done.

Chapter
thirty-nine

After some moments of sitting on the bench in silence, both pretending to listen to the Mariachi band, Maggie took off her straw hat and ran her fingers through her matted hair, all the while wondering how best to get their conversation back on track. She put her hat back on. Her hair couldn't go it alone in this humidity. It looked better covered up. She was about to ask Michael about his golf games with the captain, when he reached over and took her hand.

"I know I'm not a helluva lot of fun to be with," he said so softly she had to strain to hear even though the Mariachi band had moved to the opposite side of the square. "I've already told you that this is not a pleasure cruise. Neither is it a business trip. It's the voyage of the damned."

Huh? Maggie stared at him, saying nothing while waiting for him to continue.

"I came on this cruise to try to put thoughts of my wife..."

"You're *married?*" Maggie gasped and pulled her hand free. No wonder he'd been so cagey. No wonder he kept to himself on the ship and didn't mingle. Well, she might be a fool but she was no home-wrecker. But how on earth was she supposed to know he was married? He wasn't wearing a ring. Of course, it now became clear why he had asked so many questions during dinner tonight; it had kept her from posing any of her own. Okay, her bad luck was holding; even in foreign ports she couldn't get a break, but what had made her believe otherwise? Anyway, she immediately reminded herself that she had not come on this cruise to look for a man. She was sailing solo and enjoying it. Why was she even spending time with Michael Sanders when she could have gone sightseeing with Francine, Mildred, and Doug? She enjoyed their company. It was uncomplicated. It was comfortable.

"I'm married but I don't have a wife," Michael qualified, sensing her consternation.

I've heard that one before, she thought bitterly. Now he'll try to tell me that his wife doesn't understand him or has frozen him out of their bedroom. "You're in the process of divorcing?" she asked tersely, bracing for the predictable lie.

"No."

"Just separated, huh?"

"No. I'm a widower...I think..."

"You *think?*" Had he turned to face her, Michael would have seen an absurd frown.

"I haven't accepted the fact yet," he said.

Okay, this was a new one. Maggie waited.

"I...I lost my wife and my daughter..." Looking down at his feet, Michael was pushing some gravel around with his shoe, noise that scraped Maggie's eardrum stretched tight as it were with this awkward conversation. "Suzanne was only sixteen when she died."

"What? *Died...?*" Shocked, and instantly regretting having jumped to conclusions, Maggie wished she could think of something profound to say – some heartfelt expression of sympathy, but her tongue lay like lead in her mouth. Even if she were a poet, what fine, flowering words could she draw upon that would offer comfort? Michael had just said that his wife and daughter were dead, yet she couldn't come up with a single phrase of condolence. He had obviously suffered a terrible family tragedy, most likely a car accident. Motorists on the Los Angeles freeways had a reputation for speeding. Had he been the driver? Was he blaming himself? What could she possibly say? *I'm sorry* sounded trite in the face of such a calamity.

"Uh...how...what happened?" she finally asked.

"It's a long story."

"Was it a car accident?"

"No." Michael shook his head.

"What then?"

"I told you a minute ago that I flew for South World Airlines..."

"You were involved in a plane crash?" she interrupted, horrified and staring at him in disbelief.

"Yes."

She gave him a quick once over. It didn't appear as if he'd suffered a scratch. He must have walked away from it. "What happened?"

"It's difficult to talk about."

"I know. It was difficult for me to talk about David after he died. It was hard for his parents as well and probably the key reason they moved to Florida. They didn't want to confront their loss every time they saw me. People talk adnauseum about other people's tragedies but not their own. It's human nature."

"Maggie, are you a patient listener?"

"Try me."

"Okay." Michael gave her a thin smile, reached over and squeezed her hand. Drawing a painful breath, a few minutes passed before he began.

"When my daughter turned sixteen this past June, my wife and I planned to give her a party. But she wanted a trip, which was fine with us. Some of her friends were going to Europe for the summer and we encouraged her to join them. Her older brother had gone abroad at the same age."

"You have a son?"

"Yes. Jeffrey. He just finished law school and now works in New York City...your neck of the woods. He married a year ago. He and Carol live in Westchester...a place called Hastings. They are expecting their first child."

"That's wonderful," Maggie said while her mind was trying to remember if she'd read about a plane crashing this past June. Perhaps Michael was talking about a small private aircraft?

"Much as we encouraged a trip to Europe," he went on, "Suzanne wanted to go to South America. She had done a school project on Argentina and was enamored with the lives of Peron and Evita. She found their story irresistible and wanted to see where this fierce love or, more likely, political expediency had taken place. It was a ridiculously easy request. I flew roundtrips between Los Angeles and Buenos Aires and simply arranged for a one-week layover, reserving seats for Lynn and Suzanne on my flight. A ten a.m. nonstop. The day of the trip, I drove to the airport early as required for pre-departure checks. Lynn and Suzanne would arrive later and board the aircraft with the passengers. Shortly after nine o'clock my wife called from the car. They were hopelessly stuck in traffic on the Santa Monica Freeway. I explained that I could only delay the flight without cause for fifteen minutes at the most. Still, airport security being what it is nowadays and with early gate closings, I realized they wouldn't make it even if I could stall the departure for an hour. So I arranged for them to travel on the next flight leaving Los Angeles at one o'clock."

"South World flight 408!" Maggie gasped, suddenly remembering. "Oh, my God! I read about it. It went down in the Pacific Ocean off the coast of Puerto Escondido. What? Five...six months ago?"

"June 25th."

"Are you telling me that your wife and daughter were on that flight?" When Michael nodded, Maggie felt goose bumps crawl up her arms as she stumbled on. "I recall the newspapers saying there were no warnings of trouble, mechanical or otherwise. What happened? What brought the plane down?"

"We don't know. The aircraft simply vanished from radar. Except for an oil slick, it left very little in the way of a debris field. The black box has not yet been found. Without it, the FAA has very little to go on. The last radio communication with air traffic controllers was routine. Electronic probes were lowered around the crash site and a two-man submarine went down to explore what turned out to be a bottomless trench in the ocean floor so deep the pressure would crush the sub like a tin can. Further search of the area has now been abandoned."

Michael shuddered visibly, but a moment later went on. "Not knowing what happened makes it all the more difficult to accept. That morning, listening to Lynn's and Suzanne's talk of freeway traffic, notorious and predictable, I never guessed it'd be our last conversation. I assured them there were seats on the one o'clock flight and that I would meet them at the gate in Buenos Aires. I joked, telling them that they were lucky because Captain Wilson was a better pilot than me. They'd have a smoother ride. My daughter whined about wanting to be on my aircraft, point being that she wanted to get onto the fight deck, which since 9/11 is more difficult than breaking into Fort Knox." Michael wrung his hands. "I should have postponed their trip. I had already arranged for my layover, of course, but that could have been changed. Every waking minute since that last conversation, I wish I'd told my family to go back home. Exit the freeway, turn around and go back. Those few words and they would be alive today."

"Had you told them, would they have listened? Would they have gone home?"

"No," Michael admitted, slowly shaking his head from side to side. "Both were stubborn. They were ready and eager to go and of course Suzanne realized she'd have a chance to visit the flight deck on the return trip." Michael's voice broke, grief burning his throat; he drew a painful breath before continuing. "She was a lovely child. Enthusiastic and good-natured. She never gave us any trouble. And now...now I don't even know where she is. Where my wife is. No grave. No marker..."

"At least they are together," Maggie offered softly.

"Strange you should say that. That very thought has occurred to me many times. It's a small comfort. Neither died alone among strangers. Still, the idea of them being entombed in a crushed fuselage on the vast ocean floor is a recurring nightmare. I frequently dream that they survived the impact, freed themselves from the wreck before it sank, and are floating in the sea, treading water, calling for help. I swim toward them...swim like a madman and I see them but I can never get close. Instead I wake up in a cold sweat."

Maggie remembered burying David on Long Island, his large family around her, sharing her grief. Even after they withdrew from her life, she remembered the comfort of this initial emotional support.

"There's something very healing about collective grief," she said. "Have you met with family members of others on that flight?"

"No. South World held a memorial...a gathering hastily put together at the Ramada Inn at LAX. They supplied clergy and counselors. My wife's sister and parents went. So did Jeffrey and Carol. I couldn't participate. I was too angry. Angry at fate and angry with myself because I had put my family on the doomed plane. I was angry at rush hour traffic and whoever had stalled and created the additional jam on the freeway that morning. I was angry at airline maintenance. I yelled at the supervisors. I accused them of having overlooked some mechanical flaw. South World insisted I get therapy. I tried it for a while. It didn't work. So I decided to retire."

"And you came on this cruise to help you forget?"

"No. I came to bury my family."

"Bury them?"

"Yes, in a manner of speaking. I dropped two wreaths on the water along with some ceremonial items." Michael cleared his throat. "You know, personal things. You probably think I'm being maudlin but, in lieu of a real burial, sending those things into the deep helped me in some small way to connect with my wife and daughter; enough perhaps so I can begin to come to terms with the accident and slowly let go and feel some kind of closure. Anyway, that's what the psychiatrist claimed might happen. He chided me for not attending the public memorials and suggested I have a private one. Among other things, he said it would help alleviate the nightmares."

"Has it?"

"It's too early to tell. The ceremony took place last night."

"Oh?" Maggie remembered that after going to bed she felt the ship slow down before stopping altogether, something she figured was due to engine maintenance. "Last evening when you were called up to the bridge was that because the navigator had located the place where the plane went down?"

"Yes. The ship's officers have been extremely cooperative. I have known Captain Reyes for a number of years. Months ago he told me that The Mexican Star regularly sails past the vicinity of the crash site. After several times of inviting me onboard, I finally took him up on it. When we pinpointed the area last night, Captain Reyes took the ship off course and ordered the engines stopped once we reached the spot. Naturally, he didn't enter any of this in the ship's log."

"I was wondering about it. My cabin is on a low deck and for a while I heard no rumbling from the engines. I thought it was mechanical trouble again."

"Let's hope the rest of the passengers thought so as well or were sound asleep."

"Many were still in the Atrium at the ball. I was told it went on till three in the morning."

"Even better. They were happily occupied and probably didn't notice a thing. What Captain Reyes did is contrary to regulations. If it became known that he deliberately went off course, he could lose command of his ship."

"The secret is safe with me," Maggie promised solemnly. "Do you feel better now after that ceremony?" She remembered how she had slipped a wedding picture into David's coffin, burying it with him, a gesture that had soothed her at the time.

"Again, it's too early to tell. But for the first time in months I got up this morning without being angry with myself for being alive. I could actually look in the mirror and not wish myself dead."

"Wish yourself dead? You have a son, a daughter-in-law, and a grandchild on the way."

"Yes, without them I would have no reason to exist. They have kept me sane, such as it is. When South World flew family members to Puerto Escondido back in July and chartered a boat to the crash site for an official wreath-laying ceremony, they participated along with Lynn's parents."

"You didn't attend that memorial either?"

"No. I can't grieve in public." Without being conscious of it, Michael had again taken Maggie's hand, kneading it softly. "But I suppose that's precisely what I'm doing now."

"Yeah, Maggie Public, that's me," she quipped.

"Well, thanks for listening, Maggie Public," he said with a crocked smile and realized that except for his airline-mandated sessions with the psychiatrist, this was the first time he'd been able to put his heartbreak into words.

Chapter forty-one

Maggie and Michael boarded The Mexican Star minutes before its midnight departure. As they said goodnight on the promenade deck and prepared to head for their respective cabins, Michael lingered, took her chin in his hand and looked as though he wanted to kiss her. But she would never know. Latecomers running up the ramp seconds before the ship cast off spoiled the moment.

"Sleep well, Maggie Public," he said instead, his fingers brushing tenderly across her cheek before dropping his hand. "I'll be out and about tomorrow. I'll look for you at the lunch buffet. I hear the watermelon boats and carved ice statues are quite amazing. I have yet to see them." Suddenly he winked. "You can treat me to lunch."

Maggie grinned. Treat him to free food? "It'll be my pleasure," she said, turned and went down to her cabin, walking on air, and humming the song from Little Orphan Annie.

Tomorrow...tomorrow...got a lunch date tomorrow...it's only a day away...

She awoke unusually early the following morning, partly from the excitement of knowing that she would soon see Michael, and partly because she felt something was amiss. That built-in sensor she'd developed after a lifetime of disappointments roused her from sleep. Even before she opened her eyes she sensed that something was wrong or, if not entirely wrong, different. There was no sound coming from the engines. The ship was not moving. Why? What was it this time?

She groped for the small travel clock on the narrow shelf next to her bunk bed and, squinting at it, realized it was only five thirty. She groaned; it was much too early to get up. Nonetheless, she put her feet on the floor and went over to look through the porthole.

The ship was docked!

Hadn't it left Salina Cruz? Of course, it had. She remembered seeing the ramp being pulled away and had clearly felt the motion of the ship steaming out to sea shortly before she went to sleep. Again she peered through the porthole, her eyes adjusting to the gray morning light without recognizing the harbor. Crates of bananas were sitting on the dock; there had been no such crates in Salina Cruz.

Turning her back on the porthole, Maggie put on the same outfit she had worn yesterday, if only because it was conveniently draped across the back of the chair in her cabin. Running a brush through her hair, she went up on the promenade deck to learn where they were and why they were docked.

Due to the early hour, few passengers were up and about. Maggie spotted the dowager and her young male companion further along the deck, sitting in a couple of canvas chairs, she watching the sunrise, he watching her while massaging her shoulders. It promised to be another beautiful morning. The pink blush of a tropical dawn was slowly spreading across the horizon, lush, green, and jungle-like.

"Where are we?" Maggie asked a steward coming toward her with cups and a carafe of hot coffee. "Why are we docked?"

"*Si,*" he smiled and held out the tray.

Resigned to the lack of English, Maggie took a cup off the tray and filled it with coffee. Sipping the steaming brew, she strolled along the deck, nodding good morning to the dowager and her male companion without stopping; involved as they were with each other they probably had little information to impart. She continued toward another early riser, a woman in a yellow jogging suit, standing alone at the railing; a passenger Maggie knew by sight only.

"Do you know why we're docked?" she asked, walking up to her and taking another sip of coffee, appreciating the fine strong brew; like the cuisine onboard, the coffee was superb.

"Sure. Look!" The woman pointed to the wharf where a black car was parked among the banana crates near the ship's landing ramp. Maggie identified it as a Plymouth or Dodge station wagon. From up here on the deck it was hard to tell, except for the fact that it was an old model with a bad paint job.

"So, what's with the car?" She turned to the woman, puzzled.

"That's no car. It's a hearse."

"A hearse? Someone died?"

"That'd be my guess."

"Who?"

"I don't know. One of our passengers. Maybe a crewmember? They're obviously not announcing it on the loudspeaker. It's too early in the morning for that kind of news and the captain probably wants to keep it quiet for as long as possible. A death at sea is supposed to be bad luck. It might spook those prone to superstition."

Maggie didn't believe in bad luck, except her own. "Do you know where we are?" she asked the woman.

"Puerto Romano. We've been here for about half an hour. I got up at five for my regular jog around the deck. That's when I saw the hearse drive up."

"I see." Maggie drank the last of her coffee and signaled the steward for a refill, reveling in the fact that she was holding a lovely china cup about to be filled with freshly brewed coffee, a far cry from the reheated Starbucks she drank from cardboard containers back home. And what a view! Instead of a bleak courtyard strewn with castoff furniture, she was looking at cartons of bananas tended by Mexican dockworkers in colorful Panama hats. Today was the last day of November, no sleet, no ice; a warm tropical breeze swayed the tops of the tall palms growing along the road leading away from the harbor and disappearing into the lush rolling hills. If she were an artist this was the scene she'd paint. She took a deep breath. It was wonderful to be alive on such a morning.

Maggie looked at the hearse again and sobered. Who was it waiting for? A passenger she knew by name or one of the ship's nameless crew? She tried to think of all the old and frail people onboard and hoped that whoever it was had died peacefully, slipped into eternity from a comfortable berth as the ship lolled on the languid sea. Not a bad way to go. If she were to die today, this would be the place to do it. But after lunch. She first wanted to keep her date with Michael, the thought of which put her in a spectacularly good mood despite the ominous presence of the hearse waiting like a black vulture on the pier.

Startled from her pleasant reverie by activity on the ramp, Maggie leaned over the railing and saw a stretcher being carried off the ship by four solemn-faced stewards. The person on the stretcher was covered from head to toe in a white sheet, but one exposed, large foot identified the body as that of a man, which narrowed the field.

Maggie's ears pricked when she suddenly recognized a voice.

Sheila McKiernan?

What was she doing up at this hour of the morning? That woman never showed herself on deck until noon and after a visit to the spa and the beauty parlor. Maggie put her empty cup down on the tray of a passing steward and watched in astonishment as Sheila dressed in a pearl gray Armani suit, a wide-brimmed fuchsia hat and matching accessories, walked briskly off the ship and headed toward the black hearse. With a rapid and painful jolt, Maggie realized that the body on the stretcher would have to be Bill McKiernan. Why else was Sheila following it?

Bill? No!

Clenching her hands, Maggie pressed the knuckles against her chin. *No, please no! Not Bill! It couldn't be!* He was in fine form yesterday. Actually, she hadn't seen him yesterday. She remembered looking for him among the disembarking passengers in Salina Cruz, and she also now recalled Doug saying that the ship's doctor had been seen on the McKiernans' deck. Had Bill fallen ill? Had he swallowed his medication with scotch or martinis again? But even so, that wasn't a death sentence. It hadn't killed him the time before. It had only made him groggy.

Lost in troubled thought, Maggie didn't hear the woman in the yellow jogging suit speaking to her. She wished Francine and Mildred were up and about for surely they would know what had happened to poor Bill. But Francine was never awake at this hour and Mildred, assuredly, was still asleep. Ruefully, Maggie continued staring at the hearse and the somber cortege of stewards, watching more closely now that she knew it was Bill on the stretcher.

"Do you know the departed?" the woman asked again and more loudly than necessary in order to jar Maggie from her inattentiveness.

"Oh?" Maggie turned to face her. "Yes. I believe it is William McKiernan. That's his wife." She pointed to the unpleasant scene now unfolding on the wharf where Sheila was having a fit when she realized she was expected to ride in the modified, dated station wagon with the bad paint job.

"This is unacceptable!" Mrs. McKiernan was raising her voice to one of the ship's officers helping the stewards slide the stretcher into the rear of the car where part of the back seat had been removed to accommodate the awkward cargo. "I will not...I simply *cannot* ride in that thing! You may take my husband in this...this..." Sheila sputtered for words describing the battered hearse while her hands waved the air, rejecting the offending vehicle. "I'll follow in another a car. A real automobile! *Comprender?*" Pivoting on her stiletto heels, she walked back toward the ship. "You..." she turned to the stewards carrying her suitcases. "Stay here! Watch my luggage. I'll be in my cabin to oversee the packing and shipping of my husband's belongings."

Dismissing Sheila and her temper with a sad shake of her head, Maggie now stared in surprise when she spotted Michael Sanders walk off the ship with First Officer de la Vega in full dress uniform. Michael was wearing a gray bomber jacket, white shirt with tie, navy slacks, and black aviator sunglasses. She saw both men stop at the bottom of the ramp to exchange words with the volatile widow. Maggie strained to listen but couldn't hear because, unlike Sheila, the men were keeping their voices low. But whatever they said seemed to calm the waters. Sheila walked up the ramp and back on the ship without another outburst. The next thing Maggie saw was the back hatch of the hearse being closed and Michael and Officer de la Vega squeezing into the front seats next to the driver. The car drove off squirting gravel from its rear tires. Laborers on the dock went back to work. The scene once again became one of banana crates, palm trees, and Panama hats.

Poor Bill McKiernan. Maggie watched the hearse until it was out of sight. *That dear, dear man...*

Seeing her struggle, the woman next to her asked, "Did you know the deceased well?"

"Yes." Maggie nodded and left the promenade with a heavy heart, disappointing the woman who had hoped for some gossip.

Maggie went down to her cabin. She needed to change into some fresh clothes before breakfast. She suspected it would be a subdued food service this morning, and wondered how long the ship would remain docked. It's departure would obviously have to wait for someone to deliver a car that met with Sheila's approval, and long enough for Michael and Officer de la Vega to return to the ship from wherever they had taken the body.

She flicked through the narrow closets in her cabin for something attractive to wear. She didn't want Michael to see her in the same clothes she'd worn yesterday. In fact, she might wash them before breakfast. She had plenty of time. She changed into a pair of clean white slacks and a red tank top, then thought of poor Bill and put on a dark blue T-shirt instead. Gathering her wash together, she went to the laundry on her deck and put the clothes into a machine. Soap was provided and no quarters were needed. The laundry was free.

Chapter Forty-three

Maggie had just returned from the laundry room when someone knocked on her cabin door. Opening it, she found herself face-to-face with Sheila McKiernan and one of the ship's officers. Standing behind them was Arturo Rivas, the salesman Maggie remembered from the jewelry store. Heavy-eyed and unshaven, it appeared he had been roused from sleep.

"Kindly explain this!" Sheila was demanding, holding up a sheet of paper Maggie instantly recognized as the receipt from Bill's purchases. "Mr. Rivas tells me that you were with my husband the evening he bought me a necklace and a pair of earrings."

"Yes," Maggie said. "He asked me to help him."

"Just like you helped him the night you were taking him to your cabin for a little tryst?" Sheila had conveniently forgotten the testimony of a number of witnesses.

Maggie sighed. "I believe that incident was closed days ago."

Sheila gave a little snort. "Where are my earrings?" She tapped a lacquered fingernail on the receipt she was holding. "I bet you thought I'd never see this. Well, sorry to disappoint you, but I just found it moments ago among my husband's things. I called Mr. Rivas to ask about the earrings and he told me you were with my husband the night he bought them. I suspect you might know where they are."

"Yes. I...I have them."

"See!" Sheila turned to the officer. "Mr. Torres! What did I tell you? She stole them!"

"Do you have Mrs. McKiernan's earrings?" The officer's voice was grave as he looked at Maggie.

"Yes. Her husband gave them to me."

"Did you hear that?" Sheila looked from the officer to Mr. Rivas. "The nerve of this woman! What gall! She is not only a thief but a liar *and* an opportunist taking advantage of a old, senile man on his deathbed."

"Your husband was perfectly well the evening we went to the jewelry store," Maggie said. "Surely you, Mr. Rivas, remember that." She looked beseechingly at the salesman. He shrugged, not willing to commit himself, perhaps afraid to take sides or, more likely, preferring to stay in the good graces of a wealthy widow to that of a passenger traveling on a low deck.

"Look, Ms. Maghpye," Officer Torres was uncomfortable with this entire confrontation. "It'll be best for all concerned if you just give Mrs. McKiernan her earrings. Then we can forget this whole incident. No one will press charges. Mrs. McKiernan needs to leave the ship. She has to take her husband's body home."

Dabbing at a nonexistent tear with a lace handkerchief she pulled from a fuchsia alligator purse, Sheila nodded. "Yes, under the circumstances and being that we are pressured for time, I might be willing to forget about any criminal act."

Stung, Maggie didn't know what to say. But she knew one thing: Bill had wanted her to have those earrings.

"Ms. Maghpye," the officer said, losing patience and holding out his hand. "The earrings, please!"

Maggie had been accused of being late and lax but never of being dishonest, and now Officer Torres took her for a common thief. Would this reach Michael's ears? Of course it would. The officers on board talked among each other and were prone to gossip like anyone else.

"I...I don't have them in my cabin," she said, defeated by humiliation and worrying about what Michael would think of her; this might cancel their lunch date. "I...I put them in the s...ship's safe yesterday." She was angry with herself for stuttering, it was self-incriminating, but she couldn't help it.

"All right," Mr. Torres said. "Please accompany us to the Purser's Office. We have to hurry. Mrs. McKiernan has a flight waiting for her at the Puerto Romano airstrip."

"A flight?"

"Yes. Mrs. McKiernan has leased a small plane."

"Who's flying it?" Maggie asked, now holding her breath and knowing the answer before Mr. Torres spoke.

"We were fortunate to have a commercial pilot onboard the ship. He has volunteered to fly Mrs. McKiernan and her husband's body home."

Maggie exhaled and her heart sank. *Of course!* She had watched Michael walk off the ship with First Officer de la Vega, only the latter would return. She felt herself go limp. Any fight to keep the earrings evaporated. She no longer wanted them. She had no reason to sparkle now that she wouldn't see Michael Sanders again. Once he had flown the McKiernans to San Francisco it would make no sense for him to return to the ship where his own personal mission had already been accomplished. Volunteering to fly Bill's body home was an expedient return home for himself. Apparently he had overcome his reluctance to fly.

"All right," she said, "I'll get the earrings from the safe." She reached for her purse and keycard, shut the door to her cabin and followed Sheila, Mr. Rivas, and Officer Torres down the corridor to the elevator.

Waiting for it to arrive, Maggie felt as though the two men were standing unnecessarily close to her as if ready for action in case she tried anything funny. Acute embarrassment swept over her, nothing new, her very existence was humiliating and she ought to be used to it. However, this was the first time she'd been accused of stealing. She lowered her eyes with shame while Sheila repeatedly pushed the button although the elevator had already been summoned. When it finally groaned to a stop and the door opened, Francine stepped out.

"Maggie!" she cried, short of breath, her hands pressing against her chest. "I rushed down to find you as soon as I heard. Poor Bill has passed away." All at once Francine took notice of the three people with Maggie. "Oh?" Mystified as to why they were here, she bid good morning to Officer Torres and Mr. Rivas before mumbling her condolences to Sheila.

Maggie couldn't meet the older woman's eyes. She didn't want to see Francine's expression when told of the accusation. If Francine believed her a thief, it was more than she could bear.

"Can we move along now?" Sheila said, irritated with Mrs. Wirth's presence. The woman had clout, was seated at the captain's table, and had known Bill for years; all good reasons not to like her.

"What's going on?" Francine asked, looking around the group; this entire gathering was out of the ordinary.

"Ms. Maghpye needs to return some jewelry that belong to Mrs. McKiernan," Officer Torres spoke up. "There's been an unfortunate misunderstanding."

"How so?" Francine bristled at the officer and turned to Maggie saying, "Are we talking about the diamond and sapphire earrings that Bill gave you?"

"Yes. But maybe he didn't mean for me to keep them. He might have suffered a lapse and..."

"I beg your pardon!" Francine interrupted and pulled her shoulders back like a soldier going into battle. "Never! I've known Bill for years. He's never suffered a lapse except when..." Francine shot a dire look at Sheila and decided to curb her tongue.

"Mrs. Wirth," Officer Torres used a kind voice, "I understand your great affection for the late Mr. McKiernan. But now, and with all due respect, let's return Mrs. McKiernan's property to her so she can leave the ship and take her husband's body home."

"Her property?" Once riled, Francine was not about to back down.

"Francine, really, it's all right," Maggie said to diffuse the situation. "I don't mind. I don't need the earrings."

Impatient and growing bored with the conversation, Sheila sashayed into the elevator and held down the button to keep the door open so everyone could join her.

"Not so fast," Francine said, glaring at her. "Maggie, I remember you telling me that Bill sent a note along with the earrings. Where is it and where, come to think of it, is the steward who delivered them? Officer Torres, have you questioned any of the stewards tending the McKiernan cabin?"

"No." Mr. Torres spread his hands. "Please, Mrs. Wirth, there isn't time."

"We'll make time!" Francine snapped like a woman accustomed to having her way. Turning to Maggie, she said, "I hope you saved Bill's letter."

"I...I think so." Without ceremony, Maggie ran back to her cabin and all but ransacked it. A moment later she was holding Bill's note, having located it in a drawer where she kept her apartment keys and some postcards she intended to mail from the next port-of-call. She ran back along the corridor and handed it to Officer Torres.

After reading it aloud, he mumbled an apology. "Ms. Maghpye, it seems we've made a mistake. This clearly states Mr. McKiernan's wishes. No one would question this." He handed the letter back to Maggie. "I'm awfully sorry. Please forgive me."

"All right." She shrugged.

Officer Torres turned and looked into the elevator. "Ah, Mrs. McKiernan. I believe we..."

But before he could finish, the elevator door closed. The hum told everyone that Sheila McKiernan was on her way up.

Maggie was relieved to see her go. And she was jealous. Sheila would be spending the next several hours alone with Michael. Would the attractive young widow work her charms on him? Maggie wouldn't put it past Sheila to cry crocodile tears for his benefit. And what man could resist a young, beautiful dewy-eyed widow?

Forty-Four

Lifting off from the runway at Mexico City International Airport, now reaching an altitude of 22,000 feet, Michael realized how much he had missed flying. Admittedly, he was at the controls of a Learjet, the Porsche among aircraft, and a far cry from the ancient prop he had just flown from Puerto Romano. During that leg of the journey, he had been grateful to stay aloft at a crop-dusting altitude. In fact, when he and Officer de la Vega arrived at the Puerto Romano airstrip this morning, Michael had come to within an inch of refusing to fly the wreck parked in the grass, vines climbing up the wheel struts, attesting to the length of time it had been out of service.

But while the driver of the hearse and Officer de la Vega secured the stretcher with Bill McKiernan's body at the back of the fuselage, and while waiting for Mrs. McKiernan to arrive from the ship in a car that met with her approval, Michael carefully examined the plane and figured it might make it to Mexico City if flown at a low elevation. He wiped grime from the windshield, freed the wheels from the tangle of weeds, and kicked the tires for good measure. The lone mechanic servicing the small airstrip topped off the fuel tanks and assured Michael that the engine was as good as new, which translated into English meant take it or leave it, nothing else is available. And, inasmuch as Sheila McKiernan didn't throw a fit when she arrived and saw the prop plane, woe be it for Michael to upset the widow. He helped her board, carefully distributing the weight of her luggage.

Remaining safely on the ground, First Officer de la Vega gave Michael a jaunty thumbs-up and watched him taxi the shaky aircraft across the grassy field toward the single runway. The airport mechanic crossed himself before disappearing into a small wooden structure as if unwilling to bear witness. There was no tower, no traffic control; Michael could take off at will.

Once airborne, circling over the airstrip and heading northeast, he spotted the battered black station wagon speeding along the winding road to the harbor, delivering Officer de la Vega back to the ship.

When Michael landed at Mexico City International, a Learjet was waiting and ready for immediate takeoff with a copilot, Mr. Diomar, who worked for the leasing company. A mahogany coffin had already been stowed and received Mr. McKiernan's remains. Michael filed his flight plan to San Francisco, designating it as a mercy mission giving him tarmac access in an area where personnel from the funeral home could meet the flight.

Now climbing to 28,000 feet before leveling out, he increased the airspeed, appreciating the quick response of the Learjet, but also remembering that this was not how he had expected to spend today. His best laid plans went awry when Captain Reyes came to his cabin at four o'clock this morning, woke him, and told of Mr. McKiernan's sudden death from what Dr. Madrasso determined was acute heart failure until an autopsy could be performed in San Francisco, required when a death occurrs at sea. Captain Reyes implored Michael to fly Mrs. McKiernan and her husband's remains home. He couldn't refuse, he was in the captain's debt, and knew it was imperative to get the body off the ship as quickly as possible. As the captain explained, freezer space could be made available, but it was bound to spook the kitchen staff, while word of it might give passengers indigestion.

While Captain Reyes set an immediate course for the nearest port, Puerto Romano, as it were, Michael dressed for the flight, pocketed his essentials, leaving his luggage to be delivered to his home in Santa Monica once the ship returned to San Diego. He was handed a cup of coffee and was quickly caught up in the ship-to-shore activity associated with the leasing of an aircraft. Few were available along this lower part of Mexico's coastline, none were capable of making a direct flight to San Francisco, which was why Michael had to settle for the thirty-year-old prop from Puerto Romano to Mexico City.

Now flying over the vast Pacific, heading due north toward California, he glanced out the window on his left. Far below him the calm ocean looked like liquid mercury, the shadow of the Learjet appearing like a winged ghost skating on the placid surface. Suddenly he felt a sharp jab between his ribs. This view must have been the last Lynn and Suzanne saw. He checked his watch. The time of day coincided as well. The sun was high in the sky, not a cloud on the horizon, perfect flying conditions which he normally would have taken pleasure from but couldn't, realizing the horror his wife and daughter experienced on a day just like this.

Brooding on the tragedy, Michael's shoulders sagged under the invisible weight of *if only* while a knot tightened in his chest as if he were panicking, which he wasn't. He was a professional. He did not panic at the controls. Both engines could be on fire and he'd deal with it in a calm manner. After a few moments of wrestling his mind back to the task at hand, he gave Mr. Diomar a routine order, that of reporting their position to the air traffic controllers at Mazatlan, a seaside port similar to Acapulco, but smaller.

Acapulco...Maggie...

Michael wished he had left her a note. That would have been the correct thing to do. However, the whirlwind of predawn activity on the bridge had left no time for writing letters, and he certainly couldn't have called her cabin that early in the morning. To radio the ship now with a message for her would serve no purpose. It was three o'clock in the afternoon. She would have heard of Mr. McKiernan's demise hours ago and know the reason for Michael's absence.

He visualized her on deck in a chaise lounge, reading, her hat askew, her glasses – a poor fit because of the broken stem – repeatedly sliding down her nose while her foot twitched a subconscious rhythm. In the same manner that she had climbed to the top deck late at night, Michael had gone for short walks most afternoons, spotting her each time. Her very reticence, her contentment with being alone, had appealed to him.

Maybe he ought to drive down to San Diego and meet the ship the morning it returned? He could pick up his luggage rather than wait for it to be delivered and surprise Maggie at the same time. Perhaps they could have lunch at one of the seafood restaurants near the harbor, after which he could offer to drive her to Lindbergh Field for her return flight to New York. In the event she was leaving from Los Angeles, he could drop her at LAX on his way home to Santa Monica.

" A nyone up there want a drink?" Sheila McKiernan said from her beige leather recliner and threw the magazine she'd been reading onto the floor. When she didn't get an immediate response, she coyly repeated herself in Spanish. *"Alguien sediento?"*

"Si. Perrier, por favor," Mr. Diomar smiled over his shoulder.

"Nothing for me," Michael said.

"All right. One Perrier coming up." Sheila's mood had improved dramatically after they left Mexico City in this comfortable plane. She walked to the rear of the Learjet and took inventory of the well stocked bar. Bill had leased similar aircraft on many occasions and she was familiar with the amenities. Maneuvering sideways past the shiny casket secured in the aisle, she returned with a bottle of Perrier for the copilot and handed it to him, saying, "I'm not the flight attendant. I trust you don't need a glass."

"No problem." Mr. Diomar took the bottle and twisted off the cap.

"Mr. Sanders, are you sure you don't want anything?" she asked, leaning over the back of his seat, her breath fanning the hair at the back of his neck as she spoke. "There's champagne in the bar."

"Champagne?" He frowned. "I think not."

"Why?"

"It's against regulations."

"Oh, come now," Sheila laughed and flicked her black hair over her shoulder with a quick toss of her head. Once they were airborne, she'd kicked off her shoes and removed her hat and her jacket, exposing a sleeveless lace camisole, pearl gray like the suit. An enormous amethyst and diamond pendant hung on a heavy gold chain from her neck. "This is a private flight," she purred, taking the pendant and teasing it around the edge of his collar. Surely we don't need to worry about silly rules."

Mr. Diomar gave her a narrow-eyed look. She hadn't offered him champagne; not that he would have accepted it, of course.

"Private or commercial, FAA regulations are the same," Michael said tonelessly.

Sheila pouted and went back to the rear of the aircraft to fetch some champagne for herself. She returned and held the bottle over Michael's shoulder. She had flown on enough Learjets to know that he was on automatic pilot and had his hands free.

"Here, open this!" she demanded. "There's no rule about what a passenger can drink, is there?"

"No."

"Okay. So do the honors. Open the bottle."

"Sorry, I can't."

"Well!" Sheila sucked in her breath and turned to the copilot, pointing the bottle toward him. "Mr. Diomar! Open this!"

"*Senora*, an open bottle of an alcoholic beverage on the flight deck is prohibited. I could lose my license."

"For God's sake! Who's going to know?"

"I will," Michael said.

"You wouldn't tattle on your copilot," Sheila protested.

"Don't count on it."

Peeved, Sheila went back to the bar and, venting her anger, managed to pop the cork, spilling a great deal of the foamy bubbles onto the carpeted floor. She shrugged negligently; that was the leasing company's problem. She took two crystal flutes from the cabinet over the bar, filled both and set one down on the coffin as she passed it on the way back to her seat.

"Here's to you, Bill," she said, sitting down and raising her glass toward the coffin. "*Salute!* You know I don't like to drink alone."

The widow's irreverence, the sight of the full champagne glass perched on the coffin, made Michael ill. "Turbulence!" he warned an instant before he banked the aircraft just enough to topple the glass, forcing Sheila Mc Kiernan to now busy herself wiping down the mahogany. Even she realized she couldn't arrive with a champagne-stained coffin.

Michael landed at San Francisco International Airport and taxied the plane across the tarmac to a reserved area where a gray stretch limousine was parked alongside a black hearse with white satin draped across its windows. The hearse was attended by a number of funeral personnel, while a single chauffeur stood by the limousine. As Michael signed off with the control tower and shut down the engines, he was surprised to see several television crews exit two panel trucks parked some distance away. They surged toward the plane.

Sheila must have been expecting them. During the latter part of the flight, she'd spent a great deal of time, repairing her make-up and fastening her long black mane into a chignon, pulling some tendrils loose to frame her face, giving her a flirtatious look. But at least she had the decency not to don the flamboyant hat; her fuchsia snakeskin purse and shoes spoke loudly enough. When she stepped from the plane behind her husband's coffin, her mouth was demurely turned down at the corners, her red lips twitching with emotion for the benefit of the cameras immediately surrounding her, flashbulbs popping.

As Michael exited the plane, a reporter pushed a microphone into his face. He managed to brush it aside with a curt "No comment" before walking away, giving the coffin being placed in the hearse one last respectful glance. He left the tarmac with Mr. Diomar, both men heading toward a terminal office to file their paperwork.

That evening after dinner and a show, enjoyment of both tempered by the events of this morning, Maggie went to the casino with Francine. She needed Francine. She needed her no nonsense attitude, her stiff upper lip, and she needed to stay up as late as possible because she was still dealing with a deep sense of loss and knew sleep would elude her. The cruise seemed different without Bill McKiernan and Michael Sanders. Today had passed at a snail's pace, and at one point Maggie found herself mourning Michael's absence over that of Bill's death. She immediately felt ashamed because she ought to miss that kind old gentleman the most. He had thought enough of her to give her expensive earrings. But Michael had given her a glimpse into his soul. He had shared his innermost heartache, which to her was more significant than sparkling baubles. In fact, she would gladly toss them overboard for one more hour in his company. Not a practical tradeoff but she wasn't practical by nature; it had been forced upon her by grinding hardships.

She had counted on spending today with Michael, then *puff* he was gone. There would be no lunch, no follow through of their fledgling friendship. He had left the ship without a word of goodbye, which had the same finality as Bill McKiernan's death. Losing people she cared for was the story of her life and she ought to be used to it by now. Of course, she still had Francine, Mildred and Doug, not to mention the nice group of people at her table in the dining room. It was something to be grateful for. She had hit a bump in the road, lost some tire pressure, but was still cruising.

It was time to get back to enjoying it.

Tonight she stuck close to Francine, remaining in the casino till the wee hours of the morning. Happily, her twenty-dollar limit doubled then redoubled when she won several spins at the roulette table. Eventually pocketing her windfall, she became a spectator and watched Francine play Black Jack. At another table she saw Claudia Rasner win, then lose, then win some of it back. Her eyes black and dilated, Claudia looked like a wild woman. Maggie wondered if she was high on painkillers.

It was past two o'clock in the morning before Maggie and Francine left the gaming arena, exiting along the corridor where the row of slot machines stood idle at this late hour.

"I have two dollars left in coins," Francine said, stopping in front of one of the nickel machines. "I might as well use them up."

"Okay." Maggie reached into her own purse for some change to play a couple of games as a final distraction before the inevitable tossing and turning in her bed.

"I haven't had much luck tonight," Francine said, inserting coins and pulling the lever. "I'm due for some." The drums spun again and again.

Suddenly all manner of mayhem broke loose. The bells sounded signaling a jackpot, and nickels began pouring out. Hundreds of them or so it seemed in the heat of the moment. Laughing, Francine cupped her hands trying to catch the coins as they spilled out. Realizing she needed a bucket, she turned and was leaning over to grab one from a card table, when she lost her balance and crashed to the floor, landing on her shoulder and taking the stool down with her. She heard what sounded like the crumbling of tissue paper in her left knee, felt an excruciating pain along with the sensation of tendons rolling down inside her leg, sending chills to every part of her body. After the first shockwaves swept over her, she wondered why her knee hurt when her shoulder had taken the brunt of the fall.

Maggie had not been close enough to prevent Francine's fall and was momentarily immobilized, gaping at her friend, but the noise brought several men running out from the casino.

"What happened?" they asked, seeing Francine on the floor. One of them bent over her while another began collecting her winnings, putting the nickels into a paper bag.

"I tripped." Her lips pinched in agony, her face white as chalk, Francine tried to smile and make light of her tumble. But for all her stoic demeanor, everyone knew she was hurt as they stared at the odd shape of her left knee protruding through her slacks. "I think I broke something," she said, her brave front finally cracking.

"Please, call Dr. Madrasso!"

One man fumbled with his cell phone, punching numbers, getting no signal. Another passenger ran down the corridor to a red emergency phone.

Dr. Madrasso arrived and without a word ripped open the cloth of Francine's slacks, examining her leg right there on the floor.

"We have a problem," he said after a few moments and paged his nurse, telling her to hurry and to bring a wheelchair.

She materialized and Francine was lifted into the chair, the doctor directing the nurse to hold up the injured leg. "Keep it straight," he cautioned. "Don't let it bend."

"Good luck," the gamblers said solicitously to Francine as she was wheeled away. The one holding the bag of coins put it on her lap.

"Thanks," she said, giving a thumbs-up. "I'll be fine."

Maggie followed the wheelchair.

Once in the infirmary, Francine was placed on a gurney where the nurse finished cutting the rest of the cloth away from the injured leg, fully exposing the discolored and distorted knee. Francine turned her face away. She couldn't look at it.

There went a perfectly good pair of expensive slacks, Maggie ruminated, her frugal nature kicking in. She watched Dr. Madrasso give Francine an injection. After waiting a few minutes, he began pushing the tendons back into place with his hands, as best he could. Then he fashioned a splint on her leg.

"This is all I can do," he said, wrapping tape securely around the splint. "I don't have an X-ray machine. We're not equipped to deal with this kind of an injury. You'll need surgery. I'll alert the captain. You'll have to get off the ship." He went over to a cabinet and returned with a packet of painkillers. "Take one of these every three hours," he said, handing them to Francine.

"Leave the ship?" Stunned, she wanted to ask how and where, but the injection worked like a tranquilizer and all at once she felt disoriented; still, through the haze, she remembered that the coastline along these parts was nothing but jungle and small towns.

Half an hour later, lying on top of the bed in her cabin, and despite having been sedated, she couldn't sleep. She was worrying about a great number of things. Mostly she feared becoming a cripple.

Chapter Forty-seven

Come morning someone knocked on her door, and Francine expected it was Dr. Madrasso. "Come in!" she called out in a deceptively firm voice. "The door is not locked."

"Hi!" Maggie stuck her head in.

"Oh, Maggie!" Francine shifted heavily on her bed. She had spent the night in her clothes and the splint was pressing painfully on her swollen leg.

"How are you?" Maggie walked in, closing the door behind her. "Did you get any sleep?"

"I don't think so. But it doesn't matter. I won't be running any marathons today."

"Do you want some breakfast? I'll call room service."

"No. I don't feel like eating. Maybe just some coffee? What time is it?"

"Eight o'clock. I came to tell you that we're about a mile out from a town called Tonala. There's a hospital but no deepwater dock so we've dropped anchor. A tender is bringing a doctor from shore to look at your leg."

"Thank God!" Francine grimaced; the injection had worn off. Her leg ached. "Maybe that means I'll be able to stay onboard."

While waiting for room service, Maggie helped Francine change into a clean shirt and a pair of yellow Bermuda shorts made of a stretchy material that could be pulled over the splint. Slacks were out of the question, so were stockings even if she were disposed to wearing a skirt. Francine took one of the painkillers when the coffee arrived, the pain subsided almost immediately and she felt better. However, any hope of remaining on the ship was dashed once the shore boat brought the doctor from Tonala. He came into her cabin, examined her leg and immediately ordered her ashore for X-rays and surgery.

As disheartening as that was, she was about to experience cold fear as well, because moments later she learned what it was like to be plucked from the outside of a tall building. Sitting helpless in a wobbly wheelchair with nothing to hold on to as it was being carried down the narrow steps on the side of the ship to the shore boat far below, she was glad she hadn't eaten breakfast.

Seeing Francine's expression as she swayed in the wind like a trapeze artist without a safety net, the men grunting and swearing, making the already precarious descent all the more ominous, Maggie decided to tag along. "I can't let Mrs. Wirth go ashore alone," she told the steward manning the gate at the top of the steps. "I'm going with her." Climbing down, she was careful to leave plenty of room between herself and the high wire act ahead of her. Miraculously, everyone made it into the tender, which now sped toward the harbor where an ambulance that looked like a milk truck was waiting to take the injured American to the hospital.

The facility turned out to be a couple of rooms behind a dirty storefront where patients suffering various ailments – some with open infected sores – were sitting in chairs or lying on cots along the walls buzzing with flies. A nurse was bending over a patient, swabbing at some ugly red swelling that to Maggie looked like gangrene. The entire place smelled of fish gone bad, a veritable banquet for the flies. The physician who had come out to the ship spoke briefly with the surgeon on duty and then left, returning to a practice elsewhere in town.

Having finished treating a patient with an ulcerated ankle, the surgeon came over to Francine without washing his hands. She recoiled from this grievous lack of hygiene and eyed his blood-smeared smock with alarm as he helped her onto a gurney and removed the brace to examine her leg. Speaking in rapid Spanish, he told the nurse to wheel the new patient into the back room for X-rays. She took a series of pictures with what looked like a brownie box and once they were developed, the doctor studied them under a lamp. Economizing on conversation, the language barrier making any kind of small talk a waste of time, he now turned to the American and simply said, "*Operacion.*"

"What? Here?" Francine looked aghast. This back room was as unclean as the front.

"*Si.*" He nodded.

150

The nurse went back to the front ward, leaving the door open, and Maggie jumped up from her chair and immediately came in to hear the verdict.

"They want to operate right here," Francine told her and, tropical heat notwithstanding, suddenly felt chilled to the bone. She turned back to the doctor. "How long will it take?"

"Two *horas*. After *operacion* you...stay..." The doctor ran out of English vocabulary and held up six fingers. "*Seis quiza doce semanas.*"

"Six hours?" Francine looked confused.

"No, weeks," Maggie clarified, having deciphered the Spanish. "This surgeon is not talking in terms of hours, Francine. He wants you to stay here six to twelve weeks."

Francine gasped. "Here? I...I can't! I can't stay here six weeks. Or, God forbid, twelve! It's impossible. I have no friends here. I don't speak the language." Her eyes were wide with disbelief and an urgency to escape. The sagging mattress on an empty metal bed next to the wall was filthy and probably the one they planned to put her in. "Maggie, we've got to get out of here!"

Maggie agreed. She turned to the doctor. "We'll have to think about the operation," she said, mixing English and Spanish together. "First we have to get back to the ship. Dr. Madrasso only wanted us to come here for X-rays." She didn't know what kind of message Dr. Madrasso had relayed, but figured it didn't matter what she said because this man probably didn't understand her anyway.

The physician shrugged and was, indeed, wondering what this woman was blabbering about. The communication from the ship had been clear: an American patient was coming ashore for surgery. Still, he couldn't keep anyone here against her will. Let the ship's doctor reason with this patient and send her back. He put a cotton stocking over the leg, stirred a mixture of Plaster of Paris, and smeared a thick layer around it from Francine's groin to her toes. Then he sprayed blue foam over the entire mess to harden it.

Watching him, Francine realized she'd be carrying an eighty-pound weight on her leg. It might as well be around her neck. The result was the same: crippling.

When the doctor went over to a sink to finally wash his hands, Francine said, "Okay, Maggie, let's go! Let's not keep the ship waiting any longer than necessary."

"*Una momento!*" Drying his hands on a stained towel, the doctor came back and tapped the cast. It was rigid. "*Bueno,*" he said. "You go." With Maggie's help, he lifted Francine off the gurney and into the ship's wheelchair.

Maggie wheeled Francine toward the exit, both women thankful to be turning their backs on the festering misery in this hospital. Once outside they looked around for the milk truck that had brought them here.

"Where is it?" Francine wondered, looking up and down the street crowded with pedestrians and donkey carts. "Maybe we'd better go back inside and ask."

"I'll go. You stay here and wave it down in case it comes by." Leaving Francine on the sidewalk, Maggie went into the hospital and again employed her limited Spanish vocabulary.

"Ambulance?" The physician shrugged. "Take taxi."

Maggie came back outside. "The doctor said we have to take a taxi. I guess the ship didn't arrange for the ambulance to bring us back."

"They thought I'd be staying here. And they didn't figure on you coming along."

"I didn't either until the last minute."

"Well, I'm awfully glad you came, Maggie."

"It was a snap decision. Unfortunately, I didn't bring my bag. Do you have any Mexican money for a taxi?"

"Sure." Francine patted the small purse she had kept on her lap the entire morning. "I expected to pay the doctor but I guess the ship will bill me. But how will I get this cast into a taxi? I spotted one passing by here a minute ago. It was smaller than a Honda Civic."

"I'll go back inside and tell the doctor we must have an ambulance."

"Use a stern tone. He'll hear you better."

She did and the doctor, although inconvenienced with the request, called the ambulance. The milk truck came and drove the women to the harbor, where the ship's agent standing by the shore boat told Francine it would serve no purpose for her to return to the ship.

"I've been waiting to take Ms. Maghpye back," he explained. "You must stay here. Dr. Madrasso insists you need an operation."

"That might be. But I'm not having it here. That would be a death sentence."

"Then you'll have to go home to America. You can't come back on the ship." The agent spread his hands in a helpless gesture, but his face showed little concern for her dilemma of being dumped in a backwater town of a foreign country. "We have no facilities onboard to deal with your type of injury."

Francine bristled. "If you're telling me that I can't continue on the cruise, then please tell me how I'm supposed to get to Florida from here, wearing *this!*" She pointed to the thick Plaster of Paris around her leg.

The ship officer realized Francine Wirth was one of those stubborn Americans one had to reckon with. He also realized that she had a point; it was a rather large cast. "Look, you wait here," he said, sounding conciliatory. "I'll go back to the ship and make travel arrangements. We will get a taxi to drive you to the nearest airport. I'll see to it that your luggage is packed and brought ashore."

Francine lost all patience. It was bad enough that Dr. Madrasso wanted to admit her to an unsanitary clinic; now this agent wanted to abandon her to a local taxi that might or might *not* drive her to an airport that could easily be a hundred miles from here. On top of that, they expected to go through her belongings. Staring at the officer, she decided that come hell or high water, she was going back on the ship; if only just long enough to pack.

"I have valuables in the ship's safety deposit box and some extremely important documents in my cabin," she said, formulating her argument and pulling herself upright in the wheelchair with as much dignity as the eighty-pound blue cast allowed. "Heirloom jewelry and private papers for my eyes only. My attorneys will be furious when they hear about this. This entire episode could result in some very unpleasant legal ramifications."

The ship's agent heard her. Without another word, he and the boat operator helped Francine into the tender.

Maggie jumped in behind her.

Having survived the dizzying descent earlier, Francine felt sure heights would never again bother her. She was wrong. Getting back onboard the ship in the wheelchair, made dangerously unstable by the large cast, was a nightmare. The stewards hoisting their cargo were huffing and puffing as if she were a grand piano, while the ocean below licked the sides of the ship, waiting to swallow her. Hanging on to her precarious seat, Francine didn't dare breathe as the chair ascended one shaky step at a time. Any misstep, any shifting of her weight, and she would topple into the sea, the heavy cast sinking her like a stone. The ocean was two miles deep here. The fastest diver in the world wouldn't be able to reach her. For all her years on God's green earth, Francine had never before been this frightened.

"Shall I come with you to your cabin?" Maggie asked as she came back onboard behind the wheelchair, breathing a sigh of relief shared by all who had watched Francine's white-knuckled ascent. Passengers standing shoulder to shoulder along the railing exhaled in unison; the tender pulled away, the ship's horn bellowed, and The Mexican Star sailed on; the captain having decided to keep Mrs. Wirth onboard until the next port-of-call where air travel to the States could be accomplished more easily.

"Thanks Maggie, no, I'm fine now." Some color was returning to Francine's ashen face. "You've done enough. I'll see you later." Francine reached over to squeeze Maggie's hand just before the steward wheeled a path through the onlookers.

Amanda Olson buttonholed Maggie, asking bluntly, "So, what happened on shore?" Every soul on the ship had of course heard of Francine's unfortunate accident.

"A surgeon examined her leg and took X-rays," Maggie said, eager to extricate herself; she hadn't had breakfast yet and needed an infusion of fresh coffee. She suddenly remembered that they had left the X-rays behind. But never mind. They were probably useless to American doctors.

"And...?" Claudia Rasner wedged herself in between those surrounding Maggie. She knew about injuries and was sure a torn knee was almost as serious as a dislocated back. "Is Dr. Madrasso going to operate?"

"No. It can't be done on the ship and Francine doesn't want it done in Mexico. She's going home to Florida."

"From here? How on earth will she do that?" Mildred asked, breathless, her wig of glossy curls bouncing. Having just gotten out of bed, she had come running, but not fast enough to see Francine before she was wheeled away.

"I don't know. I guess the ship will arrange something from Tapachula. Our next port-of-call."

"I find it hard to believe that a cruise ship this size doesn't have a doctor who can operate," Dorothy chimed in with a troubled frown.

"It's not that simple," Dr. Hellman explained. "An operation requires an anesthesiologist and, in this particular case, an orthopedic surgeon. Dr. Madrasso is a general practitioner. I'm sure the ship's insurance is involved as well."

Amanda smiled at his wisdom and plucked at his sleeve. "Come," she said, growing bored with the subject, which had quickly taken priority over that of Bill McKiernan's sudden death. "Let's go finish our run." She drew him back toward the deck's jogging path.

Maggie and Mildred went up to their usual poolside spot. It was eleven o'clock. The breakfast buffet was being cleared, but an accommodating steward brought freshly made scrambled eggs and French toast from the ship's kitchen.

"Poor Francine..." Shaking her head, Mildred's worry for her fallen comrade was so genuine that she could hardly eat. "I slept later than usual this morning and couldn't believe it when Doug called my cabin and told me what had happened."

The dowager and her young male companion stopped at the table a moment later to express their concern. "Too bad about Francine," the dowager said, clucking her tongue. "The McKiernans are gone, and now I hear that Francine will be leaving us as well. The captain's table will be dreadfully empty for the remainder of the cruise." Under the shade of her wide-brimmed hat, she looked quite perturbed, developing a whole new set of wrinkles in her recently "done" face.

"I'm sure the captain will select someone suitable from another table to join you," Maggie said curtly, thinking the woman should be grateful that *her* only loss was dinner companions.

"You are right," the dowager nodded. "Commodore Reyes is extremely accommodating. This morning he graciously gave tours of the bridge while the ship sat idle. Mildred, did you go?"

"No. I slept late. This is the first I hear of it." Avoiding salt, she sprinkled some pepper on her scrambled eggs and took a small bite. "Anyway, I've been on too many cruises to suddenly develop an interest in visiting the bridge. I'm sure it's just a row of computers."

"No, it's far more than that. It's extremely interesting. One has a bird's eye view of the entire sea. It was marvelous." The dowager took her companion's arm. "Well, we've got to run. A marine biologist is giving a lecture at eleven-thirty."

"Enjoy." Mildred waved them off.

As soon as Maggie and Mildred had finished eating, they went to Francine's cabin where a Do Not Disturb sign hung on the door. Dr. Madrasso had probably given her another injection.

When they returned later, Francine was sitting in a straight chair, her cast propped up on the bed where her suitcase lay open. She was packing with the help of a steward. She was still dressed in the same top and yellow stretchy shorts, which made sense; no pair of slacks would fit over the cast. A tray of food on the table in her spacious cabin had not been touched.

Seeing Francine immobile and helpless, Mildred's emotions went into overdrive. She hugged her, blubbering how unbelievable that a double calamity could happen. "And to think that I convinced you to come along on this cruise," she cried. "I practically forced you. Now I wish I hadn't. Just look at you. Will you ever travel with me again? First we lose Bill. Then you."

"Please, Mildred!" Francine had grown up in a family of five sisters and had an aversion for clinging females. She threw off the fleshy pink arms encircling her neck and gave her friend a withering look. "Unlike Bill, I'm not dead. Not yet, anyway."

"No! No! Of course not!" Mildred realized her poor choice of words. "I didn't mean that." She fumbled in her pockets for a handkerchief. "I just can't believe you're leaving the cruise. I will miss you."

"I know. I'll miss you too," Francine said, regretting her stern tone and patting Mildred's arm, consoling her, even though she was the one who needed comforting. She was a long way from home and terribly worried about the trip ahead of her. Earlier she thought of telephoning her son, but decided against it, remembering that Richard and Anne were in Colorado, skiing with their married daughters and families. Francine was not one to spoil their fun. Besides, she took pride in her independence. She fended for herself and would continue to do so as long as there was breath in her body. If not for being confined to a wheelchair, traveling home would be a walk in the park. People took her to be in her sixties when she was actually in her seventies, something she attributed to good genes. She retained a thick head of hair peppered with gray, a youthful posture, amazing energy, and excellent health despite a twice broken heart.

She had buried her husband twenty years ago, and only last year her younger son succumbed to overwhelming medical complications associated with diabetes. Losing Andrew was the worst thing that had ever happened to her, a heartache from which she would never recover. She'd cried until she had no tears left, and even if she had some now, she certainly wasn't going to spend them on herself. Likewise, she wasn't going to run to Richard for help as long as she was able to manage her goal of getting home to Florida. Besides, if she called Richard he would insist on flying down here to meet her, which would only delay the entire process of getting home to American doctors who washed their hands.

The ship's agent knocked on the door and entered, holding Francine's itinerary to Miami.

"Your flights have been arranged," he said, handing her a thick envelope he said contained her airline tickets and assorted paperwork. "We have reserved a taxi to take you from the dock at Tapachula to an airport at Comitan. Just give this envelope to the driver. Instructions are in Spanish and local currency for the cab fare is enclosed. You have nothing more to worry about now." He shook her hand, wished her a pleasant journey and nodded to Maggie and Mildred as he left.

Francine put the envelope in her purse for safekeeping. She wanted to believe that her troubles were over, but had grown distrustful. The ship's staff had conspired to leave her in Tonala, something that had hardened her against them. She unleashed some of her frustration on the steward.

"For God's sake, put creams and lotions into plastic bags before you pack them," she said, pointing to several small zippered clear bags on top of the bureau. "And double bag everything. Suppose the bottles break in transit."

"*Si*," he nodded, placing the plastic bags into the valise and putting the bottles and jars on top of them.

Rolling her eyes, Maggie stepped in and showed him what to do before Francine could upset herself further. Maggie also made a decision. She would get off the ship with Francine. She could not let her travel the long way back to the States alone, in a cast, and with no knowledge of Spanish. Besides, since Michael's departure, the remaining days held little magic. The time now would simply amount to more of the same rich food, sun, and shows. She was done with that. She had her airline ticket from San Diego to New York and surely the route could be adjusted. She could go see the ship's agent who had handled Francine's affairs. If Francine could get to Miami from Tapachula, Maggie could get to New York. Returning home a few days early meant she could get a head start on her job search and perhaps lock-in a position before Christmas. No harm in that.

Chapter fifty

Francine and Maggie left the ship the following morning when it docked at Tapachula. As promised a taxi was waiting to take the ladies to the airport near Comitan some fifty miles away. Like all taxis in Mexico it was small and the brawny female driver loaded Francine – still dressed in the stretchy yellow shorts but with a clean shirt – into it as if she were a sack of potatoes, leaving her half sitting, half lying across the back seat with the cast protruding through an open window. Maggie got into the front seat. A steward stowed their luggage in the trunk but the wheelchair belonging to the ship remained behind. Francine handed the envelope from the ship's agent to the driver who was leaning heavily on the horn as she negotiated the streets choked with morning traffic.

They were soon driving on a narrow country road. The landscape was ambrosial with overgrown vegetable gardens surrounding the occasional cluster of adobe houses and whitewashed farms. It was only nine o'clock but the sun was already relentless. The open window accommodating Francine's cast turned out to be a blessing because Maggie's was jammed shut. She cranked the handle, it rotated but the window didn't budge. She took off her white jacket and folded it across her lap. She was wearing a sleeveless red top over beige cargo pants, her bare feet in sandals; still, she felt overheated and her hair was plastered to her head. She took off her sunhat and now used it to fan herself. Again she tried the window handle.

"*Parabrisas*," the driver said, pointing to the windshield peppered with flattened sticky bug remains that looked like bird droppings. "*Ventana*...how you say in English? Best keep closed. *Si?*"

"*Si*," Maggie said, realizing why the driver had set the passenger window in a permanently closed position. Insects were worse than heat.

They had gone approximately ten miles when the driver suddenly pulled over to the shoulder and stopped. Having used her elbow to steer the car for the past mile or so, veering all over the road while attempting to open the ship's envelope, she finally had the good sense to stop to read the instructions and, more importantly, make sure her payment for this long drive was included. It was. But where were the plane tickets?

"No ticket," she said, examining the envelope. She killed the motor and turned to Francine spread-eagle on the back seat. "You have ticket?"

"No." Francine pulled herself upright as far as the cast allowed. "My tickets are supposed to be in the envelope. The ship's agent said he included everything."

"Not here." The driver shook her head and again rummaged through the envelope containing cab fare, instructions, and a passenger release form from the ship. "You have tickets?" She looked at Maggie.

"Yes. My own." Maggie opened her purse and held up the ones the ship's agent had issued her last night.

"Okay, my traveling companion has her tickets," Francine nudged the driver. "Keep going. I'll get mine at the airport. We're on the same flight."

"Need ticket," the woman insisted. "I call ship."

"That's ridiculous," Francine sputtered. "For heaven's sake! Let's just get to the airport."

"Can't go." The driver pulled a shiny neon-blue cell phone from the glove compartment and started dialing. "No ticket. Can't fly."

Snazzy cell phone, Francine mouthed the words to Maggie. The car was a rusty wreck but the phone was brand new. Typical. In Florida those who could least afford it invariably had the latest in expensive electronics.

"Okay," the woman said a moment later, disconnecting the call. "We wait."

"What? Here?" Francine said, shocked. Who was this driver kidding? She looked around. This was a perfect place for a stickup. "Look, just drive on," she said. "We can wait at the airport."

"No. Ship say we wait here. They bring ticket." The driver forced her side window down, lit a cigarette, leaned back, and settled in for the duration, now dialing a friend's number and chatting in Spanish on the neon-blue contraption.

Maggie and Francine exchanged looks and checked their respective watches.

"I hope we don't miss the flight," Maggie ventured after a while, clutching her small white purse. It held the box with the precious jewelry. She remembered her experience in Acapulco and felt vulnerable out here in the middle of nowhere. She didn't want to lose a second pair of earrings.

"Look, we've got to make this flight or we'll miss our connections," Francine said after half an hour of exercising patience. "I can't imagine there are regular shuttles to Mexico City from Comitan." She signaled the woman to please hang up the phone and drive on. "Really, come on! I'm telling you, I will get my tickets at the airport. I'll buy new ones if I have to."

"No ticket. No go." The woman repeated, took a stubborn drag on her cigarette, but finally put her phone away.

"It's hard to believe the ship's agent could be so careless," Maggie said over her shoulder to Francine.

"It's partially my fault. I should have checked the contents of the envelope. This whole thing has been handled so poorly from the beginning that I should have been more suspicious." Francine sighed, inwardly thinking that this was the final straw. She was probably going to miss her flight while sitting on this remote roadside where anything could happen. The surrounding fields might be supporting a marijuana crop. She couldn't identify the greenery, but it wasn't corn. Perhaps someone was watching the car this very minute, wondering why it was stopped. Suppose some local cannabis farmer with drug cartel connections came along and accused them of spying on his harvest.

Just when she was giving up all hope of making the flight, another taxi roared up behind them, skidding to a stop in a cloud of dust. The ship's agent jumped out, rushed over and apologized profusely. He handed Francine her tickets and told the driver to "step on it!"

The woman closed her window and after a few false starts, the old engine sputtered to life. She put the car in gear and peeled away from the shoulder, the sharp smell of burnt rubber in her wake. It became a suicidal road race. Indianapolis 500 without inflammable suits and safety barriers. The car exceeded speeds of 90 mph on a road built for donkey carts. Peasants on foot jumped for their lives, burros scattered, and chickens were maimed. Come dinnertime, there'd be a pullet in every pot along these parts.

The taxi screeched to a halt in a plume of red dust at an airstrip on the outskirts of Comitan. A commuter plane was sitting on the runway, its engines running. A wheelchair was parked at the edge of the field; the ship's agent got that one right. Seeing the latecomers, the pilot along with a male passenger exited the aircraft and helped Francine into the wheelchair. While they pushed her toward the plane, the taxi driver unloaded the suitcases, shut the trunk, and with a wave to the Americans, drove off behind a slow-moving bus servicing the airport.

Francine was carried onboard; the chair was left behind in the grass where the local clinic, which had provided it, would reclaim it. After depositing Francine in the rear of the plane, the pilot collected their tickets and stowed their luggage. Closing the cargo hatch, he climbed back into the cockpit. Both Maggie and Francine now realized why tickets were essential. This was an airstrip. Not an airport. There was no ticket counter. No skycap. Not even a burrito stand. A small Quonset hut at the edge of the field served as a terminal that only provided shelter.

Within minutes the plane was airborne. Francine's cast straddled an empty seat, other than that the flight was full. A quick head count told Maggie there were fourteen passengers in addition to herself and Francine, all of them locals, some traveling with small caged domestic animals. A thin woman who looked more Indian than Mexican sat across the aisle from Maggie and proudly told her that she was bringing the two pygmy piglets under her seat to her sister's birthday celebration. The sister lived on the outskirts of Mexico City; they hadn't seen each other in five years, hence the generous gift. The woman pointed to her husband snoring next to her.

"He scared to fly," she giggled. "Doctor give sleep medicine."

Maggie wondered at this woman's command of English and finally asked her.

"I work in America," she said. "Three years. I go home to marry. Never go back. Someday I show husband America. Is nice."

"Yes, it is," Maggie agreed, suddenly homesick.

Chapter fifty-one

A wheelchair, unfortunately one without a leg extension was waiting for Francine at the arrival gate in Mexico City. Praying their checked luggage would be transferred to the Houston flight in good order, Maggie took charge of their carryon bags. A skycap pushed Francine, who was left holding up the eighty-pound cast, bracing it on her good leg the entire length of the terminal, through passport control and check-in. At the gate to the Houston flight, the skycap put her cast up on one of the plastic chairs bolted to the floor, that done, he pocketed his tip and disappeared. Her good leg trembling from the strain of the weight it'd borne, Francine was perspiring despite her light clothing. She wiped the back of her hand across her forehead in a tired gesture.

"Can I get you a soda or something?" Maggie asked.

"No. I'm afraid to drink anything. I don't know how I will manage to use a public restroom."

"I could help you," Maggie offered.

"Thanks, but no." Pride prevented Francine from accepting that kind of personal help.

"By the way, do you have someone meeting your flight in Miami tonight?"

"Oh, I totally forgot. My handyman doubles as my driver and I left him with instructions to pick me up on Friday. I don't believe my cell phone works from here. I'll have to call him from Houston. I'm glad you reminded me."

"He's reliable?"

"Absolutely. Alberto has worked for me for many years."

The flight to Houston was uneventful but uncomfortable. The plane was full and although Francine was in an aisle seat by the bulkhead, the serving cart repeatedly rammed the cast, sending pain through her entire body. The only thing that kept her from falling apart was knowing that with every passing minute she was closer to home, her own doctors, and getting this monster off her leg. She was long past caring what her knee looked like. An ugly mass of purple pulp wouldn't turn her stomach. Her ordeal had hardened her.

They landed in Houston where Francine was again helped into an airport wheelchair at the exit door. Thankfully, this one had a leg extension. Of course the skycap's English was no better than his counterpart in Mexico City; the two might have been brothers.

Collecting their luggage and passing through customs, Maggie had to declare her earrings. In the column marked value, she simply put a question mark and in parenthesis: *gift*. She showed the custom agent Bill's note written on the ship's stationery, which she prayed would serve as sufficient proof that the earrings were duty free. Luck was on her side. The agent looked at the paperwork, didn't ask to see the earrings, and let her pass.

Her flight to New York left ahead of Francine's to Miami and Maggie now had to hurry to catch it. They had already exchanged telephone numbers and again promised to keep in touch. Knowing that Francine was safely on home soil and would be met in Miami by a trusted individual, Maggie bent down and hugged the older woman before dashing off, pulling her suitcase behind her and keeping her eyes on the arrows pointing to the American Airlines concourse.

Francine waved and watched her run.

fifty-two

The lines at Delta's check-in area were astonishingly long, but Francine finally reaped the advantage of being in a wheelchair when the skycap bypassed the crowd and took her to an empty counter. While he swung her luggage up on the scale and pressed a button, she dug out her cell phone and placed a call to Alberto. When he didn't pick up, she left a message on his answering machine about her arrival in Miami tonight. She had just disconnected the call when a ticket agent brushing crumbs from her chin materialized through a door marked *employees only*.

Francine placed her envelope on the counter. "I'd like to upgrade to first class," she said, having decided that she'd been jostled around in enough tight spaces for one day. She took out a credit card for the additional charge.

The agent, a heavily made up young woman with straight blond hair fanning over the shoulders of her blue uniform, raised herself on tipped toes and leaned over the counter to get a better view of the wheelchair-bound woman dressed in a rumpled shirt, stretchy yellow Bermuda shorts, and an unsightly blue cast. "Sorry," she mumbled, retreating to her keypad, now furiously typing. "The first class cabin is booked solid. But I see that you are in row twenty-three. I can try to move you up a bit." Having managed to eat a corn muffin in the employee lounge without disturbing her fire engine red lipstick, she ran her tongue along her teeth to make sure they too remained pristine. "Um, yes, here we are. We're in luck." She finished typing. A boarding pass popped up. "I got you a nice window seat in row twelve."

Who was she kidding? "A window seat?" Francine said, pointing to the Civil War canon on her leg. "With this?"

"Oh, yeah, I see what you mean." The agent tore up the boarding pass and started from scratch. "Okay, I'd better put you in the last row of the aircraft where there's a chance a seat will be vacant next to you."

The last row! Accepting her lot, Francine was too miserable to argue.

A new boarding pass popped out of the computer. "Here you are," the agent said cheerfully, circling the gate number and tagging the suitcase, placing it on the conveyor belt. "Your flight to Fort Lauderdale leaves from Gate 7C." She attached the baggage claim stub to the ticket envelope and handed it back across the counter.

"Fort Lauderdale?" Francine said, thinking the agent had made a slip of the tongue.

The young woman smiled. "Yes. Have a pleasant trip."

"But I'm not going to Fort Lauderdale. My ticket is from Houston to Miami."

"Miami? No. Look, it's right here." The agent took back the envelope, lifted out the ticket, and pointed. "See?"

Sure enough, the ticket was to Fort Lauderdale. Preoccupied with her crippling injury, Francine had again taken too much for granted and not double-checked her itinerary. "But I'm supposed to fly into Miami," she said, lamely. "Someone is picking me up there tonight."

The agent checked her computer. "The next flight to Miami is tomorrow morning at eight o'clock."

Defeated, Francine dropped her shoulders. "Okay," she sighed. "I'll go to Fort Lauderdale." It meant a much longer drive for Alberto who lived near Miami, but so be it.

While the skycap wheeled her toward security, she rummaged in her purse for her cell phone and again dialed Alberto's number, leaving an updated message about her arrival in Fort Lauderdale.

The lines at the security check point snaked around the entire terminal, airport employees patrolling the crowd, chatting with weary passengers to keep the peace, while announcements blared over the loudspeakers: *Unattended bags will be confiscated. Have your boarding pass and picture ID out and ready for inspection.*

Eying the crowd, Francine checked her watch, wondering if she'd make her flight. She was about to mention her concern to the skycap, when one of the agents manning the line came over. "The chair won't fit through the metal detector," he said in Spanish to the skycap. "You need to take your passenger to the far side of the security area to be searched manually." He looked at Francine's boarding pass.

167

"You'd better hurry. That flight is already boarding."

Once inside the roped-off area, Francine parted company with her purse and carryon. They went in one direction to be fed through the X-ray machine while she was wheeled over to two uniformed women, who proceeded to run a wand and their hands over every part of her body, including the airport issued wheelchair. *Don't they trust their own equipment?*

Fascinated with Francine's cast, the women tapped it and tested it with separate instruments. One of them spotted the shoe on her good leg, removed it and brought it over to the conveyor belt. No surprise. Passengers were expected to go barefooted. Once Francine's belongings had passed through X-ray, they disappeared from sight, something the loudspeakers repeatedly warned about. Craning her neck, Francine turned in her chair as much as she was able, but her view was blocked.

Don't leave your bags unattended, the loudspeaker droned overhead.

"I can't see my bags," she said to the female attendants taking liberties, the electronic wand now passing between her legs as she sat, helpless, in the wheelchair.

"They're safe," one of them said while running her hand down the back of Francine's thin top that couldn't conceal as much as a sheet of paper. The other agent was still testing the cast.

"What are you looking for?" Francine finally mumbled to the latter whose face was puckered in curiosity with the blue Plaster of Paris. "There's nothing inside but a mangled knee. Believe me, there's no b...." Francine stopped herself before uttering that terrifying word, which would result in a complete airport lock down.

The two stony-faced agents finally grew bored and motioned to the skycap, giving him the go-ahead just as the loudspeaker could be heard paging passenger Francine Wirth.

Please proceed to Gate 7C! Last call for passenger Wirth!

"Oh, my God! That's me!" Francine looked at the non-English speaking skycap and gestured frantically.

He understood sign language, grabbed the handles on the wheelchair and broke into a sprint, dodging dangerously between passengers getting dressed after having been searched.

"Wait!" Francine screamed at him. "Stop! Where's my carryon? My purse? My shoe?"

The skycap realized his neglect, stopped on a dime, set the brake on the wheelchair and raced back to the security checkpoint to fetch the forgotten articles. Returning, he dumped everything into her lap before again plowing toward the gate. Holding her breath in terror, Francine clutched the cast and her belongings, praying nothing would shift and upset the apple cart, sending her rolling on the floor.

Arriving as the gate was being closed, she was transferred to a small narrow chair that fit the aisle inside the plane. Now quickly wheeled down the ramp, a male flight attendant took charge of the latecomer, securing the door to the aircraft behind her. Reading Francine's boarding pass, he wheeled her to the very rear of the plane and asked two passengers to please move up a row, creating three empty seats. Stowing her carryon in the overhead bin, he helped her from the wheelchair, placed her cast across two seats, and fastened a safety belt around her waist. As the plane pulled away from the gate, he fetched some extra pillows, put them under her cast, and secured everything with a belt.

Hogtied across three seats, Francine counted her blessings.

fifty-three

Arriving in Fort Lauderdale shortly before midnight, having lost two hours to time zones, Francine was again helped off the plane and into an airport wheelchair manned by a skycap. They left the arrivals area via a crowded elevator down to the baggage carrousel. She looked around for Alberto. The buzzer sounded, the carrousel started to spit out luggage, and people surged forward, lunging for any piece that looked familiar. Happily Francine's luggage was among the first to appear on the conveyor belt.

The skycap retrieved it. "I'll get you a taxi," he said, putting her stuff on a cart.

"No. I'm being picked up. Just wheel me over to the glass doors where I can look for my ride."

He parked Francine and her luggage near the exit doors. She tipped him and he left to assist other passengers.

Eventually the area emptied of travelers, even of skycaps, and once the car rental counters closed for the night, Francine felt like an abandoned orphan. There were no more flights till morning and the airport became eerily silent. Stoically, she waited, wondering what was keeping Alberto. A lone sheriff guarding the area eventually came up to her.

"Do you need a cab?" he wanted to know.

"No, I'm waiting for someone." Francine checked her watch. Alberto was now more than an hour late, which was very unlike him. "I'd better call my ride," she said, digging into her purse for the cell phone.

"Hello?" Alberto's voice was heavy with sleep.

"Alberto? Where are you?" she shouted.

"Huh! Oh...Mrs. Wirth? Is that you?"

"Yes. I'm at the Fort Lauderdale Airport, waiting for you."

"What did you say? Fort Lauderdale?"

"Yes. I came in on a Delta flight. Didn't you get my message?"

"No."

"I called twice from Houston. I left messages on your answering machine."

"Oh...?" Alberto sounded bewildered and coughed, holding a hand over the receiver to muffle the sound.

"Alberto, you sound awful. What's wrong?"

"I've got the flu or something."

"Don't tell me you didn't check your messages today."

"I...I guess I forgot. I've been asleep most the time. My phone's been off the hook."

"Are you really sick?"

But sick or not, Alberto was sufficiently alert to realize that Mrs. Wirth wouldn't be calling him at one o'clock in the morning unless she was in trouble. Before she could tell him to remain in bed, that she'd go ahead and get a taxi, he had hung up, saying, "Sit tight. I'll be right there."

Bless him! Francine settled down to wait. It was worth it. Alberto's town car had plenty of room for the cast. She didn't have the heart to squeeze into a cramped taxi again.

fifty-four

It was almost an hour before Alberto arrived – the longest hour in Francine's life, and although the poor man was wheezing and coughing, he was a sight for sore eyes.

Leaving the car idling at the curb, a definite *no-no* at airports, he rushed into the baggage claim area as fast as his legs and sickness could propel him. He spotted Mrs. Wirth sitting in a wheelchair by the exit doors.

A wheelchair? "Welcome home," he uttered, raking a hand through his hair. "My God! What happened to you?"

"Ah, excuse me!" The sheriff approached briskly, addressing Francine and giving Alberto a critical eye; dressed as he were in pajamas and an old terrycloth robe. "Ma'am? Is this the man you're waiting for?"

"Yes," Francine said, gratified by the sheriff's diligence. He must have kept an eye on her the entire time. For once she appreciated airport security.

Alberto wheeled Mrs. Wirth outside to where his car was now surrounded by two police officers eying it suspiciously. Of course once they spotted the wheelchair-bound woman, there seemed to be no point in calling the bomb squad or a tow truck. They walked away, stopped and watched from a distance as the man in the bathrobe put the luggage into the trunk, pushed the front seat of the car back as far as it would go, and helped the infirm woman into it.

"This is the best we can do about leg room," Alberto said, panting and struggling to fit the straight cast under the dashboard. "Would you rather lie down on the back seat with your leg up?"

"No. This is fine." Francine shuddered as she remembered the ride this morning from the cruise ship to Comitan, her leg out the window. "Believe me, this feels good. I'm sitting in an almost normal position for the first time today."

Alberto closed the car door, doubling over with a rasping cough as he returned the wheelchair to the terminal.

"I feel terrible about dragging you out of bed," Francine said solicitously once he slid in behind the wheel, put the car in gear, and pulled away from the curb. "How long have you been sick?"

"A few days. But never mind that. Tell me, what happened to your leg?"

"It's a long story. Just get me home."

"Okay. Have you called your son?"

"I'll call him tomorrow after I see the doctor."

"Your son doesn't know about this yet?" Alberto frowned and glanced at the large cast. He knew Richard Wirth and figured he'd be plenty angry about not being informed immediately about something as serious as this.

"I didn't want to worry him," Francine said.

"Okay, you know best." Alberto became practical. "I think you need a wheelchair. How else will you get into your house? And once inside, how will you move around? Maybe you ought to have some crutches."

"You're right. How will I get around? I guess I've been too preoccupied with just getting home to think much beyond that. But where do I get a wheelchair at this hour?"

"I know a woman in Pompano. She has some equipment stored in her garage. She broke her hip last year. Her place is on our way. I'll stop by and borrow some stuff."

"Now?"

"Sure." Alberto shrugged. "I'm not going to ring the doorbell or anything like that. I won't wake her."

"You have a key?"

"No."

Half an hour later, Alberto had jimmied the lock on the garage door and entered his friend's cluttered domain. Using a flashlight he found on a workbench, he moved stealthily around a battered Toyota and some old paint cans, finally locating the folded wheelchair in a corner. He put it into the rear of his car. Then he went back to look for some crutches.

Watching Alberto and worried some silent alarm might have been triggered, Francine could only hope that the local sheriff would be as kind as the one at the airport. She eyed the neighboring houses, expecting floodlights to go on at any minute. She began perspiring, something she blamed on the warm, humid night because she had no experience with breaking and entering.

"I couldn't find the crutches," Alberto finally said, getting into the car after carefully closing the garage door. "Maybe they're inside the house." Stifling a raspy cough, he put the car in neutral, silently coasting down the driveway, starting the engine only once he was out in the middle of the street.

Francine felt like a thief slipping away in the night.

Fifty-five

At long last Francine arrived home. The approach to her house on the grounds of the Polo Club in Boca Raton was a welcoming sight. The night gatekeeper on duty smiled and waved the car through, saying, "Welcome home, Mrs. Wirth!"

Palms on each side of the winding road were bathed in pink light from lamps hidden among the shrubbery, and in the middle of her circular driveway, the dancing waters in an ornamental fountain sprayed a fine mist on the surrounding flowerbeds, adding a glossy sheen to the blooms.

Never before had Francine felt happier about arriving home.

Alberto parked by the front door and helped her from the car and into the borrowed wheelchair after first wiping it down with a rag he found in the trunk. At this point all Francine could think about was getting to the bathroom. She hadn't visited a restroom facility since leaving the ship this morning. By now she was in pain.

"Do you want me to stay here tonight?" Alberto asked once they were inside the wide entrance hall. He walked around the exquisitely furnished home, turning on lights and adjusting the thermostat on the air conditioning.

"No. Go home and get some sleep. If you feel well enough come back tomorrow. I'll need to see my doctor first thing in the morning. But only come if you're up to it. I can always get someone from the manager's office to drive me."

"I'll be here at nine o'clock," Alberto promised, squaring his shoulders, belying his illness. He had been Mrs. Wirth's right hand man for years and didn't want to chance her finding another. She paid well and with the Christmas holidays approaching, his wife was counting on his bonus.

"Before you go, Alberto, wheel me to the bathroom and wait outside just long enough to help me into bed. Having made it this far, I'd hate to fall and not be able to get back up."

"Sure. No problem." Alberto wheeled Mrs. Wirth down the hall and into the bath connected to her bedroom. The home had three bathrooms; this was the largest and accommodated the wheelchair with ease. It was also the prettiest with full-length beveled mirrors, lovely silver-speckled wallpaper and crystal sconces.

Alberto closed the door behind Mrs. Wirth to give her privacy, but kept his ear to the door in case she fell. She didn't. A few minutes later, he wheeled her into the bedroom. Still dressed in the cruise wear, she decided she was too tired to change into nightclothes. Alberto pulled back the bedspread and helped her into bed, putting a pillow under the cast.

"Are you absolutely sure you don't want me to stay?" he asked after he had fetched her a glass of water, putting it on the night table.

"I'm sure. Go home. Get some sleep. I'll see you in the morning."

"Okay." Alberto turned off the lights and left, locking the front door behind him.

Exhausted, home in her own bed, eyes clamped shut, Francine fell into a deep sleep. When the gray morning light began filtering through the white plantation blinds, and she heard the lawn sprinklers being turned on at the same time birds began chirping in the magnolia tree outside her bedroom window, she awoke feeling rested but with no feeling in her injured leg.

Chapter fifty-six

A s the flight from Houston began its approach into La Guardia Airport, Maggie's mood descended right along with the plane. Below, New York City lay in a sea of bright lights and passengers sitting on both sides of her craned their necks to get a glimpse of Manhattan's skyscrapers. But the splendid view did nothing to stabilize Maggie's plummeting spirits. While traveling home from Mexico, Francine's predicament had kept her from thinking about her own. Feeling her friend's pain and, in a small way, knowing that she was helping her cope, she had managed to keep a stiff upper lip. But about to land in New York, all she could think about was the cruise and now regretted leaving the ship early. She thought back on the musical evenings in the Atrium. She envisioned Ms. Olson and Dr. Hellman on the deck, holding hands in the moonlight. She pictured the wild-eyed Claudia Rasner gambling, and Rose Burke pursuing Ronald Cohen with the exact same look. Maggie recalled the big-haired Dorothy playing that nice gentleman, Paul Hopkinson, for all he was worth. And, if she lived to be a hundred, she would never forget Bill Mc Kiernan and his generosity. The earrings he gave her might well mean her survival because she could sell them.

A hollow pit in her stomach – no food was served during the flight and Maggie hadn't purchased any – brought back memories of the deck buffets and the five course meals served in the beautiful dining room by waiters wearing white gloves. Each meal had been something to look forward to; each day had passed pleasantly without a care in the world except deciding which nightly entertainment to attend. Each and every minute on the ship had been a wonderful adventure. The only thing she could now look forward to were fingers cramped and ink-stained from filling out job applications, along with headaches brought on by the stress of interviewing for positions the agencies would rather fill with someone twenty years younger than she. During all those wonderful days on The Mexican Star she had been able to set aside her personal woes; now they rushed her like a mugger from a dark alley. She felt robbed, cheated of the final days on the ship as well as a chance to see a little bit of San Diego between docking and catching her flight home.

She was back to square one. Back to where she'd started. And why not? Why should she have believed that a cruise would change anything? She was the same Maggie. Loser Maggie. Unemployed Maggie. No references Maggie. Of course, beating herself up served no purpose. Tomorrow others would do it for her. Tomorrow might as well be a rainy Monday, blue Monday; black and blue as far as she was concerned, because she would take her first beating at that agency Vera had recommended.

Maggie sighed. At least she had an apartment to return to and thanks to Lisa was not in arrears on the rent. But how long might Lisa stay? Could they coexist in that small space until Maggie collected her first paycheck? Had Lisa, herself, found a job? An apartment? Selfishly, Maggie hoped that she hadn't because it would mean that she would be moving out and no longer be helping with the rent.

The seat belt light came on. Maggie buckled up, put away her reading material, put her backrest in its upright position, and listened to the captain's confident voice saying he would have the aircraft on the ground and at the gate in approximately ten minutes. As he signed off with a few additional pleasantries, Maggie felt a sudden longing to hear Michael's voice. From his flight deck, he must have uttered those same comforting words a thousand times to his passengers. Yet there had been no opportunity for him to offer any sign-off to her, not even a standard goodbye. There had been no chance to suggest that they stay in touch, no opportunity to exchange telephone numbers, which was par for the course. Her life was paved with lost chances, a depressing chain of sad events, yet she never stopped believing that things might change. Of course she would never see Michael Sanders again. She was not foolish enough to believe in fairy tales. They lived on opposite coasts. Shipboard romances didn't last and theirs hadn't even been a romance, just a short friendship, the hours of which could be counted on one hand. Nonetheless, the idea of never seeing him again depressed her far more than being broke and jobless. She should have gone to Florida with Francine, helped her get all the way home, a detour that would have postponed her own return to New York for a few days – postponed the inevitable – that of having to start over and look for a job at the age of forty-four.

Landing at La Guardia, Maggie caught the Port Authority bus to Grand Central Station in Manhattan. The bus was only nine dollars, whereas a taxi would have been twenty plus tolls and tips. At Grand Central, and although she generally avoided subways, she took the Lexington Avenue Line to 86th Street. The subway was pretty empty at this hour of the night except for a loud group of young men whose legs were spread-eagle over three seats each. Maggie remained standing by the door, not making eye contact and ready to exit at the next stop in case of any funny business.

Getting off at 86th Street and in order to avoid being entombed in one of the subway's derelict elevators, she dragged her luggage up the stairs toward the street, steering clear of two foul-smelling homeless individuals sleeping on a landing against bags of plastic recyclables. She held her breath until she reached the sidewalk where she discovered that her cotton jacket was no match for the bitter December cold. As she started to walk the three blocks toward 83rd Street, she desperately missed her old overcoat and wool cap. The day she left for the cruise, she was picked up in front of her building by an airport shuttle bus, a convenience she had reserved ahead, which meant she hadn't needed to wear warm clothing.

Rounding the corner of her street and turning down toward Second Avenue, she was hit by a blast of air screaming up from the East River, ripping at her thin jacket and sending her straw hat flying. She rescued it at the foot of the doors to a Duane Reade Pharmacy, which was open around the clock, catering to New Yorkers wanting to buy toothpaste and cough syrup at any hour. Other hardy souls were simply out on the streets, walking their dogs, owners and pets warmly dressed; the former eying Maggie's white cotton jacket and straw hat with suspicion until her suitcase came to their attention, at which point they smiled knowingly.

A dumb tourist on the loose in Manhattan.

After some initial surprise with the activity at this hour, Maggie remembered that New York was a city that never shut down. Something was always open; people were always out on the streets even at midnight. It was one of the reasons she loved living here. Tonight, however, trudging along the sidewalk, she felt no emotion and no fondness. Numbed by the cold, her steps were slow and sluggish as though she were walking in water, while her shoulders were hunched with a depression embedded too deeply to be written off as the normal low one might experience when returning to the real world after a holiday.

Stopping in front of her brownstone, fumbling for her vestibule key, Maggie gave herself a mental shake. Just get upstairs, she told herself. Unpack. Go to bed. Get up early. Put on the gray suit still in the plastic bag from the cleaners, and get to the first employment agency by nine o'clock.

Climbing the five flights to her apartment had never before been this difficult. Of course it was unusually late and Maggie normally didn't carry luggage. By the time she reached the fourth landing she stopped to catch her breath *and* to listen.

Music? She cocked her head. At this hour?

She tackled the last flight of stairs and put her key into the lock. She needn't have done so because the door was open. She walked in and discovered a loud party in progress. A party? She turned back toward the hall, believing she had mistakenly walked into a neighbor's apartment.

"Maggie!" Someone rushed from the din in the living room and took her suitcase, setting it down in the narrow hall with a thud and no concern for the downstairs tenant. "You're home? Hi!"

Maggie found herself staring at spiked hair, a nose ring, and ears with no less than five glittering stones in each. "Lisa?" she mumbled, struggling to recognize Simone's niece whose hair had gone from brown to red; not auburn red, lipstick red with white streaks that made it look like peppermint candy. Okay, so far so good, Lisa was here for at least another month. Looking like a freak, she couldn't possibly have landed a job yet unless it was with a Rock Band.

"Hi!" Lisa said again, shouting above the noise behind her. "You're home early. I didn't expect you till later this week."

That was obvious. "I cut my trip short," Maggie said.

"Okay. Glad to see you. Hope you don't mind this?" Lisa gestured over her shoulder before turning to her friends and yelling at them to pipe down. There were a dozen or so, a mixture of the sexes, though they all looked the same, males distinguished from females only by their facial hair. Levi's torn at the kneecaps and T-shirts displaying a myriad of politically correct messages was the evening's dress code.

"Hey! You guys! Tone it down!" she hollered again.

No one paid any attention.

"My mom's home!" she finally shouted.

That got results. Someone lowered the volume on the CD player.

"This cast will make a fine umbrella stand," Dr. Holtz joked Wednesday morning in his office in Boca Raton while sawing through the heavy plaster around Francine's leg. Of course, his joking stopped abruptly the minute he saw the condition of her injury. He made quick work of his examination and rewrapped the leg with fresh gauze bandages.

"You'll have to see a specialist right away," he said, now fastening a light metal brace around the leg. He turned to his nurse and told her to make an emergency appointment with Dr. Kennedy, a well-known orthopedic surgeon with a practice a few blocks away. "Dr. Kennedy will take some X-rays. Once he studies them, he will know exactly what needs to be done. He's the best in the field."

Despite Dr. Holtz's urgent and grave tone, Francine felt better. She was finally getting top-notch medical attention, the kind she was familiar with.

Alberto drove her to Dr. Kennedy's office. They had half an hour to spare and stopped along the way for coffee and some take-out breakfast food. Francine ate just enough so Alberto wouldn't nag her about keeping up her strength.

An assistant took a series of X-rays, and after studying the film as well as the injury, Dr. Kennedy told Francine what she already knew. She needed an operation and it had to be done sooner rather than later.

"I'll have to break your knee bone, drill three holes, stretch the tendons and pull them back up and reattach them," Dr. Kennedy said matter-of-factly, failing to notice Francine's pallor with his vivid description. "But first we'll need to run a battery of tests." He glanced at a time chart on the wall. "We can admit you to the hospital today for the preoperative work and schedule your surgery for tomorrow.

But first, you need to sign some consent forms."

"I have to talk to my son before I sign anything," Francine said. "He will kill me if I don't call and discuss this with him first."

"Then I suggest you call him immediately because we can't proceed without your signature. We also need the signature of a family member. Your next of kin."

"I don't have any family here in Florida. Can a friend sign? Or my handyman? He's right outside in the waiting room. He's like family. He has worked for me for many years."

"It has to be a blood relative."

"My son is in Colorado at this time of year."

"All right, we will accept his signature by facsimile."

Chapter Fifty-eight

As soon as Francine arrived home, she dialed Richard's number. It was eleven o'clock in Florida so it'd be nine o'clock in Colorado. The two-hour time difference meant she would catch him before he went up on the ski slopes. Richard was an extreme skier with the stamina to spend an entire day on the trails, Anne at his side. Skiing was a sport they both loved. They had taught their three daughters to ski almost before they could walk, and it was no surprise that each of the girls had been Olympic material. But much to Francine's relief, they married and instead of medals produced children.

Richard's reaction was pretty much what Francine expected. He was angry at having been kept in the dark. "You injure yourself on the cruise and you don't call me?" he shouted. "You don't pick up a phone for two days?"

"I had to leave the ship in a hurry," Francine kept her voice calm to diffuse his fury. "They couldn't treat my injury onboard and wanted to admit me to some Godforsaken hospital. My only concern was how to get out of there before they strapped me down for surgery. I had little time to think. Let alone make phone calls. Besides, my cell phone didn't work in Mexico. And since I didn't really know what was wrong with my leg, why upset you until I got home and had something to report?"

"Upset me? Not calling *that* upsets me!" Richard was still venting his spleen, his way of showing concern. Since his younger brother's death last year, he had become overly protective of his mother, calling her every day except when she was on a cruise where telephone connections were, admittedly, difficult. "You schlep yourself home in a wheelchair *alone* from God knows where..."

"I wasn't alone," Francine interrupted him. "I had a lovely travel companion."

"Well, whatever. I could have sent a plane to pick you up. Amy's and David's Cessna is sitting right here at the Vail-Eagle Airport. They came out yesterday. Now, listen to me. And listen carefully. I'm on my way. I want to speak with the knee surgeon. Don't do anything till I get there."

Richard arrived that evening on his son-in-law's plane. The following morning he went to see Dr. Kennedy who spelled out the need for an immediate operation, followed by twelve weeks of recuperation. Richard didn't argue with the diagnosis, but was bothered by the postoperative period where his mother would be flat on her back. Neither he nor Anne could remain inactive in Florida for that long.

"I would prefer to take my mother to New York for the surgery," he told Dr. Kennedy, "because my wife and I will be around to see her through it."

"Family is the best medicine," Dr. Kennedy agreed.

"If it were your mother, what would you do?"

"I guess I would take her to New York."

By two o'clock that same afternoon, Francine wearing the slim metal brace, a far cry from the bulky Plaster of Paris, was lifted onto the Cessna for the flight to White Plains near Richard's and Anne's spread in Greenwich.

The aircraft arrived at the Westchester County Airport three hours later. As Francine was helped off the plane, a blast of cold air paralyzed her unaccustomed lungs. She held her breath until they were inside the terminal, crossing it to a sheltered overhang where Richard's car and driver were waiting. Francine hadn't been in the northeast at this time of year for ages and had all but forgotten about ill-tempered weather. However, once she was settled inside the heated car, now driving along the dark winding roads toward Greenwich, she had to admit the view was pleasant. Lights spilling from the windows of the pretty suburban homes they passed, cast warm glows across frozen lawns and hedges. Many of the homes had colorful outdoor holiday lights strung in trees and around mailboxes, adding to the ambiance.

Francine thought of Maggie in nearby Manhattan and decided she would give her a call as soon as the operation was behind her.

Chapter *fifty-nine*

Anne Wirth had left Denver that same day on a commercial flight to La Guardia and, arriving in Greenwich by taxi minutes ahead of Richard and Francine, was determined to make her mother-in-law comfortable.

Francine didn't want any special treatment and wished Anne hadn't rushed home to smother her with kindness. But, like it or not, there were flowers on the supper tray brought into the guest room that evening and again on the breakfast tray the following morning; each meal a feast that the housekeeper whipped up on short notice, given the fact that she hadn't expected the family to return from Colorado for several weeks. She certainly hadn't expected to wait on an invalid.

But despite everyone's good intentions, Francine was for all practical purposes a prisoner in the guestroom. Unlike her own one-level home in Florida, Anne's and Richard's house had several flights of stairs, so any wish for a change of scenery required two strong individuals to carry her up and down. She realized that, following surgery, this would not be the place to spend her recovery.

The next morning Richard took his mother to New York City for a consultation with Dr. Owens, a world-renowned orthopedic surgeon at Columbia Presbyterian Hospital. Later that afternoon he brought her to a specialist at their local hospital in Greenwich for a second opinion.

"I recommend immediate surgery," Dr. Farber said after his examination and after studying Dr. Kennedy's X-rays that Richard carried along. This diagnosis was the same as the one earlier in the day in New York, but Dr. Farber added a warning. "If you wait much longer and allow the injury to repair itself you might never again be able to bend your knee."

Francine looked stricken. "Do whatever you have to and do it right away," she said, unwilling to waste another minute. She certainly didn't want to consult with additional specialists, something she knew that her son – being a stickler for perfection – was planning to do. Besides, she had taken an immediate liking to this young Greenwich surgeon and her instincts about people were generally good. "Richard! Sign the consent forms! Let's get this over with."

Dr. Faber smiled at her eagerness. "It's only fair to let you know that I have never operated on a person your age. I specialize in sports injuries. I generally work on young athletes."

"Does that mean you'd rather not?" Richard shot back.

"No. It only means that because of age issues there might be some question as to the final outcome." He looked squarely at Francine. "I must warn you that your leg may never be a hundred percent again."

"Will I be able to walk?"

"Yes, but you might experience a slight limp."

"How many of these operations have you done?" Richard now asked. He wanted an experienced surgeon. Dr. Farber looked to be in his mid thirties and might not have honed his skills sufficiently.

Dr. Farber thought a minute. "Off hand, I'd say I have probably done forty."

"Dr. Owens, the specialist we saw this morning in New York City, has done over two hundred," Richard said.

Dr. Farber smiled. "Well, he's older than I am."

Richard had to admit there was an advantage to younger, steadier hands.

Chapter

sixty

Friday in Los Angeles dawned with the typical marine layer hanging over the Santa Monica hills; fog from the Pacific Ocean that rolled in overnight and burned itself off before noon.

Michael padded down the stairs to the kitchen, turned off the alarm system, plugged in a pot of coffee, and walked through the family room to open the doors to the terrace where he stood a moment, inhaling deeply. The morning air was heavy with ocean mist and a heady fragrance from the gardenia bushes growing around the foundation at the back of the house.

Michael's home was a two-story beige Mediterranean with a red tiled roof and black wrought-iron window shutters. A narrow, second-story balcony ran the length of the front of the house and was accessible through verandah doors from the master bedroom. A neat lawn grew to the edge of the curb where several tall Jacaranda trees ensured privacy from traffic and passersby. There were no sidewalks on Miranda Drive. Generally speaking, Los Angeles was not pedestrian-friendly. People walked on treadmills or they strolled inside air-conditioned malls; the rugged jogged along the beaches, water bottles bouncing in their belts.

The house sat on a picturesque half acre of paradise and Michael couldn't imagine living anywhere else. The ground floor had a sunken living room with a beamed ceiling. There was a fireplace at one end and a domed picture window at the other. To the right of the center hall was a dining room and a small library; kitchen with family room completed the downstairs. He and Lynn had bought the place twenty-five years ago with financial help for the down payment from both sets of parents. Back then the price tag of two hundred thousand dollars had seemed a princely sum but in the long run turned out to be a bargain. In today's market similar homes in the area fetched from between one to two million.

The coffee maker gurgled, signaling the brew cycle was finished. Michael filled a cup and brought it outside on the terrace. A green and white striped awning kept the moist sea breezes from condensing on the patio furniture; still, he tested a chair before sitting down. A row of evergreens and several tall eucalyptus trees fenced-in the back garden and pool, the latter being a standard accessory in Southern California. From his seated position Michael could see the tops of his neighbors' roofs, all of which were identical to his own. After the canyon fires of four years ago, most residents along Miranda Drive had invested in Spanish tile. This house was originally built with those tiles, something Michael was grateful for because, according to his neighbors, their new roofs didn't come cheap.

Leaning back in the patio chair, he put his feet up on a chaise lounge, sipped the coffee, and noticed some leaves floating in the pool. He was about to get up and fish them out when he remembered that the gardener was coming later today for the weekly moving and trimming. The gardener's wife, Martha, came twice a week to clean and do the laundry just like she'd done when Lynn and Suzanne were alive. During the past six months Michael had occasionally asked her to do some grocery shopping, and she soon took it upon herself to put a chicken in the oven along with a vegetable and rice dish. He had never asked her to do any cooking but suspected it was her way of assuaging his grief, at the same time making herself indispensable. Whatever her motivation, he began to look forward to the dinners she left on the days she worked here.

Finishing the coffee, he realized that he felt unusually alert this morning and was increasingly excited about today's prospects. The idea of meeting the cruise ship when it docked in San Diego had first occurred to him the morning he flew Bill Mc Kiernan's body home to San Francisco. However, it wasn't until last night that he decided to actually follow through with his plan. According to the most recently updated ship arrivals posted in the newspapers, The Mexican Star would dock this morning at eleven thirty.

Since so abruptly leaving the ship, Michael had weighed the pros and cons of trying to reconnect with Maggie. Although he hadn't quite decided to pursue a long distance relationship, he was keen on seeing her again and only hoped there would be enough time to have lunch before she had to catch her flight to New York. He was familiar with flight schedules. Non-stops from San Diego to the East Coast left in the mornings, too early for her to be booked on any of them. She was probably on an afternoon flight connecting in Chicago. Or better yet, a red-eye, which would give them more time.

Mostly, he hoped that she would be glad to see him. He felt sure she had enjoyed his company and trusted nothing had changed since Salina Cruz and their open and frank dialogue, which he suspected had been therapeutic for both of them. Thankfully, she had not offered the clichéd brand of grief therapy that others had. Nor had she told him to "get on with his life;" advice regularly given to him by the women his friends rammed down his throat, claiming he was becoming a recluse. After each of those encounters, he had decided that a hermetic lifestyle had a lot going for it.

Michael realized he could never again be completely happy. There was a hole in his heart that an eighteen-wheeler could pass through. He often wished himself at the bottom of the sea, never more so than on the mornings following one of his nightmares. But he wasn't there, he was in the here and now and had to try to make the best of it, at least go through the motions of living.

He got up from the chair and went back inside, leaving two iridescent hummingbirds buzzing at the feeders his daughter had hung on the terrace and which he now kept filled. The misty morning air was chilly and damp and the kitchen felt warm in comparison. He had a second cup of coffee at the breakfast table, popped some bread into the toaster, and turned on the small flat screen TV attached to the underside of a cabinet. Flipping channels he searched for some news. There was another suicide bombing in Afghanistan. Two American marines were killed. Michael shivered. After graduating from college he had spent six years in the Air Force.

He turned off the TV, had second thoughts about the toast, and went upstairs. Flicking through his closet, he chose some beige corduroy slacks and a blue open collared shirt. He was eager to get going. With no traffic the drive to San Diego should only take an hour and a half, but low volume on the freeways was something one could never count on; he needed to give himself plenty of time for any eventuality. If he arrived late, he might miss Maggie.

Much to his chagrin, his heart began beating a little faster as he envisioned her walking down the docking ramp in that silly straw hat, the tip of her nose pink where the brim hadn't protected it from the sun. She was probably wearing the camp shirt with the cargo pants he was familiar with. She was not a fashion plate who traveled with a different outfit for each day. Among the disembarking passengers he figured he would have no trouble recognizing her. And in the event she and Francine Wirth were still joined at the hip, he was prepared to invite Mrs. Wirth to lunch as well, counting on the fact that she would decline.

Michael shaved, ran a comb impatiently through his hair, momentarily wondering what had happened to the brown color he seemed to have lost overnight, strands of gray now getting the upper hand. But never mind, at least he still had plenty of it. Anyway, this past year he had turned the corner on fifty so some signs of age were inevitable. He threw a suede jacket over his shoulders and went back downstairs. Grabbing the car keys, he unplugged the coffee maker, reset the alarm, and walked through the kitchen door into the garage.

Backing his olive green jaguar convertible out into the driveway, he eyed Lynn's silver SUV, a car he couldn't part with because of the memories of her at the wheel. She had loved that gas-guzzler; justifying the low mileage to a feeling of safety the day Suzanne got her learner's permit.

Michael hit the remote. The garage door closed and he backed into the street and headed for the Santa Monica Freeway, which would connect to the southbound Interstate. By the time he got to San Diego the fog would have lifted and he could put the top down. By noon it would be a bright day – picture perfect – typical of Southern California. If the lunch with Maggie went well, perhaps she could be enticed to stay on for a few days. The sun should clinch it; after all, she'd mentioned how she had fled the cold weather in New York. She had also told him that she had no job to return to, so getting back to Manhattan could certainly be postponed for a day or two while he showed her the sights, such as Hollywood Boulevard, which in spite of it's tacky souvenir shops, pseudo porn shops, and rundown street corners, was always a favorite with out-of-towners.

Michael often wondered why some studio moguls didn't band together and raise funds to beautify the landmark street, home to the old classic movie theaters like Grauman's Chinese, El Capitan, and The Egyptian. The Walk of Stars had been a good idea, but was high maintenance; spilled soda, gum, and other discarded litter regularly marred the brass stars in the sidewalk. Building the new Kodak Center and restoring the old Roosevelt Hotel was another good idea but a drop in the bucket. Basically, the film industry left most of Hollywood Boulevard to decay like an abandoned back lot. Maybe he should show Maggie Rodeo Drive in Beverly Hills and the attractive sidewalk cafés along Sunset Boulevard instead. Perhaps she'd like to tour the Getty Museum or attend a concert at Disney Hall. Personally, he would enjoy that. But, whatever her preference, it'd be fun to show her around.

He suddenly felt a strange tingle in his spine; strange because it was something he hadn't felt in months. It didn't take long to identify it as happy anticipation. He pressed his foot down on the accelerator, signaled, and pulled into the fast lane.

The Mexican Star was docking, and people meeting passengers were gathering on the wharf. Men in black livery uniforms stood poised as well, holding up signs displaying the names of those they had come to collect, pretty much like at any airport arrival gate.

Standing on the edge of the crowd, Michael watched as passengers started down the landing ramp. Being careful not to miss Maggie, he barely blinked. Eventually he spotted Mildred Fischer and Doug Collins disembarking together and felt sure Maggie would be right behind them. She wasn't. There was no sign of Mrs. Wirth either.

Once everyone was off the ship, Michael wondered how on earth he could have missed seeing Maggie. He pushed his way through the passengers to where the luggage was unloaded and placed in alphabetic order for easy retrieval. She was not near her section. Again he saw her friends, Mildred and Doug, the latter already in possession of his suitcase and wheeling it toward the F sign where Mildred Fischer's valise would be placed.

"Mrs. Fischer!" Michael called out to get her attention. She was dressed in a pink pantsuit and the same western hat with the glittering rhinestone band that he remembered her wearing in Salina Cruz.

"Yes...?" She turned, stopped, and studied the figure approaching her.

"Welcome back," Michael smiled and nodded to Doug Collins. "We met on the cruise. I'm Michael Sanders."

"Oh? Mr. Sanders? Yes, of course. What are you doing here?" Mildred looked puzzled. "Didn't you leave the ship? We heard you flew poor Bill's body home."

"I did. I'm here today to meet Maggie."

"Maggie?"

"Yes, but I must have missed her in the crowd on the ramp. I didn't see her come off the ship."

"She left with Francine."

"I didn't see her either."

"Oh, of course, you haven't heard. You left the ship before it happened."

"Before what happened?"

"Francine had an accident." Mildred squinted against the sun as she tilted her head to look up at Michael. "She tore up her leg something awful."

"I believe it was her knee," Doug corrected. "She saw a doctor in Tonala and was put in a cast. She and Maggie left the ship."

"They left the ship in Tonala?"

"No. In Tapachula." Doug Collins eyed the suitcases being placed in the F section, anxious to reunite Mildred with hers so they could be on their way. Her flight left for Chicago at two o'clock. His to Miami left an hour earlier, a departure that didn't give him time for idle conversation.

"Francine needed an operation," Mildred said, gesturing toward her valise. "That's mine, Doug. Over there! The one with the pink ribbon on the handle." Doug was quick about retrieving it.

"Are you telling me that Maggie and Mrs. Wirth are in Tapachula?" Michael asked, disappointment settling in hard and fast.

"No. They flew home from somewhere near there. Francine wanted her own doctors in Florida to operate on her leg."

"Maggie went to Florida with her?"

Mildred looked unsure. "I don't think so. I believe she wanted to go home to New York. When I get to Chicago tonight, I'm going to call Francine." Mildred opened her purse and pulled out her address book. "I neglected to get Maggie's telephone number but I have Francine's right here. Do you want it?"

"Yes. Just a second. Let me write it down."

Mildred read it aloud as Michael pulled a pen from an inside pocket in his jacket and scribbled the number on the back of his parking stub.

"I'm sorry I forgot to get Maggie's number," Mildred said, putting her address book away. "Everything was so confusing before they left. But call Francine. She'll have it."

"I'll do that." Michael bid goodbye to Mildred and Doug. "Have a pleasant flight home." He shook hands with both of them, turned and left the wharf.

Crossing the street, he walked over to the parking lot where he'd left his car. Before relinquishing the stub, he transferred Mrs. Wirth's number to a slip of paper the attendant let him have, then he headed north on the San Diego Freeway back to Los Angeles. His mind on Maggie, he realized too late that he could have boarded the ship and retrieved his belongings. But never mind. As pre-arranged his gear would be delivered to his home.

Maggie was back in New York. Damn!

When would he next be on the East Coast? Probably when Carol's baby was born. But that was not for another four or five months. A lot of water would pass under the bridge before then. The cruise would be ancient history and Maggie might have forgotten him.

Chapter
sixty-two

As expected, the fog had burned off. It was a brilliant, sunny day but it might as well have been raining because Michael didn't put the top down; the motivation to do so was gone.

He returned home, deciding he'd swim some laps and perhaps go to a movie. Maybe he'd drive over to the club, do some putting or get in on a golf game with some of the old-timers. His regular group only played on the weekends; weekdays they worked. Suddenly Michael realized that he hated being retired. At fifty he was too young to be put out to pasture. Swim? Golf? A movie? The choices were pathetic, unless it was Sunday.

Fingering his keys, he left his car in the driveway and walked around the flagstone path to the front door to pick up the mail. Unlocking the door, he disarmed the alarm, dropped the mail on the hall table and went into the library to check his answering machine. The red light was blinking. Maybe there were some interesting calls? He pressed the button and listened. The first call was from a colleague, a fellow pilot who regularly called to set him up with a sister, cousin, friend, foe or stranger. He erased the call. The next two messages were both from Connie, her chipper voice suggesting he come to her place tonight for some home-cooked lasagna; her second call indicating tomorrow would be fine as well. Giving him an alternative date was the same as giving him no way out, because how could someone with no social life possibly be busy two nights in a row? He erased the messages. He would call Connie back later after first making some plans so he could be truthful when giving his regrets.

Connie had been Lynn's best friend since high school, and they had gone on to

UCLA together. Divorced, Connie was a successful real estate agent, and after Lynn's death had taken it upon herself to look after Michael, occasionally stopping by with a casserole and regularly inviting him to various social events. He liked Connie, if only because she'd been Lynn's friend, but her manner was becoming increasingly constrictive. Although he never encouraged her, she acted as if they were an item, which was ridiculous.

He heaved a deep sigh. Despite Connie constant calls, he felt lonely. He missed his life with Lynn and Suzanne with a vengeance. He no longer looked forward to coming home. A house that had always been full of activity was much too quiet now, his movements echoing eerily within its walls. And, although all the drapes were open, it always seemed dark. He missed the regular gatherings of friends and family and he missed the high-pitched laughter when Suzanne and her pals hung out around the pool. He even missed the mundane, such as giving the kids a ride to the mall. He missed enforcing curfew on school nights, checking homework, and bringing picnic supplies to Griffith Park when Suzanne's class had an outing. He missed driving to Hancock Park Sunday mornings to fetch her after a sleepover at a friend's house. His job had never been nine-to-five. His flight schedule left him with free days to be involved in his daughter's activities, in Lynn's as well. He had accompanied her on many a midweek hunt through the flea markets in Long Beach for "antique" bric-a-brac, afterwards stopping for lunch at a seafood place where, rather than having a table with a pleasant water view, Lynn insisted on sitting by a window overlooking the parking lot in case someone decided to break into the car and steal her new "treasures."

He grimaced with the memory and struggled against a searing ache in his chest. God Almighty, he missed his family! He'd been told that the pain would lessen with time. Not true. It had been six months and it was as bad as ever. The ceremony at sea had helped a little but it had no permanency; just a band-aid that was already falling off, laying his wound bare.

Truth be known, he also missed flying and the purpose that went along with it. He missed coming home after a layover, changing out of his uniform, and having a glass of wine on the terrace with Lynn, allowed when he wasn't flying for the next eighteen hours.

Maybe he should go back to South World, test his reflexes in the simulator and if he was as sharp as before, talk with Bill Knight, old friend and flight coordinator. Perhaps he could get back in the air or at least go on the reserve list and substitute for pilots who called in sick. The powers-that-be at South World would no doubt insist that he first have another go at some therapy with the psychiatrist they kept on the payroll. Okay, he could do that. He really ought to give it another try.

Michael wiped his hand across his eyes. His musings about Lynn and Suzanne had brought him near tears. He hadn't cried since the age of ten, but during the past six months it happened frequently, which was something he needed to control if he expected to pass muster with the airline psychiatrist and fly commercial jets again.

He stood up, raked a hand through his hair in a restless manner and checked his watch. He felt like talking with someone. He needed to hear someone's voice. His brother in Arizona? Jeffrey and Carol? Maybe he ought to call Lynn's parents, or her married sister, Allison. They all lived nearby in Brentwood. He could invite the entire gang out for dinner. Take the whole family, including the kids, to Spago's. Then again, maybe not? His relationship with the senior Emersons had been strained since the crash. It was as though they blamed him even more than he blamed himself. Also, it was still difficult to see Allison's and John's children, their daughter in particular. She and Suzanne were the same age, had been as close as sisters, and even resembled each other. The last time Michael had seen her, he had not handled it well.

He decided against calling the Emersons. It would be more uplifting to talk with Jeffrey and Carol. It was now two o'clock in Los Angeles so it'd be five o'clock in Hastings. Jeffrey wouldn't be home yet, but Carol would. She taught school in nearby Dobbs Ferry and was usually home by four. He might encourage her to give the Emersons a call. Married to their grandson, she would soon give them a great-grandchild, which should provide all concerned with some happy conversation.

But before he called Carol, he'd better call Bill Knight and secure a time slot in the flight simulator. Then he'd have something new to tell Carol.

Chapter
sixty-three

The week following Francine's surgery, and while she was confined to the hospital, Richard and Anne looked at nursing homes. Dr. Farber insisted they find one because Francine would be flat on her back for weeks and require care around the clock. But each facility they visited was more depressing than the previous. One smelled abominably of bathroom odors masked by the scent of Lysol, the combination assaulting them the minute they entered. They turned around and left the premises before going to the director's office to keep their appointment, Richard calling from the parking lot to cancel as they drove on to the next one.

That home was no better. The infirm sat in wheelchairs, shoulder to shoulder along halls like limpid sentries guarding their individual sleeping cubicles. The smell of meat loaf and creamed spinach permeated the narrow corridors painted a dull green to match the 1940 vintage linoleum on the floors. Some patients were asleep in their chairs; others were slumped over in a state of boredom, drooling, while some stared vacantly into space. Those who were alert looked at Richard and Anne, smiled and tried to recognize them, wondering if they were family who had finally come to visit. Those were the saddest cases.

After seeing half a dozen convalescent homes in Westchester and Fairfield County, Richard and Anne finally found an acceptable facility in the town of Rye. The rooms were large with views of well-tended grounds, and the main corridor had floor-to-ceiling glass facing a center courtyard planted with shrubbery and evergreens. Best of all, it didn't smell. The staff reacted to an accident with the same zeal they'd react to a fire. After five minutes in the place, Richard signed on the dotted line and hired a private nurse to supplement the regular staff. Days later when Francine entered the facility, flowers, plants, boxes of chocolate, books, chimes, trinkets and cards arrived from friends near and far. After a week in the place she could have opened a gift shop.

Richard and Anne visited daily; their daughters alternated on weekends, often bringing along their small children to cheer her. Friends from bygone years still living in the New York area also came to keep her spirits up, redundant as it were because Francine was a woman with a positive attitude and regularly entertained her visitors by recounting the perils of being hoisted up the side of the cruise ship, wearing an eighty-pound cast. Repeated and revised, the story eventually became a world-class comedy.

Still, with all the visitors and all the attention from the staff, Francine wished herself back in her own home in Boca Raton. Twice a week she telephoned Alberto, reminding him to water her houseplants, check her answering machine, forward the mail, and oversee the cleaning service.

Chapter sixty-four

"Why are you no longer with Goodman, Barr & Noune?" The interviewer at Jobs Aplenty looked over the rim of his reading glasses, and studied Maggie sitting ramrod straight in her chair, ankles crossed, the pleats in the gray skirt covering her knees demurely. Under her suit jacket she wore a tailored white blouse, no gold jewelry – not that she had any – and her hair was sprayed down flat so it wouldn't curl in a flirtatious manner. She looked every inch the proper paralegal. The only strike against her was her age and the fact that she had to fudge the truth about the circumstances surrounding her last job. But lie she must. It would be the kiss of death to admit she was fired.

"After twelve years with the same firm, I quit," she said and looked at the man without blinking. "I needed a change. A new challenge." Keeping eye contact with the interviewer, she put great emphasis on that key word because wanting a challenge could mean any number of things, all of them positive.

"I see..." Mr. Roberts' face showed no expression. His complexion was pasty. A rumbled suit covered his fleshy frame; he was obviously a fast food addict and, although he looked to be in his mid thirties, had the used appearance of someone much older. When he remained silent, it was a signal that he expected Maggie to continue.

She obliged him. "Goodman, Barr & Noune is a small law firm," she said. "Three partners and a couple of associates. I would prefer working for a larger organization. A Wall Street firm. One with a hundred attorneys and a handful of paralegals." Maggie forced a smile. "You know the old scenario. Swim in a big pond."

Nodding, the interviewer took off his glasses and rubbed his eyes. It was only ten o'clock in the morning, but he was tired. "Did you give the required two weeks notice before you quit?" he asked, replacing his glasses.

"Certainly." Maggie felt her cheeks burn.

"I see on your application that you stopped working back in November. Have you been job hunting since then?"

"No. I went on a cruise. I decided I'd better take a vacation before interviewing and starting a new job."

This answer seemed to satisfy him. For the most part he was suspicious of applicants who quit one job before they had another.

"Very well." He stood up, indicating the interview was over. "I'll check your references. Ms. Laura Noune was your last boss?"

"Yes," Maggie said, inwardly reminding herself to alert Vera about her promise to intercept the call.

"Good. Now, as I said initially..." Mr. Roberts reached across his desk and shook Maggie's hand, "it's awfully close to the holidays and firms generally don't hire right before Christmas. January is more active. I will definitely be able to get you an interview then. I will call you as soon as I have something."

Thanking him, Maggie left his cubicle, walking past other job applicants in the reception area, filling out reams of paper. She grabbed her coat off the rack by the front door, buttoning it in the elevator as she rode down the eighteen floors, all the while fighting claustrophobia and wishing she had walked down. But just back from vacation, eighteen floors were a bit much and she had to see several more agencies today.

At the end of the week, having left applications at half a dozen employment offices, her gray suit was no longer fresh and needed to be pressed. Mr. Roberts at Jobs Aplenty had been right. December was a slow month. One agency blamed not only the holiday season but also the stagnant economy, telling Maggie that even large law firms were downsizing.

She wondered if she ought to go ahead and just take some temporary work as a salesperson in a department store that might be hiring in anticipation of holiday sales. However, before exploring that avenue, she kept a lunch date with Simone.

"Okay, now I want to hear all about it. Each and every delicious detail," Simone said the minute they slipped into one of the small booths at their favorite sandwich bar on 57th and Sixth Avenue. "Oh, and thanks a million for the postcards. Acapulco looked particularly spectacular. But first tell me...did you meet anyone on the cruise?" Simone was a hopeless romantic. "You look wonderful. I like the light streaks in your hair. Did the sun do that?"

"No. I spent a fortune at the hairdresser before the trip."

"Well, it looks great. And, you don't look as though you gained any weight." Simone gave Maggie's trim figure a once over. "People go on cruises and invariable pile on the pounds. The ship had a gym?"

"Oh sure. And I took exercise classes every morning. It helped because I ate like a horse the entire time."

"Without getting fat?" Simone slapped down the menu. "Howard and I are going on a cruise."

"I'm sure the benefits are temporary. Another frustrating week of job hunting and I'll be back to my frumpy, lumpy self."

"Yeah, looking for work can't be much fun. The economy is bad. My father-in-law had to let two people go. I still say you ought to sue Ms. Noune for unfair dismissal." Simone picked up the menu again, pursed her lips, and perused the list of pita sandwiches. "For crying out loud! You worked there for twelve long years."

"I'd rather sell my diamonds," Maggie blurted just as a waiter came to their table.

"Sell your *what?*"

As soon as the waiter had taken their order and left, Maggie told Simone all about Bill McKiernan, his gift, and how it came about.

"The earrings are *genuine?*" Simone sputtered. "Real?"

"You bet. They cost twenty thousand dollars. I saw the price tag."

"Twenty grand? *Wow!*" Simone sucked in her breath. "That's serious money."

"Yes, and since they've hardly been worn, I can probably sell them as new."

"I don't know. I think jewelry is like a car. Once you drive it from the showroom, it's considered used. Actually, come to think of it, I believe I've heard of your sugar daddy and his trophy wife. I saw an article a while back in Forbes Magazine. My father-in-law has a subscription at the print shop. Occasionally I leaf through an issue during my coffee break. It's always interesting to read about the filthy rich." Simone took a sip of coffee and looked pensive. "I wonder if The New York Times ran an obit on your friend? I can't imagine I would have missed one about a tycoon's sudden death at sea. That kind of stuff is always interesting. Do you think maybe his wife had a hand in it? Do you think foul play was involved?"

"No. She neglected him. That's all I know. Is that a crime?"

"I don't think so unless it's a child being neglected."

"Poor generous soul..." Maggie mumbled, shaking her head. "I still can't figure out why Bill was so nice to me."

"Bill?" Simone raised her eyebrows.

"Everyone used first names on the ship."

"Oh, sure." Simone winked, teasing her. "You really expect me to believe you did nothing *special* to earn the fancy jewelry?"

"Come on! Stop it!"

"Hey! Simmer down." Simone held up her hands. "I'm only kidding around."

The sandwiches arrived and the two friends ate for a few moments in silence, both gesturing toward their empty cups when a waiter walked by with coffee.

"So, seriously, are you going to keep the earrings or sell them?"

"I'll probably have to sell them."

"Well if so, I suggest you go see Frankel's Jewelers on 53rd Street. Howard bought me a diamond pendant there for our fifteenth wedding anniversary. He knows the owner. Use Howard's name and they won't cheat you. Some places advertise they pay high prices for estate jewelry and then rob you when you bring it in. They figure you're desperate and take advantage of you. Discuss it with Howard before you do anything."

"Thanks, I will."

"In fact, he can go with you. How about that?"

"Let's wait and see. If Lisa stays in my apartment long enough, I might not have to sell."

"How is the roommate business?"

"Terrific. Lisa is always out. If it weren't for two dozen bottles of grooming lotions and her wet socks on the radiators, I'd never know I had a roommate."

"I heard she had a couple of parties while you were away."

"No problem. No one damaged anything. Not that there's anything to damage. Lisa is welcome to have a party any time she wants. I'll just make myself scarce and go to a late movie."

"Well, you'll have plenty of peace and quiet during the holidays. Lisa will be going home to Pittsburgh for Christmas."

"Yes, I know. She told me. I only hope she comes back. Splitting the rent is a huge help. This sounds selfish, but I hope she stays till I get a job."

"She'll stay. From what I hear, she loves your place. Her friends around the city invariably live in grungy basements. She's happy to be in a fifth floor walk-up. Besides, she's got to first find a job. Without that, no landlord will give her a lease."

"Unless she gets rid of the peppermint hair, I doubt she will find employment."

"Well, unlike you, she doesn't want full time work in a respectable firm. She's just looking for something temporary like waiting on tables in a celebrity café. No pasta joint for her. And she doesn't want to work at Kinkos. Of course that's where the jobs are. But no! She wants to rub elbows with Broadway types and film stars. She figures she'll be discovered if she looks sufficiently quirky while serving lattés. To her credit, she's taking some acting classes down in the Village."

"Yes. I wish her all the luck in the world." Maggie sighed, remembering how youthful dreams have a way of crashing when you aren't looking.

"Well, if it doesn't pan out, she'll go back to college next year. Anyway, on a different subject," Simone finished her sandwich and pushed her empty plate aside. "Since you missed our Thanksgiving feast, I'm going to insist that you come out for Christmas dinner. How about it?"

"I'd love it," Maggie said. It was no use pretending she had other plans. Besides, since the cruise, she didn't like being alone nearly as much as before.

"Good. No presents. We keep it simple."

"How about a pecan pie?"

"Pie gladly accepted."

Chapter sixty-five

Early Sunday, after running down to the corner newsstand to buy *The New York Times*, Maggie reminded herself to call Francine. It was high time. It was almost a week since both had returned home.

It was cold and rainy and coming back with the bulky newspaper, Maggie climbed the five flights of stairs slowly, shrugging out of her wet poncho on the landing before unlocking the door. Entering quietly, she put the paper on the floor in the hall while she tiptoed to the kitchen to reheat some Starbucks coffee. Lisa had been out till all hours and was still asleep on the living room couch. All Maggie saw of her roommate was a tuft of frizzy peppermint hair; the rest was buried under a fluffy eiderdown her parents had sent her from Pittsburgh. Maggie smiled. For all of Lisa's attempts to impress and shock, and despite her somewhat privileged background, she was comfortable sleeping on a lumpy sofa in a generic living room that had seen better days. The furniture was old and worn. The TV set didn't work. The blinds were broken. None of this bothered Lisa. She was easy to live with. Except for the assortment of bottles and jars in the bathroom as well as her habit of washing her underwear in the kitchen sink, leaving it to dry on top of the radiators, she was a dream.

The telephone was in the living room, there was no phone jack in the bedroom, and not wanting to disturb Lisa's sleep, Maggie decided she'd wait a while before calling Francine. It was ten o'clock. Lisa would probably be up by eleven.

Sipping the coffee from its cardboard cup, Maggie went into her bedroom, sat down on the bed and opened the paper, separating out the various sections according to interest; there were pounds of pulp to weed through. A mixture of rain and sleet was pelting the small window where the shade still hung on its disabled spring, but it would serve no purpose to raise it manually; no measurable light would enter anyway. Maggie simply turned on both lamps in the room, plumped up a pillow behind her back, and began reading the Book Review, jotting down titles of new books that caught her fancy. Tomorrow she'd call to see if they were available at the 79th Street Library where, unfortunately, there was always a waiting list for *best sellers*. Maggie dreamt about the day she could walk into a Barnes & Noble and plunk down $27.99 for a hardcover. The day she could do that, she would consider herself rich. Longingly, she remembered the well-stocked library on the cruise ship. No sign-up sheet. Help yourself. Borrow as many books as you want. What luxury!

Eventually she put the paper down and glanced at the clock radio. It was past eleven. It was time to call Francine. If Lisa woke up now, so be it.

Walking into the kitchen to discard the cardboard coffee cup, she took a bagel from the freezer and while waiting for it to thaw, tiptoed back to the living room for the telephone, stretching the cord into the hall as far from the couch and its sleeping occupant as it allowed. From a sitting position on the floor near the front door, she dialed Francine's number in Boca Raton.

After four rings, a man with a distinct Spanish accent answered. Believing she had gotten the wrong number, Maggie immediately hung up and now redialed each digit more carefully. The same male voice answered. This time she didn't hang up. Instead, she waited and listened to the entire recorded message: "Hello. You have reached the home of Francine Wirth. She is not here. Until further notice she can be reached at..." Crawling on her hands and knees back into the living room, Maggie quickly grabbed a pen and pad from on top of the TV set and jotted down the number the man repeated twice in a slow and deliberate voice; the 203 area code indicating it was a number in Connecticut. Maggie realized that Francine must be visiting her son and daughter-in-law, which was good news, because if she was able to travel up north so quickly her injury obviously wasn't all that serious. Nonetheless, Maggie decided to let a few days pass before calling the Connecticut number. If Francine had just arrived, it might be intrusive to call her family this soon.

Despite her intentions, Maggie let almost an entire week slip by before calling Francine, reason being that she was too preoccupied with her own affairs. So far only one law firm had scheduled an interview, and the appointment wasn't until January the 3rd, confirming what Mr. Roberts at Jobs Aplenty had predicted. Maggie also learned that, flush with temporary help, the stores were not hiring for the holiday shopping season.

Having written the Connecticut phone number into the margin of her address book, Maggie looked at it several times but was never quite in the mood to call because she would have to sound upbeat and that would be a strain. It wasn't until the following Sunday that she finally pulled herself together and dialed Francine's new number.

A pleasant female voice answered. "Hello?"

"Hi! My name's Margaret Maghpye. I'm trying to get in touch with Francine Wirth. I got this number from a message on her Florida answering machine."

"Are you a friend of hers?"

"Yes. She and I were on a cruise together. The Mexican Star line."

"Oh, of course! You're Maggie?"

"That's right."

"Francine told us about you. You left the cruise with her. I'm Anne Wirth. Her daughter-in-law."

"Hi! I guess she's staying with you? May I speak with her?"

"Oh, dear! You haven't heard?"

"Heard what?"

"Francine is in a nursing home."

"A nursing home?"

"Yes. She's had a very complicated and painful operation. We pray she'll be able to walk again. Her leg was horribly mangled. And now after the surgery it's proving slow to heal."

"My God! I'm sorry to hear that. I knew her knee was in bad shape, but she didn't complain much on the trip home."

"That's my mother-in-law. True grit. The John Wayne in our family. She's a brave woman. We were in Colorado when she called and told us what had happened. My husband flew to Boca Raton and brought her back to Connecticut. He didn't want her operated on in Florida and we both wanted her here where we could keep an eye on things."

"So the surgery itself went well?"

"Yes. But we won't know the outcome until the incision heals and she can begin to bend her knee. She's getting physical therapy and the doctor examines her every day. That's why she's in the nursing home."

"I'd like to call her."

"Do you have a pen handy? I'll give you the number."

"Yes." Maggie pulled out the pen she'd wedged in the spine of her address book. "Okay, I'm ready," she said. "Can you also give me the address of the nursing home? Maybe I can visit her."

"That would be nice. I know she'd enjoy that."

After writing down the information, Maggie thanked Anna Wirth, hung up, and immediately dialed the number she had given her.

"Rye Convalescent Home!" a crisp voice announced.

"Hello. I'd like to speak with Mrs. Francine Wirth."

"One moment, please."

Maggie waited, hoping she wasn't calling at a bad time because it took a while before the line was picked up.

"Hello?" In spite of the sound of children shrieking in the background, Maggie recognized Francine's voice.

"Hi, Francine! It's me. Maggie."

"Maggie! How nice to hear from you. How are you?"

"I'm fine. But how are *you*? I just spoke with your daughter-in-law. She told me you've had a horrendous operation."

"Yes, that pretty much describes it. It was no picnic. My son insisted I come north for the surgery. But no matter the venue, surgery is dreadful. What can I say? But at least the doctors believe I won't be a cripple."

"Thank God for that."

"I'll say. I've been thinking about you, Maggie. I was planning to call you but they're keeping me so busy here with physical therapy and a host of other routines. Not to mention visitors, which I adore, of course. Without visitors my days would be awfully boring."

"I'll come out and see you. When are visiting hours?"

"Anytime. Right now I've got one granddaughter here along with her two toddlers."

"I can hear them in the background."

"Yes, the kids are noisy, but I love them," Francine laughed.

"How about if I come out on a day when you're not expecting anyone else. Perhaps an afternoon during the week?"

"That would be lovely. On weekdays, my son visits every morning. He always stays till lunch. He's such a dear. He and Anne were supposed to be in Colorado all this time. They're missing their ski holiday on my account. I've told them they ought to go back, that I'm perfectly fine, but they won't hear of it. Anyway, why don't you come out some early afternoon? That's usually a quiet time around here. You pick the day."

"How's Tuesday?"

"Perfect. Let me give you the address."

"I already have it. Your daughter-in-law gave it to me."

On Tuesday Maggie took the Lexington Avenue bus to Grand Central and bought some flowers at the station before catching the noon train to Rye. Arriving in Rye, she was lucky to run into two other people from the train, also going to the convalescent home. They shared a taxi, Maggie gauging the distance by counting the blocks as they drove, deciding that unless these people left at the same time she did, she could easily walk back. Suburban taxis were far more expensive that city cabs.

Expecting a dreary environment, she was pleasantly surprised when the taxi let everyone off at a facility that from the outside looked like a country club, complete with sloping lawns. Stopping at the front desk in a circular and cheerful hall, wide corridors fanning out in several directions, Maggie was told that Mrs. Wirth was in Suite 602. Heading in the direction the nurse pointed to, Maggie quickly found the room.

"Hi!" she said and stepped through the open door.

"Maggie! You made it. It's so nice to see you." Francine was all smiles and raised her head, the rest of her remaining flat on a typical and unattractive metal hospital bed. But, otherwise, the room was homey, decorated with tasteful furniture, pretty curtains, plants and family pictures. A nurse was sitting by the window, reading, but immediately got up and took the bouquet of pink chrysanthemums, promising to put them in water.

"Darlene, this is Maggie," Francine said, lifting herself carefully up on one elbow. "My friend from the cruise. The one I told you about. "Maggie, meet Darlene. My guardian angel."

"How do you do?" Maggie smiled at the woman whose skin was the color of milk chocolate and as smooth. It was impossible to guess her age.

"Nice to meet you," Darlene said, adding, "I'll go get a bowl of water." She left the room.

Maggie stuffed her gloves and scarf into the pockets of her coat before hanging everything, including a new vinyl shoulder bag, on a garment rack behind the door.

"It wasn't necessary to bring flowers," Francine said. "But thank you."

"You're welcome." Maggie noted two colorful arrangements on the coffee table as well as the red poinsettia on the dresser; another was perched on the windowsill. She wasn't the only visitor who had thought to bring flowers. She sat down on a straight chair next to the bed. "So, how are you feeling?" she asked, her eyes traveling the length of Francine's leg encased in what looked like an aluminum brace with adjustable metal gadgets on both sides. Though bedridden, Francine was dressed in a colorful red jersey top and matching jogging pants, one leg cut to accommodate the brace. The room was toasty warm. Maggie began to feel hot in her blue turtleneck, wool slacks, and boots.

"Except for being immobile I'm fine." Pointing to a patch of gauze on her knee, Francine added, "Once that spot heals I'll be able to bend my knee. In increments of course. But it'll mean more mobility."

"Your daughter-in-law said the surgery was very complicated."

Francine shuddered. "Thank God, I didn't have it done in Tonala. I'd be dead by now. I still wonder if Dr. Madrasso had any idea what that place was like."

"Had he known, I can't imagine he would have sent you there."

"By the way," Francine made a snorting sound, "I got a courtesy call from the ship's agent a few days ago. He tracked me down to offer me a two-hundred dollar voucher redeemable for my next cruise on The Mexican Star."

"What?" Maggie gasped. "In view of everything that happened he's trying to lure you back with a puny voucher? That takes a lot of nerve."

"Precisely what I told him. Between you and me, Maggie, I don't think I'll ever go on another cruise. I just want to get on my feet and go home to Florida."

Darlene came back into the room, carrying the flowers in a bowl of water.

"Put them on the table by the window where I can see them," Francine said and told her to take a coffee break while her visitor was here. "Before you go, just give me an extra pillow so I can sit up a bit." Turning her head toward Maggie, she asked, "Do you want some coffee?"

"No thanks."

"A piece of chocolate?" Francine nodded toward several boxes of Lady Godiva on the table by the sofa.

"No. I'm fine. I ate a greasy hot-dog at Grand Central while waiting for the train. I'm still trying to deal with it." Maggie laughed. "I sure miss the ship's wonderful food. But, tell me, how do you spend your time here?" It was difficult to imagine the dynamic Francine flat on her back.

"Oh, time passes somehow. Visitors make it bearable, and I have physical therapy every day. My main concern right now is the incision. It's being stubborn. Darlene has started to put GranX in between the stitches."

"GranX? I never heard of it."

"It's a new miracle medication that's supposed to induce healing."

"And not available in Tonala, I suspect." Maggie glanced around Francine's pretty room. "I still shudder whenever I think of that Godforsaken place. You wouldn't even have had a TV to help pass the time." She nodded to the large screen television.

"Actually, I can do without that. I prefer to read. And of course we have lectures."

"Lectures?"

"Yes, twice a week the library at the end of this corridor becomes a classroom. A variety of speakers volunteer their time. Some of their topics are quite interesting. Others border on the ludicrous. But whatever the subject, everyone is wheeled in to listen. Yesterday the topic was *How to Land a Man*. The speaker spent an hour, telling the bedridden, the crippled, and those suffering from various degrees of senility, how to become sexually active and keep their partner happy."

"What?" Maggie squelched a grin.

"It's the honest to goodness truth. How the speaker managed to keep her composure is beyond me. Most of us can barely move. Others have a foot in the grave. Romance is the last thing anyone is looking for. Everyone is happy just to breathe without a ventilator. Any woman here interested in a man is simply pining for one in a white coat with a stethoscope around his neck." Suddenly Francine looked as though she was remembering something. "Speaking of men," she said, "I had a strange call a couple of days ago. Do you remember a Michael Sanders from the cruise?"

Did she ever! Nodding, Maggie held her breath.

"Well, can you imagine, he called me out of the blue. Apparently Mildred gave him my home number in Florida and he tracked me down. Anyway, more importantly, after solicitously inquiring about my welfare, he asked for your telephone number."

"He did?" Still holding her breath, Maggie was turning blue.

Misinterpreting the expression Francine immediately put her fears to rest and said, "Oh, don't worry! I didn't give it to him."

"You didn't?" The air trapped in Maggie's lungs escaped in an audible gasp of disappointment.

"Well, first of all, one can't be too careful nowadays and I couldn't recall how well you knew him. Frankly, I could barely remember him. I only remember him as being a bit odd and tightlipped."

Reeling from the fact that Michael had wanted her number and angry that Francine hadn't given it to him, Maggie pinched her lips together, afraid a shrill comment might slip out.

"Besides, I figured your number was unlisted," Francine went on. "Mine certainly is. I don't give it out to just anybody."

Just anybody? Michael wasn't just anybody. "Actually, my phone number is unlisted," Maggie finally said in an even tone. "I got fed up with calls from telemarketers and other strangers."

"I know exactly what you mean. That's why I thought it was best to ask for his number. I told him I'd give it to you and if you wanted to speak with him, you'd call."

"You got his number?"

"Yes. It's right here somewhere." Gingerly turning on the bed, Francine reached for a small loose-leaf address book on the nightstand among a clutter of necessities: Kleenex, water goblet, books, and magazines. She tore a page from the back of the booklet and handed it to Maggie. "I hope you can decipher my handwriting. It's not easy to write from this prone position."

Michael's telephone number!

Maggie looked at the slip of paper and thought she'd never before seen anything more beautifully written.

"I can read it," she said, thanking Francine. "It's fine."

It was more than fine. A certain amount of intimacy was attached to it because all she had to do was pick up a phone, dial those numbers, and she would hear his voice.

Afraid to lose the piece of paper, Maggie immediately committed the number to memory. Also afraid of disappointment she put off making the call, figuring that maybe Michael just wanted to explain why he hadn't kept their lunch date, which was redundant because she knew why: Bill McKiernan's body had to be flown home. It was the captain's good luck that Michael was able and willing, the flip side being Maggie's poor luck. But after a lifetime of it, she had come to expect it. Bad luck stuck to her like a hungry puppy.

By December the 23rd, she had still not made the call to Los Angeles and now it was too close to Christmas, so she decided it could wait till after the holidays. It could even wait until after her job interview in January when she might feel better and sound more positive over the phone. Besides, the holidays were depressing enough without overloading the situation with an unnecessary explanation for a broken date followed by a polite sign-off where Michael might say something vague like...*maybe we'll run into each other again on a cruise some day.* Or...*give me a call if you ever find yourself in Los Angeles.*

Lisa left for Pittsburgh and suddenly the apartment seemed cold and melancholic, not helped by the fact that no heat came up through the radiators. Maggie opened the pipes as far as they would go to no avail and made a mental note to call the super.

Trying to keep warm, she went to bed early that evening and while snuggling under the covers felt something under her pillow. She groped the spot, reached over to turn on a bedside lamp, and discovered that Lisa had left her a present. Sitting up, Maggie stared at a box wrapped in a colorful red and green Santa Claus paper. It had been ages since anyone had given her a Christmas gift, but she should have suspected that Lisa would do something sweet like this. She immediately felt guilty that she hadn't thought to give her roommate anything; it hadn't even occurred to her. Years ago, she and Simone had sworn off exchanging gifts, coming to the conclusion that the time spent shopping could be put to better use. Taking a walk together, seeing a movie, was far better than waiting in line at a cash register.

But Lisa? That was a different matter altogether. Maggie tore at the wrapping and found a beautiful, scented candle in a stained glass votive. It was exquisite. Each piece of colored glass was beveled. Getting out of bed and throwing a bathrobe over her shoulders against the chill in the apartment, she went into the living room, found some matches, lit the candle, put it on the coffee table and sat down in the sofa to admire it. The sparkling jewel tones looked out of place on the table's scarred surface, but the glow worked its magic, softening the worn décor in the entire room. Delighted with the votive, Maggie decided that it was not too late to make amends. She could have a little welcome back present waiting for Lisa when she returned after the holidays. Lisa loved to take snapshots around the city. Her pictures were quite good. An interesting frame for one of her photographs might be just the ticket.

The following day, since it was no use pestering anyone for a job on December the 24th, Maggie took care of some errands, first stopping in at Zitomer on Madison Avenue where she found a quirky frame, the type Lisa would die for. She had it gift wrapped in an overall pattern of fireworks and wrote "Happy New Year" on the small card that came with the wrap. Next, she went to the public library on 79th Street for some books to read over the holidays, including a copy of *The Da Vinci Code*. Years ago when everyone was reading it, it was never available, but it was not too late to learn what all the excitement had been about. To counter it with a dose of reality, she checked out a memoir that promised to be brimming with hard luck and abuse. Leaving the library, she put the books into the shopping bag from Zitomer and continued to Eli's on Third Avenue to pick up the pecan pie she was bringing to Queens tomorrow. While there, she also bought a prepared dinner for tonight: meat loaf with mashed potatoes and a small salad in a separate plastic container. This year she was spared from buying Eli's individual turkey platter, and thanked her lucky stars that she was going out to Simone's. If her Christmas dinner was anything like past Thanksgivings, it promised to be a feast, a lively one to boot, because the crowd always included a colorful assortment of family members.

Walking toward home, Maggie once again reminisced about the wonderful Thanksgiving on the cruise. She thought about the tropical seas, people she had met, and particularly the Captain's Ball where she had danced with Michael. Thinking about it made her feel warm all over. Maybe once she landed a job, she could start saving up for another trip. The thought put an extra spring in her step. She didn't feel the icy wind, nor did she feel the weight of the books and other purchases she carried. In fact, she felt so good that she decided to walk to 64th and Lexington where a store called Pylones sold interesting gifts, gadgets, toys and tools in wild designs and outrageous colors. She would bring each of Simone's three sons a present tomorrow. Why not? In the New Year she could go to Frankel's, sell her earrings, and be awash in money.

On December the 28th New York got a foot of snow. The storm began shortly after midnight and didn't let up till midmorning. Maggie heard the details when her radio alarm sounded at six a.m.

*It's six o'clock. This is 1010 WINS...*the announcer's perky voice said. *It's twenty-three degrees in Manhattan and snowing. Nine to twelve inches are expected before the storm tapers off sometime before noon. Expect morning delays on the Metro North and Path Trains. Subways are running on or near schedule. And now...1010 WINS news from around the world...*

Maggie grunted, turned over and prepared to hit the snooze button before changing her mind and switching the radio off. With that much snow falling, she might as well sleep in this morning. It was no use rushing out to employment agencies. Offices across town would open late, if at all. Maybe she was destined to wait for that one and only job interview Mr. Roberts had scheduled for the third of January. With that gloomy thought, she sank back into a despondent sleep, a semiconscious slumber, where her personal woes precluded any real rest.

She awoke at noon with a start and realized that she'd slept six hours since her alarm originally sounded. Disoriented, she glanced at the clock radio, willing it to be wrong. But it wasn't wrong. Angry and dismayed, she raked a hand through her matted hair. Only the severely depressed slept like the dead. She had read about people going through their entire life feeling tired, never believing they got enough sleep, although they regularly spent twelve hours in bed.

Sleeping too much was a bad sign!

Maggie put her feet on the floor. The ice-cold linoleum sent unpleasant shivers up her spine, she gritted her teeth and considered it part of her punishment. Groping around for her slippers, she decided she would take a shower and get dressed as if she were going job hunting, which she might actually still do. Blackouts shut the city down, whereas snow only gummed things up a bit. She padded over to the window and peeled back the limp paper shade. She couldn't see a thing. The window was covered with frost. She forced it open.

Numbing air rushed in, nonetheless, she stuck her head out and looked down. The weatherman was right. Snow concealed the old furniture and other discarded stuff in the courtyard and a layer covered the neighboring roof where pigeons huddled under the ventilation pipes and window ledges. But at least it was no longer snowing. As predicted, the storm had run out of steam. Soon the clouds would break, the sun would shine through and perhaps melt some of the snow.

After showering and washing her hair, letting it air-dry, Maggie made some instant coffee and plunked down on the sofa, which was all hers while Lisa was away. Forgetting her good intentions about getting dressed, she pulled a terry cloth bathrobe around her, kicked off her slippers, tucked her feet under her, and found the place in *The Da Vinci Code* where she'd left off. She would go out later; skip the employment agencies and just take a walk through Central Park and watch Manhattan skiers in full alpine attire schuss across Sheep Meadow, their flushed faces shining with a sense of personal triumph.

"Buzzz...buzzz..."

What? Frowning Maggie put her book down on the coffee table. Who was buzzing her? She was not expecting anyone, nor was she expecting a delivery. She shrugged. One of her neighbors must have forgotten his keys and needed to be let in downstairs. She rose from the sofa and walked barefooted over to the intercom by the front door.

"Yes?" she said, holding down the button.

"Buzzz...buzzz..." Someone unfamiliar with this building's ancient intercom system was fooling around with it.

"Who's there?" she snapped, hoping whoever it was would let go of the button long enough to hear her.

Chapter Seventy

Earlier that morning, Michael had gone over to the dormer windows in the guest bedroom in Hastings and pulled back the curtains. He was not accustomed to seeing swirling snow erasing the landscape and for a long time just stood there, admiring it.

Jeffrey's and Carol's house was a small 1870 vintage colonial in Hastings-on-Hudson without actually being on the river. They had bought it several months ago when they decided to move out of the city in anticipation of the birth of their baby. The house was quaint, retaining the original details, and the furnishings were of a bygone era as well. Like Lynn, Carol loved anything old. But whereas Lynn had shopped in flea markets for antique milkglass pitchers and pewter collectibles, Carol went all out, scouring garage sales for bureaus, tables, and Victorian love seats. The guest room Michael occupied was a veritable museum without the price tag because it was mostly second-hand reproductions that Carol had refinished.

Spending Christmas in Hastings had been a last minute decision when Carol's obstetrician discouraged air travel, which ruled out both Los Angeles and Michael's brother's house in Phoenix where everyone had gathered last year. In retrospect, Michael was relieved not to be visiting the venue of his final Christmas with Lynn and Suzanne; the memories might overwhelm him. Besides, he wasn't crazy about Bob's wife. Ruth personified the proverbial bleached blonde who spent weekends in Las Vegas, which thank God she didn't. Her addiction was daytime Soaps with a pack of Camels until a routine X-ray discovered a spot on her lung. After radiation treatments, she stopped smoking and also quit watching the Soaps, claiming the association was too much to handle. She and Bob had no children, a disappointment she often admitted contributed to her need for cigarettes. Bob ran a thriving dental practice and worked six days a week, although he and Ruth didn't need the extra income generated by being open on Saturdays. Except for a trip to Italy every summer they spent very little and definitely nothing on their home. The furniture was the same they had acquired after their marriage thirty years ago, supplemented over time by inherited pieces as both sets of parents passed away. Ruth did the gardening, most of which consisted of raking the green-colored gravel that simulated grass around their low-roofed hacienda. A boulder and a tall cactus sat in the middle of this "lawn" at the front of the house. The back was a rocky hillside that needed no tending. A swift stroke of a broom got rid of any desert sand that occasionally blew onto the terrace, and since no one used the pool there was no need to spend money on chemicals, the result being pond-like water that lured small animals mostly of the reptile family.

Visiting Jeffrey's and Carol's new home this Christmas proved cathartic. Hastings was a world away from Santa Monica, and the snow today made it appear even more foreign. The change of scenery worked wonders and Michael was already looking forward to returning here in April for the birth of his grandchild. He and his daughter-in-law got along well. The day after he arrived, she delighted in showing him her school in Dobbs Ferry. It was closed for the holidays, but a custodian let them tour the place. The following morning they went into New York City, first going down to Wall Street where Jeffrey showed-off his law office, after which Carol and Michael took the subway to Grand Central and walked to the Palm Court at the Plaza where they enjoyed a leisurely lunch. Later, Carol joined the holiday shoppers in the stores on Fifth Avenue while Michael visited the Metropolitan Museum, whiling away the afternoon until six o'clock when he was to meet Jeffrey and Carol at The Oyster Bar back at Grand Central Station for a quick dinner before catching the train to Hastings.

While in the city that day Michael found himself studying the people hurrying along the sidewalks, half-expecting to bump into Maggie. He also looked for her among the crowd at the museum. Of course the chance of spotting her was eight million to one, unless the population had changed significantly since last count.

As he again pulled back the lace on the windows in the guestroom and looked out into the garden, he wondered if this snowstorm was severe enough to close the airports. He was due to fly out to Phoenix tomorrow. Bob and Ruth were having a New Year's Eve party and since he hadn't spent Christmas with them, he figured he'd join them for that. No memories were associated with it because last year

Lynn, Suzanne, and he had gone back to Los Angeles immediately after Christmas.

With only one day left before leaving the East Coast, Michael made a decision. He would go into the city once more, this time on his own. Francine Wirth had been uncooperative the day he called to ask for Maggie's telephone number. When she refused to reveal it, he had left his and had diligently checked his answering machine each and every day. But now that almost three weeks had passed with no message from Maggie, he suspected that Mrs. Wirth had not given her his number. Of course there was more than one way to skin a cat. The next time he played golf with Commodore Reyes, he might ask him to check the ship's passenger records. Unfortunately, that golf game would not take place until after the holidays and patience was not Michael's long suit; he did not like loose ends. Everything had to be accounted for. He carried an internal checklist, part of his training as a pilot, where every item, critical or not, had to be checked and rechecked before pulling away from the gate. With that deeply ingrained precision, came his need to try once more to contact Maggie, and what better time than now while he was in her approximate vicinity. He remembered her saying that she lived on East 83rd Street and he also remembered something about Second Avenue. If he went into the city and walked up and down both sides of that block, surely a local business, a grocer, a dry cleaner, would know her. Even in Manhattan one could not live on a street for a number of years without being known to somebody. His only concern now was the weather, which might prevent him from going into New York. He listened carefully to the forecasters on the TV in his room and hoped the storm would, as they predicted, taper off by midmorning.

It did. Snow blowers across Hastings were soon going full blast as neighbors cleared their driveways. Street cleaning trucks followed an hour later; government services were generally a step behind private initiative. As a new homeowner, Jeffrey had not thought to invest in a snow blower, so father and son went out to clear the driveway the old-fashioned way, using shovels.

By twelve o'clock, once the Metro North trains were again running on schedule, Michael and Jeffrey walked to the station. It was a long walk but it was too risky to take the car because municipal salt spreaders had left behind a layer of thin ice that the ecologically friendly mix refused to melt.

Arriving in New York at Grand Central, father and son split up, Jeffrey taking the subway to his office down on Wall Street, Michael taking a taxi to a destination he hadn't revealed. Jeffrey might think him on a fool's errand. Or worse, think him heartless.

It hadn't been a year yet.

"Buzzz... Buzzz..." The sound was becoming irritating.

"Let go of the stupid button long enough to listen!" Maggie shouted into the intercom, clenched her teeth and wondered why neighbors who misplaced their vestibule key invariably rang her apartment as if she were the doorman-in-residence. It was as though they knew she had no life and was always available.

"Buzzz..."

"Yes! Who is it?"

The buzzing stopped, replaced by the normal sound of static and the wail of a fire engine screeching along Second Avenue. Again she shouted, "Who is it? What do you want?"

"Maggie?"

Huh? She pulled back from the intercom as if a surge of electricity had jolted her.

Michael? It couldn't be...

"Maggie? Is that you?"

Despite the static of the intercom and street noise in the background, she recognized his voice. Her heart jumped into her throat, disabling her tongue.

"Is this the apartment of Margaret Maghpye?"

"Y...yes," she croaked, swallowing past an obstruction that felt like a tennis ball in her throat. Finally, and although she knew perfectly well who was downstairs, she asked, "Who is it?"

"Michael Sanders."

"Oh, yes...hi," she mumbled.

Michael crimped his brow. Perhaps he shouldn't have come. This wasn't quite the greeting he had expected. There was no enthusiasm in her voice. Maybe she had company? He should have called first. But how could he? Her number was unlisted and Mrs. Wirth had refused to divulge it. Still, having come this far, he persevered.

"I'd like to see you," he said despite the lukewarm reception. "Can you come down? Or shall I come up?"

"Ahhh..." Maggie's mind was racing so fast it interfered with an immediate response. "I...uh..." *She wasn't dressed! The apartment was a mess!*

"If this is a bad time I can come back later."

"No!" she almost shrieked into the intercom. The last time they'd made plans to meet later he had left the ship and disappeared from her life. She wasn't taking that chance again. "You c...can come up," she said, her voice jittery, something she hoped he would attribute to the static in the intercom. "My door is on the left as you reach the top floor."

After buzzing him into the vestibule, she ransacked the hall closet in a panic, trying to decide between the brown and the navy suit, before she caught herself. *A suit?* For crying out loud! She wasn't thinking clearly. This was not a job interview. She turned and flew into the bedroom, grabbing a pair of black gabardine slacks hanging over the back of a chair. She put them on and began rummaging through the dresser drawers. Except for the red Christmas sweater she'd bought several years ago to wear to the annual office party, all the others were in deplorable condition. The blue wool she'd worn the day she visited Francine was at the cleaners. It was the red sweater or nothing. Oh, God, she wished she had something better to wear. But how was she to know that Michael would show up today? He lived in Los Angeles. Never in her wildest imagination could she have imagined he'd suddenly ring her doorbell. She brushed her still damp hair with violence and with a few fast strokes applied some lipstick, glad for once that she lived on the fifth floor because it would take time for him to walk up, giving her a few precious minutes. She found some clean socks, got down on her knees and located some brown loafers under the bed and was hopping toward the front door, stuffing her feet into them, just as Michael knocked.

A heartbeat later she opened the door. The dash to get dressed had left her winded and, seeing him standing there – big as life – further depleted her of oxygen. Dear God, he was handsome!

"Hi Maggie!" He was smiling.

"Hi, come in." She stepped back to allow him to enter the small space of her foyer. "Here, let me take your coat." She drew a couple of shallow breaths to regain her balance and tried on a smile that, unfortunately, just made her lips twitch.

"It's nice to see you again," he said, pulling off his gloves and shrugging out of his trench coat – California weight; he must have been freezing outside in that light garment. She hung it on Lisa's newly installed rack behind the door, now empty while she was in Pittsburgh. Under his coat Michael was wearing a gray corduroy jacket, navy turtleneck, and charcoal slacks; sufficiently warm clothing yet he was shivering. "I'm not accustomed to this climate," he grinned, rubbing his hands together and huddling his shoulders inside his jacket, all the while studying Maggie with an intense look.

Noting his stare, she wondered if a thread was unraveling her sweater? Was her lipstick smeared?

"So...how are you?" he went on. "You look lovely." Okay, she was properly dressed with no lipstick on her teeth. "I'm glad I caught you at home. I guess the weather kept you in today?"

"Yes," she said simply without elaborating on the sorry fact that she had nowhere else to go, snow or no snow.

"Lucky for me," he said. "Traveling into the city, I was actually surprised to see that most of the streets were cleared and traffic was moving pretty well. I gather Manhattan recovers quickly from a snowfall."

"Where did you come from?" *Stupid question.* "I...I mean...what brings you to New York?" she quickly amended and without waiting for an answer, showed him into the living room, apologizing for the mess. "I wasn't expecting company," she said lamely, shuffling some newspapers together so he could sit down on the sofa, which had once upon a time been a sleek brown tweed that had metamorphosed into an orangey humpbacked whale. "Would you like some coffee? Tea?"

"Nothing, thanks." Instead of sitting down, Michael walked over to the window, searching for points of interest to generate some small talk to help take the edge of his unannounced visit. "Nice place you have here," he finally said when nothing in particular was unusual enough to comment on. The window was covered with frost, but even without the feathery layer of ice, he figured there was no view to speak of at the back of a brownstone. He returned to the sofa and sat down opposite Maggie who took the straight-backed chair facing him. "Ah...The Da Vinci Code." He nodded toward the book on the coffee table, glad to have found a topic of conversation. "I read it years ago. Are you enjoying it?"

"So far it's very suspenseful."

He picked up the novel, noting her bookmark. "The conclusion will be something of a let down, I'm afraid. Of course, I shouldn't be saying that since you're still reading it."

"That's okay. Even the best writer can run out of steam after three hundred pages. Either that or the reader gets anesthetized by the continuously fast pace and reaches a point where no ending will satisfy."

Michael agreed and put the book down, his gaze again settling on Maggie. He didn't want to talk about books just now. He wanted to talk about her. And he wanted to look at her in that silly Christmas sweater with the appliquéd bells and angora snowman. Connie wouldn't be caught dead in one of those; not even Ruth wore such a thing. Christmas sweaters were déclassé where he came from, but for some reason it looked nice on Maggie. Still, she'd look smashing in a simple green cardigan; green would compliment her hair color. That said, he was not disappointed; the vision he'd kept in his mind since leaving the cruise was intact. There was a fresh and natural look about her, just as he remembered.

Maggie felt herself grow hot under his stare. Sitting opposite Michael was a mistake. It afforded him a front and center view, which was not to her advantage. She reached for the matches on the coffee table, again appreciating Lisa's present as she lit the votive, its glow immediately softening the room. Maybe it would be kind to her appearance as well?

While she was busying herself with the candle, Michael took another look around. In Salina Cruz she had been frank about her circumstances, but he hadn't expected something quite this sad. Perhaps she wore that bright red sweater in an effort to compensate for the lifeless décor of the apartment. He wondered if she had ever heard of *feng shui*.

"Where's your roommate?" he asked instead, remembering that she had told him about a girl who lived with her.

"She went home to Pittsburgh for the holidays," Maggie said, again offering some refreshments. "Are you sure I can't get you anything?"

When he again declined, she got up to tinker with one of the radiators; if her guest didn't want coffee, she ought to at least make sure he was warm. She tried the handle. The radiator hissed. The valve was fully opened. This was as good as it was going to get. Grateful that at least Lisa's wet socks weren't draped over the pipes, she went back to her seat. "You haven't told me what brought you to New York."

"I came to spend Christmas with my son and his wife. "

"Oh, of course. They live in Hastings. Right?"

"Yes. Carol's doctor advised her against traveling. So I came east for a few days. It was a last minute switch of plans. I'm leaving tomorrow."

"Too bad the snow came late. It would have been nice for you to experience a white Christmas. Still, it must have been lovely in the suburbs this morning."

"It was heavy."

"Heavy?"

"I helped Jeffrey shovel the stuff." Michael grinned and rotated his arm, attesting to the unusual workout. "Henceforth, I better remain in California during the winter months. Our winter is like April in New York."

"Sounds wonderful." Maggie sighed.

"Some call it monotonously beautiful."

"I'll take it at any name."

"How did you spend Christmas?"

"With a friend and her family in Queens."

"Sounds ideal."

"Noisy is a more apt description. Fifteen people at the table and fifteen different opinions on just about everything. And we never even got around to politics."

Michael laughed, acknowledging that he had been in similar situations. A moment later, he turned serious. "I'm awfully glad to see you, Maggie," he said. "I hated to miss those last days on the ship."

"You did a good deed for the captain and the McKiernans."

"Nonetheless, I'm sorry I missed the opportunity to spend more time with you. At least long enough to get your telephone number. It would have spared me from calling Francine Wirth. She wouldn't give me the time of day, let alone your number. I gave her mine. Did she ever pass it on to you?"

"Yes. I was planning to call you right after the New Year."

"I'm glad to hear that. I was beginning to wonder. Your silence was not encouraging. I took a chance, dropping by unannounced today. Not the proper protocol and I apologize. I hope you're not annoyed with me."

"Of course not. But how did you find me?"

"That day in Salina Cruz you told me you lived on East 83rd Street. I took it from there."

"A thousand people live on East 83rd."

"You also mentioned Second Avenue, which narrowed it down a bit. After some footwork, I stopped to chat with an old fellow shoveling snow two buildings down. He pointed the way."

"That must have been Mr. Kramer. He's been the superintendent of several brownstones along this side of the street since the neighborhood was called Germantown. He's very suspicious of strangers. I'm surprised he talked to you. Let alone gave you information about a tenant."

"I told him I was from the FBI."

"You did *what!*" Maggie burst out laughing. "He believed you?"

"The trench coat clinched it. It was cold. I had the collar rolled up."

"You've ruined my reputation," Maggie said, still laughing. "Old Mr. Kramer is probably still down on the street, ignoring the cold and keeping busy just so he won't miss seeing me taken away in handcuffs. By now he's probably gathered a crowd of onlookers."

"Sorry," Michael grinned. "But it was the only way I had of finding you. I drove down to San Diego the day the ship docked, hoping to see you."

"You *did?*" Maggie said, surprised that he had gone to so much trouble.

"Luckily, I spotted some of your friends on the dock. They told me what happened to Francine and how the two of you left the ship in Tapachula. It must have been quite a stressful journey home."

"Only for Francine. But she had a good attitude."

"Not the day I called her. When I asked for your telephone number, I think she believed I was planning to murder you."

Maggie laughed. "She guards her privacy and was just guarding mine as well."

Watching Maggie, Michael caught his breath. She was beautiful when she laughed. She ought to do it more often. He wondered if she had landed a job, but didn't want to ask; better wait for her to tell him.

"I have an idea," he said, glancing at his watch. "Are you hungry? It's past lunch and too early for dinner, but I believe the Palm Court at the Plaza serves an English tea in the afternoon. Finger sandwiches, scones, cakes...the works. Carol and I had a wonderful meal there earlier this week. The menu has something for every taste and appetite. How about it?"

Maggie hadn't eaten all day, mostly due to the fact that she'd slept till noon. "I'd love it," she said, and realized she was very hungry as well as eager to see the Palm Court. It had been years since she had been to there, but remembered it as a beautiful restaurant with real palm trees and lots of flowers. The only fly in the ointment was the fact that she also remembered that it was Ms. Noune's favorite spot. A short walk from the office, she and her law partners regularly entertained clients there because it was quiet, discreet, and the light cuisine didn't overwhelm their conversation. Maggie ran a hand across her sweater and glanced down at her slacks, little of the pleats remained. "Do I need to change?"

"No. You look wonderful," Michael said in all honesty and rose from the sofa. "I like your outfit. It's seasonal. Cheerful. Perfect."

Chapter seventy-two

It was half an hour later when the maître d' showed them to a table in the fashionable center court restaurant at the Plaza Hotel. Tall palms were stationed throughout the room and there were fresh flowers on every table. Maggie felt as though she were back on the cruise. When Michael ordered a bottle of champagne, the lovely memories came flooding back, as sparkling and effervescent as the bubbles rushing to the surface in the tall flutes as the waiter poured.

While sipping champagne and eating smoked salmon and cucumber sandwiches, they talked about a great number of things. Michael related details of his visit in Hastings, explaining he would be back in mid April when Carol's baby was born. Maggie hoped that meant she would see him again and was making a mental note of the date, when a familiar and shrill voice caused her to glance around.

She stiffened. *Oh, God, no!*

Her nemesis was walking into the Palm Court with Mr. Goodman and two gentlemen who were obviously clients. Lightning fast, Maggie looked away, pretending fascination with some tumescent whipped cream pastries on a serving cart nearby. Unfortunately, the restaurant was half empty and since her red sweater probably stood out like a sore thumb, it was futile to think that Ms. Noune wouldn't see her.

Michael noticed Maggie's sudden distraction and checked the room for what might have caused it. "Who are those people?" he asked, nodding in the direction of the newcomers taking their seats nearby. He suspected they were the reason for Maggie's troubled look, because nothing else in the restaurant had changed.

Jerking her attention away from the pastry cart, Maggie leaned across the table and whispered, being careful not to turn her head and make eye contact with anyone at the table in question. "It's my former boss and a senior partner, Mr. Goodman," she said. "He's the heavy-set man in the dark pinstriped suit. I don't recognize the other two. But I'm sure they're clients." Maggie glanced at her watch. It was three o'clock. "My guess is that they were supposed to have had a business lunch here and were delayed because of the weather." She lowered her voice even further with her next remark. "Ms. Noune hates me. She's the one who fired me. Do you remember I told you about that in Salina Cruz?"

"Yes. I'm sorry if she makes you uncomfortable. Do you want to leave? We can have coffee and dessert elsewhere."

"No. Ms. Noune chased me from the office. She's not going to chase me from a public restaurant." Without being aware of it, Maggie stuck out her chin.

"That's the ticket." Michael said. "Stand your ground like a good soldier."

Despite the brave words and stubborn chin, Maggie didn't feel like a warrior and silently owned up to the fact that she couldn't enjoy herself within a mile of Ms. Noune, nor could she retreat and give her the satisfaction of seeing her slink away.

"Look at it this way," Michael said when Maggie remained silent. "If she hadn't fired you, you wouldn't have taken the cruise and we wouldn't have met. Maybe we ought to go over and thank her."

"What?" Maggie sputtered with that outrageous suggestion, sputtering again as she inadvertently took a large a sip of champagne. It was a moment before she could speak. "I...I guess being fired *did* have a silver lining," she allowed, coughing into her napkin.

"Meaning you're glad you took the cruise? Or glad you ran into me?" Michael grinned. "Literally. You almost flattened me on that road in Acapulco."

Maggie's eyes shone with the memory. Having her purse snatched had definitely been worth it because she had befriended Michael. She began to relax. After all, her former boss was of no account anymore. She was just another person in the restaurant, having a meal with business associates. Maggie was here with Michael. She'd won the lottery.

Ms. Noune was flipping her blond pageboy over her shoulders, scouring the room for a certain waiter who always bowed and scraped when she came in. It was crucial that Carlos was here today to show obeisance because this was an *impress important clients* session. Unfortunately, he was nowhere to be seen. However, as she repeatedly looked around the restaurant, she spotted her former paralegal sharing a table *and* a bottle of expensive champagne with an incredibly good-looking individual. Carlos was immediately forgotten as Laura Noune now craned her neck to study the person with Maggie. The expensive cut of his jacket didn't escape her notice. He looked casually elegant with a natural confidence that spoke volumes. Who was he? Why was he keeping company with Ms. Maghpye? Had she already found another job and was this her new boss treating her to an orientation tea? A get acquainted session? Upon closer inspection, Ms Noune decided it was not Maggie's boss because he was looking at her with warmth not defensible in a professional relationship. Besides, she couldn't remember receiving any employment verification calls. While lost in burning curiosity, Ms. Noune was neglecting her clients before finally torn from her silent and inquisitive deliberations by Mr. Goodman's surprised voice.

"Oh, my! Isn't that Ms. Maghpye over there? Our paralegal? Alas, our former paralegal." Without waiting for Laura Noune's response, he excused himself and pushed back his chair. "Carry on. I'll return in a minute." As he got up and approached Maggie's table, Ms. Noune saw the gentleman sitting with Maggie rise from his seat. He was not only handsome, but had fine manners.

"Ms. Maghpye!" Mr. Goodman offered his hand. "How nice to see you!"

Puzzled by his effusiveness, Maggie smiled tentatively, shook his hand and managed a proper introduction between the two men.

"How do you do, Mr. Sanders? Please, sit down. I don't mean to interrupt, but I suspect you're the reason we lost the best paralegal we ever had, in which case I ought to enjoy spoiling your meal." Mr. Goodman figured this was the competing attorney who, according to Ms. Noune, had lured Maggie away from the firm back in November.

Michael was wondering about Mr. Goodman's odd remarks, when Maggie quickly spoke up.

"No. Mr. Sanders is visiting from Los Angeles," she said, similarly bewildered with Mr. Goodman's comments.

"Ah, Los Angeles. Great place. I've been there many times. I assume it's sunny and 79 degrees there today."

"That's a safe bet."

"Well, I hope you're enjoying our snow and ice," Mr. Goodman said and turned his attention back to Maggie. "We miss you. I wish there was some way we could entice you to come back."

"Come back?" Maggie looked confused. "Don't you know?"

"Know what, Ms. Maghpye?"

"I was fired."

"Nonsense! I didn't fire you. And I can't imagine Mr. Barr did. He thought the world of you."

"No, he didn't fire me." Maggie realized that both of the senior partners were unaware of the circumstances surrounding her sudden dismissal, and she certainly didn't want them to think that she had left without giving notice. They had always been nice to her. "Ms. Noune fired me," she said simply.

"She *did?*" Mr. Goodman's eyebrows shot up. "I see. Well, I'm awfully sorry about that. Wish I'd known. Are you already working elsewhere?"

"No."

"I'll tell you what. Come back and work for me. I'll increase your salary and throw-in a signing bonus. We need you."

Yesterday Maggie would have lunged at the job and had she met Mr. Goodman in private today, would have kissed the hem of his coat for such an offer. But she didn't want to appear overly eager in front of Michael; she wanted no hint of desperation showing along her seams. Besides, she wasn't ready to work under the same roof as Ms. Noune again, even in another part of the office. She wasn't that wretched yet.

"May I think about it?" she simply said.

"Of course. Come see me right after the New Year. The job will be waiting for you." Mr. Goodman took both of Maggie's hands in his before turning to Michael, saying, "It's been a pleasure meeting you, Mr. Sanders. Enjoy the rest of your stay."

"Thank you. I will."

Mr. Goodman walked back to his table and sat down, smiling at his clients. When he looked at Ms. Noune he was no longer smiling.

Maggie saw her squirm.

It was past four o'clock when they left the Palm Court, Michael now suggesting that they take a stroll along Fifth Avenue. He was in no hurry to catch the train back to Hastings, which suited Maggie just fine. She had no plans and wasn't eager to return home either. In fact, when the time came for him to leave, she would walk him all the way to Grand Central Station to prolong his visit because it would have to last her till April.

Winter days were short and it was already getting dark. Stepping carefully off the curb in front of the Plaza Hotel where the snow had become a brown slush, Michael took Maggie's elbow as they crossed the street to the square. Before walking along Fifth, he held back, stopping to admire the huge, impressive fountain. It was drained of water at this time of year but its statue was covered in a mantle of snow that glittered in the holiday lights strung around the evergreens placed in the empty pool at the foot of the fountain. The tall, sleek General Motors Building on the far side of Fifth Avenue faced the old classic architecture of the Plaza Hotel; a study in contrast and to someone from Southern California it was a spectacular sight. Deep in thought, Michael remained standing on the square, admiring the buildings and oblivious to the people rushing past in their hurry to cross with the traffic light. When the signal changed, pedestrians kept crossing anyway; motorists beware.

"Maggie," Michael finally said, turning to her, his hands reaching over to adjust the scarf around her neck, done for no other reason than to occupy his hands. "I want to invite you to a New Year's Eve party."

"I thought you said you were leaving tomorrow."

"I am. The party is in Phoenix. At my brother's house. I'd like you to come with me."

"To Phoenix? Tomorrow? Are you serious?"

"Yes. In fact, if you say no, you'll force me to stay here and celebrate the New Year just to be near you. Which means I'll wear out my welcome with my daughter-in-law, straining a good relationship. You wouldn't want that on your conscience, would you?"

Maggie shook her head and grinned, still wondering if he was being serious. "But how can I possibly go to Phoenix? I...I mean...just like that?" It seemed totally out of the question on such short notice. "I'll have to first..."

Michael took her face in his hands, his fingers sliding across her lips to silence her. "Not only Phoenix, darling. After Phoenix I want you to come to Los Angeles. I want to show you Santa Monica. Hollywood. The mountains. The beaches. The works."

Darling? Maggie allowed herself to savor the sound of that endearment for a moment before becoming practical. Last minute tickets cost a bundle. She would have to sell the earrings right away. At least I have a wardrobe, she thought. The cruise wear should do fine in both Arizona and California.

"I haven't told you this yet," Michael went on when she remained silent, juggling practicalities around in her head. "I have been reinstated at South World Airlines. My first flight will be on January 15th."

"Really? Same route?"

"No. It'll be between Los Angeles and Honolulu. That was the airline's decision. The perks stay the same."

"Perks?"

"Free flights, just to name one."

"A free seat? Anytime?"

"Two," he corrected. "One for me and one for a companion of my choice."

"When did all this happen? When did you know you wanted to fly again?"

"During the flight from Mexico City to Fan Francisco. After I returned home I had a number of long sessions with South World's psychiatrist. Plus I put in some mandated hours in the flight simulators. After a couple of dry runs over the Pacific I received my clearance and the new assignment. Though I'm loath to admit it, the psychiatrist deserves a lot of credit. Among other things, he helped me see that there are things and there are events in our lives that we have no control over and it's counter-productive, completely useless, to try to place blame. Life is unpredictable, sometimes tragic and sometimes wonderful." Smiling ruefully, he added, "You're looking at a new man, but a very lonely one. I need you with me. And I think you need me. I hope you do because I believe two tattered souls can be good for each other." He reached out and put his arms around her, drawing her up against him.

Michael needed her!

Maggie felt a powerful surge of happiness. Mr. Goodman wanted her back in the office and Michael wanted her with him.

There was no contest.

As she tilted her face up, her answer shining in her eyes, Michael bent his head down and in a brief and wondrous moment touched his lips to hers.

Along with the exquisite flutter of excitement with this sudden intimacy, Maggie experienced an instant of self-consciousness. She had lived in the shadows of life for so long that coming out into the open would take some getting used to. She pulled away and, embarrassed, lowered her eyes to the sidewalk as though she had sinned; after all, they were on display in the middle of a busy city square.

Michael obviously didn't feel the same way. Without hesitation, he pulled her close again and a heartbeat later kissed her like she'd never before been kissed. This time she didn't pull away. She remained in the circle of his arms, lingering in his warm embrace.

This is New York, she reminded herself.

No one will blink an eye.

epilogue

When she received the wedding invitation, Francine was living in Florida and was perfectly capable of flying out to the West Coast. She arrived for the festivities on Miranda Drive in Santa Monica, proudly walking with only the help of a cane.

The marriage took place over the Labor Day weekend. Carol and Jeffrey came from Hastings with their baby boy. Simone and Howard came from Queens with their teenaged sons, who were more exited about seeing Disneyland than attending a wedding. Bob and Ruth came from Phoenix, and Bill Knight came, representing South World Airlines, along with several of Michael's colleagues and their wives. The Emersons attended with Allison, John, and their brood. Their presence, in particular, meant a great deal to Michael.

Connie, too, was invited. Since meeting Maggie back in January, she had made it her business to help the transplanted Easterner adjust to Southern California. Maggie was happy with this instant friendship and was delighted to assist Connie whenever she hosted an Open House for a new real estate listing.

Best of all, Maggie was finally part of a real family. She had a husband, a son, a daughter-in-law, and a grandchild.

CPSIA information can be obtained at www.ICGtesting.com
Printed in the USA
BVOW011800300712

296580BV00001B/4/P